OAK CLIFF

OAK CLIFF

JACOB GROVEY

Library of Congress Control Number: 2026901571

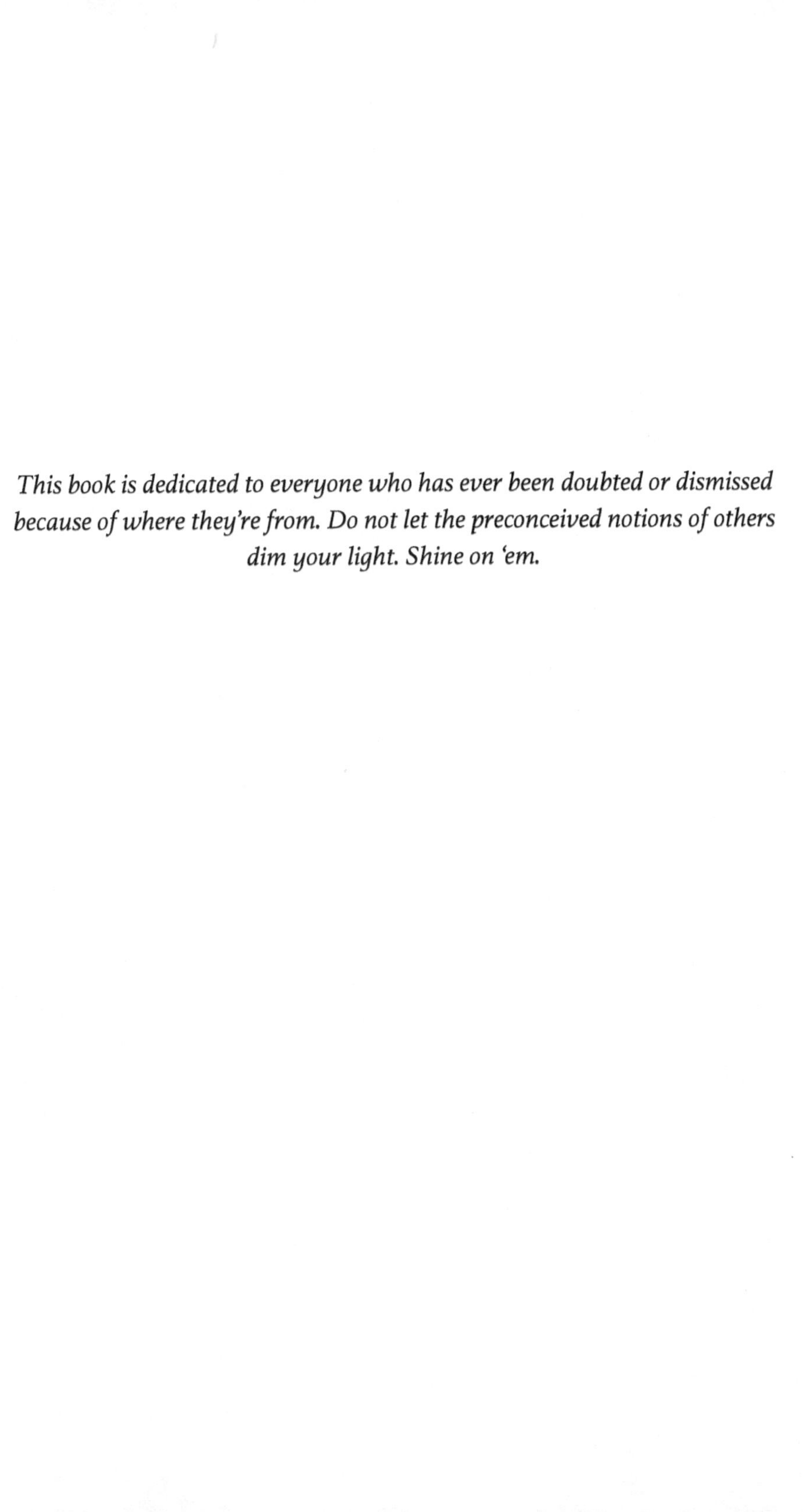

This book is dedicated to everyone who has ever been doubted or dismissed because of where they're from. Do not let the preconceived notions of others dim your light. Shine on 'em.

Do not seek revenge or bear a grudge against anyone among
your people, but love your neighbor as yourself.

— LEVITICUS 19:18

CONTENTS

1

———————

"You are the cancers that are plaguing this neighborhood."

Those words were the verbal grenades hurled into our car's rolled-up windows by a nearby street preacher. My family was passing him by when we were driving down Beckley Avenue on a Sunday afternoon.

We were in our Plymouth Sundance, which my father always spent a few hours washing at a neighborhood car wash each Saturday. It was our tradition to listen to old gospel music on the radio station, Soul 73, every Sunday, so that's what we were doing.

Pops normally focused on the music, so we were surprised he wanted to hear the preacher. Since our car didn't have power windows, we had to manually roll ours down to get a better listen to what the tall and scrawny preacher was saying.

I thought we'd take a few minutes to stop and listen, but we kept moving. I turned in an attempt to hear more of what he had to say, but it was like all the rest of his words were muted. I figured that meant I heard the part of the sermon I was supposed to hear.

As I thought more about what he said, two people, maybe in their 20s, randomly started yelling directly in front of where the preacher was.

"Quit talkin' and square up," one of them told the other.

The preacher sighed deeply before he started pointing as if to say, "See, this is exactly what I'm talking about."

I turned back around and all I could do was shake my head.

"Man, O'Cliff crazy than a mug," I said aloud.

The term, 'than a mug,' was something we all said. It was perfect for every situation because it was so diverse. Seeing people fight was crazy, especially on a Sunday, but seeing them fight in front of a preacher... that was crazy than a mug.

My eyes closed as I continued thinking about the only words I heard the preacher say. I knew about cancer as a sickness, but I was too young to understand the correlation between the illness and the community. I could've asked my parents what he meant, but I had convinced myself I should've known. So, when we made it back home, I made sure I did.

Back in the day, in order for me to find the info I was looking for, I had to use the dictionary my parents kept on the bookshelf in the living room. They kept it on the bottom shelf because they always said they wanted it to be easy for us to gain knowledge. While searching, I found a few different definitions of cancer, but the one that stood out said it was a "practice or phenomenon perceived to be evil, or destructive, and hard to contain."

I read the definition several times before it started to make sense. Understanding it was one thing, but knowing someone felt that way about the people in my neighborhood was sickening. The preacher's words made me feel condemned, but I couldn't comprehend why. I just knew his opinion gave me a bad feeling in the pit of my stomach.

I believe bad things can happen everywhere, but that doesn't mean the people should be thought of as destructive beings. I especially didn't think those thoughts should've been conveyed by someone delivering the word of God. I disagreed with what he thought, but he was entitled to his opinion, just as I was to mine.

Regardless of if I agreed or not, I knew some of my neighborhood's wounds were self-inflicted. We were used to pain, so perhaps we were conditioned to make sure there was an abundance of it. Additionally, many of us dealt with issues that were caused by factors beyond what we had done to ourselves. Our dilemmas spread like cancer, but is that why he thought we were comparable to it?

The preacher's words lived rent-free in my mind before that was a phrase people used. I should've let them go after I processed them, but I couldn't. Instead, I gave them the opportunity to add unneeded weight to the already heavy feelings I carried with me.

By the time I was 16, I had seen despair well beyond my years. I questioned why my neighborhood forced me to see things those from other parts of the city didn't. At times, I thought about how life would be if I lived somewhere else. Coincidentally, whenever I did, I felt guilty because of how much I love where I'm from. That's also when I started wondering if there would ever be any reciprocity between me and my hood.

When you love someone or something, you sometimes become so comfortable, you never want to leave, even if it would benefit you. Over the years, I discovered that's why a lot of people never left the neighborhood they grew up in. Sometimes, the comfort level they had with being familiar, caused a level of fear that froze them. When you're frozen, you're forced to see things you don't necessarily want to. For many people who lived in neighborhoods like mine, seeing lives get cut short was one of those things.

Logic would have you believe seeing death would make someone want to change environments, but we sometimes feel like there's no point because ultimately, the grim reaper never loses. Some don't think we'll be around for long, so we believe you might as well stay near the danger you know, instead of getting to know a new one.

I wasn't immune to that mindset. Death was common to people like me. So, even before I made it to Oak Cliff, I'd been given a death sentence. I was a premie baby, so people assumed I wouldn't make it. My prenatal care was non-existent because my folks didn't even know they were having me until late into the pregnancy. I learned I was unplanned, or a "happy accident" as the late Bob Ross would say.

Being unplanned, while living in a neighborhood where your trials and tribulations are right across the street from safety and salvation, can make you believe God's plan isn't for you to live long. It's easy to think negatively, but when I saw the glass as half full, my mind would make me imagine a world outside of my zip code.

I dreamt of seeing my mother and father sitting on their porch in rocking chairs, watching their grandkids play. In spite of the differences between a future I'd sometimes dream of and the reality I lived in, I've always had love for Oak Cliff because I wouldn't be who I am if I would've grown up anywhere else.

Oak Cliff is an area in Dallas, TX, with a bunch of smaller neighborhoods within it. O'Cliff, as a lot of us pronounce it, used to be its own city, but it eventually became a part of Dallas. Through it all, we've always kept our own identity intact.

Everything we do in The Cliff is different than the rest of Dallas, and that's how we want it. I love my hood, but the love isn't always reciprocated. Sometimes, I feel like I'm in a toxic relationship I can't break free from. Whenever you're in a relationship people don't think you should be in, you find yourself defending your significant other; that's how it's always been with me and Oak Cliff.

Before my sophomore year at Kimball, I started seeing the relationship with my hood differently. During the summer, I had one of the most tumultuous moments of my life. I probably wasn't mentally prepared to go back to school, but we all know time waits for no one.

When I saw the sun disrespectfully break through the windows in my bedroom, and I heard my alarm clock yell, I knew summer vacation was over. I had to act like I had forgotten what I had experienced, so I could get into my school routine.

Once I got dressed, I stared at myself in the mirror. I had a noticeable scar that snuck out below my du-rag. It was a reminder of the incident, but the elders in church said, "I don't look like what I been through." It's good I didn't because I had been through a lot.

I took my wave cap off and started brushing my hair. Having 360° waves was crucial to the overall look, so I had to make sure I was right. I was using a brush with boar hair bristles my T-Jones got from a beauty supply store 'round the way. T-Jones, or T-Lady, was something we called our moms in Dallas. I still don't know one person who can tell me why, but that didn't matter.

I pulled the top off of the Royal Crown grease most of us had in our cribs back then and I put some on. I brushed some more because I had to make sure my waves got the proper attention they deserved. I had just gotten my hair cut a few days before by Cedric, the owner of Cedric B's Barbershop. My dad had been taking me and my brother there since we were younger, so every hair on my head was laying in formation.

My father gave me a gold herringbone that summer, so I had to put it on. It added to the allure of my outfit, and it was sitting perfectly under the collar of my brightly colored Polo shirt. My pants had so much Stay-Flo on 'em, they were almost able to stand up by themselves. And my shoes, bruh, don't even get me started.

I worked all summer at Minyard Food Store, or as we all called it, Minyards, just to start saving up enough to buy them. When summer vacation started after freshman year, I went to Red Bird Mall and those 7s sat high on the shelves like they were looking down on every other shoe. They were calling out to me like they were acquaintances I was running into, but didn't acknowledge.

"You really not gon' speak? You actin' real different," they said.

I begged my folks to get them, but I knew they didn't have any extra money to spend on shoes. Plus, they had to get some stuff for my brother Elijah, and my sister, Lexi. My brother was an introverted 13-year-old with a great sense of humor. My sister, Lexi, who was 12, was an ambitious girl who was always making random requests for things she said she needed. That's what made me start looking for ways to get my own money in the first place.

Those shoes served as my motivation when I didn't want to go to work. When I was finally able to purchase my dream shoes, it felt like I had accomplished something.

"You would've been happy if we got them J's for you, but you get a different feeling when you get it done yourself," Pops said when I brought the shoes home.

I never would've thought paying for my first pair of Jordans would've given me such a sense of pride, but Pops was right. You have a different sense of responsibility when it involves something you truly had ownership in. I was so careful with the shoes, going to school was the first time I wore them, outside of trying them on in the store and around the house.

As for school, it wasn't my favorite thing. Even though I was dyslexic, I didn't have any problems with it, either. It was something I had to deal with, so I didn't fight it. As the morning progressed, I made an effort to focus on how I looked. I figured if I did, I would have less opportunities to think about what happened that summer.

When my morning routine was complete, I was ready to go. My parents were still getting ready for work while they made sure my brother and sister were good. I kissed Mom on the cheek, gave Pops our secret handshake, and hugged my siblings before I headed out of the door to walk to school.

"Please be careful," my mom requested.

We lived a few blocks away from my school, so telling a 16-year-old to be careful may seem like a bit much, but it wasn't. After what happened, Mama feared for my safety whenever I left the house. If she could've, she would've taken me everywhere I needed to go, but neither of my parents were able to do that. I didn't mind having the space to be alone with my thoughts for a little while, though.

Once I got outside, I looked at our crib for a little bit. We lived in an older home that my dad inherited from my grandparents after they passed. Most people, especially in our neighborhood, didn't have houses gifted to them, so we knew we were blessed.

We'd been living there as long as I could remember, since both of my father's parents passed away when I was around two. We never had any major issues and, for the most part, we felt safe whenever we were at home. The fear my mom had was something new, though. It wasn't there before that summer, but it arose after tragedy grabbed me by the arm and didn't want to let go.

The day my life changed seemed like it was going to be another regular day. Nothing extraordinary had happened, and I was cool with that. I was walking with my best friend, RaShawn, not too far away from our neighborhood. We had just finished watching our boys play basketball at the park.

As we were about to leave, two people snuck up on us. They demanded we empty our pockets. None of the people around us made a single move to help us. In fact, they ran off as if we weren't all just joking around together minutes before.

When the demand came, I threw the $20 I had in my pocket, but RaShawn wasn't so quick to give in.

"Bruh, let us make it to the crib," he said, his voice calm, but firm.

RaShawn usually spoke confidently, but that time, his words were more of a plea.

"Ain't nobody makin' no deals wit' you. I know you got bread, so give it up," one of them yelled.

RaShawn turned his back. To them, that was the ultimate sign of disrespect. RaShawn barely took three steps before one of the guys pulled out a gun. Before I could react, shots rang out. RaShawn froze. He looked like he wanted to move, but his body wouldn't cooperate because he had been hit multiple times.

RaShawn stumbled and tried to apply pressure to his wounds, but his actions didn't last long. He didn't have the strength to do anything, so the two guys just stood there, watching as his life slipped away. I ran toward them, not knowing what I was going to do.

One of the guys introduced the same gun used against RaShawn to my forehead, knocking me to the ground. As I tried to get up, I saw them reaching into RaShawn's pockets, taking whatever they could find.

"That's it? You risked it all for that?" One of them asked, leaning over RaShawn.

They enjoyed our pain, but we couldn't do anything about it.

"It didn't even have to be like this, but folks gotta make better decisions," one of them added.

The distance between us grew as they eventually walked off. My vision started to blur, but I kept trying to crawl over to RaShawn, hoping to help somehow. Before I could reach him, I passed out.

When I woke up, I was lying in a hospital bed.

"Where's RaShawn?" I managed to choke out, my voice hoarse.

"Please calm down," a nurse said in a calm and soothing voice.

"Where's my friend?" I asked again.

She gave me a look — the kind of look that told me everything before she spoke.

"I'm sorry young man, your friend didn't make it," she said gently.

I grabbed the pillow beneath me and screamed into it. I couldn't believe RaShawn was gone. The guys who took his life thought his life was worth less than the little bit of money they stole from him. It hurt knowing how little they valued life.

Every time I closed my eyes, I saw RaShawn's final moments replay in my mind. The nurse, seeing I couldn't calm down, placed a hand on my shoulder.

"I'm going to give you some time alone. Is that okay?" She asked, her voice full of empathy.

I nodded, but I was far from okay. When my family eventually came in with RaShawn's parents, one of the worst things I'd ever seen, was the look of hurt on their faces. Mr. and Mrs. Henderson were carrying the weight of losing their son, and it was more than I could bear.

"Are you okay?" Mrs. Henderson asked, her voice trembling.

"Yes, ma'am. I'm so sorry. We were about to come home, I promise. I tried to protect RaShawn and I thought everything was gonna be alright. Please forgive me."

I felt guilty for being able to talk, breathe, or even exist when the same couldn't be said for RaShawn. Mr. and Mrs. Henderson looked at my parents as if asking permission before they walked over to me.

"There is no need to apologize," Mr. Henderson said, his voice steady, but heavy. "You did nothing wrong, but I'm sorry you witnessed what you did. We'll be praying for you and your family for the rest of our days. Damian, this neighborhood may take a lot from you, but never let it take away your hope."

They said I didn't do anything wrong, but that wasn't true. We all do something wrong. RaShawn and I were no exceptions. I never thought anything we did up to that point would lead to his life being stolen, but it did.

I could feel the strength of his parents in their grip as the hugged me, but I also felt their pain and anxiety. They talked with my family for a while before they left, but their voices were low, like whispers in a room where words couldn't carry the weight they needed to. The moment they left, everything changed.

Outside of my room, I heard anguished cries that sent unnerving chills through me. The sound of their pain still haunts me. I wished I could've done something to take it away, but all I could offer was prayer. So, I did what they asked and tried my best to press forward while keeping RaShawn's memory alive.

Moving forward wasn't easy. RaShawn wasn't just my friend, he was my brother. Seeing his life ripped away from him hurt, but I didn't let myself grieve. Even at his funeral, I held my emotions inside because I didn't know how to release them. I wouldn't even talk to my family about how I was feeling, and I know that must've worried them.

Every day, my mom asked me how I was doing, but I always avoided talking to her about how hard it was for me to cope with the loss of my friend. My emotions built up like pressure in a bottle, and I knew it was only a matter of time before that bottle exploded. In a way, it did when I walked to school for the first time since RaShawn passed. I started hearing his voice in my head.

"D, can you believe we going to the 10th grade? I remember when we first met in kindergarten. That big kid tried to take my Chili Cheese Fritos at lunch, and you stood in between me and him like you knew me. You became my brother right then, 'cause any kid who's willing to fight for my Fritos is family, you feel me? You still got me, right?"

Hearing him hit me like a ton of bricks. I lost it for the first time since I'd heard the news he was gone. I stopped walking because my feet felt like they were stuck in the sidewalk. My legs refused to move, and my eyes started leaking uncontrollably.

I sat down on the sidewalk, unable to move. After a few minutes, I looked up to see an old Chevy Caprice rolling toward me. I could hear "I Love School" playing. It was the song they always played on the Skip Murphy & Company Morning Show on K104.

If you grew up in Oak Cliff in the '90s, that song was part of your routine, and if you didn't hear it, it was like the rhythm of the day would be off. Even though it was a little crazy hearing it right then, somehow it felt like I was supposed to—like a sign the world was still turning, even though mine had stopped.

"You good?" The driver asked as he turned the radio down.

It was Sterling. He was a year or two older than me, but we were in the same English class freshman year.

"Yeah, I'm a'ight," I said.

"Nah, for real, you good?" He asked again.

He didn't know what I was going through, but he could tell something was wrong. He waited for me to say something, but I couldn't bring myself to open up.

"Yeah," I told him, lying once again.

"A'ight then. Don't scuff up them J's sittin' on the ground," he joked, nodding at the shoes I worked so hard to get.

I didn't speak again, and neither did he. He turned the radio back up and drove off. I was so afraid to show the pain I was carrying, I chose not to be honest with someone who offered me an ear.

Whoever started the "emotions equal weakness" narrative, created a lie we've been passing down for far too long. I hoped as I grew, I would be able to change the way we, as Black men, looked at our emotions, but I didn't know if that was realistic.

I wish I had a better grip on my life at that age, but I was still a kid. I didn't have the ability to understand what I was going through. So, instead of doing what was been best for me, I continued walking to school as if everything was okay.

When I got there, I looked around like it was my first day all over again. RaShawn and I thought 10th grade would be our year, but we never thought the hood would take one of us in the summer. Whenever someone from Oak Cliff was killed, we always said, "The hood got 'em."

The "hood" wasn't just our neighborhood. It was the mentality that consumed it—the negativity that sometimes acted like a villain in a horror movie. It moved slowly at times, fast at others, but if you were its target, it would find a way to get you.

2

———

Life was feeling pointless. My surroundings made it seem like no matter what I did, the hood would get me just when I was on the edge of doing something great.

I put a fake smile on my face so I could make it to through the first day of school.

"Okay, D, I see you! Them shoes are dope," a girl said.

"Already!" I replied.

For us, "already" was a word that did everything we needed it to. It was a compliment, but also a response to one. It could be a question, a statement, or something in between. My reply showed her I appreciated her noticing me, but I already knew how good I looked.

"You a fool, D. I'll see you later, though. We need to talk," she said.

I acted like her compliment was nothing. If anyone else had said it, it would have been, but that was Kamaria. She was special, and I knew it when I met her in the third grade.

She and her mom moved to Oak Cliff in the second semester. I was sitting in Mrs. Armstrong's class, and to this day, I'm still thankful I had her as a teacher. She had an incredible ability to make every subject interesting, even the ones we didn't think we cared about. When the staff at the school said I needed to be in special ed, or take medication to help me focus, Mrs. Armstrong spoke up for me. She'd always say, "All children can be reached, it just depends on how far you're willing to stretch to get to them."

She celebrated every student's success and made us feel like we could achieve anything. When we failed, she helped us see the lesson in it and made sure we knew it was okay not to be perfect. She changed my life in many ways, and I'm grateful for her.

That day, Mrs. Armstrong called Kamaria to the front of the classroom to introduce herself. I was at my desk, quietly tapping out a beat with two pencils I bought from the machine at school. As she walked up, I switched from being the world's greatest music producer to the most prolific visual artist. My notebook came to life with characters as she got to where Mrs. Armstrong wanted her to be.

When she started speaking, her confidence shook me out of my seat.

"Hey, y'all. I'm Kamaria. It's Ka-mar-i-a. I play video games, I like to skate, and by the end of the year, I'll have the best grades in the class. I'm a cool girl and uh... well, I guess that's it."

Her intro was enough for Mrs. Armstrong to let her go back to her seat. I wanted to get back to drawing, but I couldn't stop staring at her. She was moving in slow motion — just like one of those cliché scenes in a romantic comedy I probably only knew about because my mom used to convince my dad to rent them from Blockbuster all the time.

She had long, beaded braids that swung from side to side, clicking with every step she took. I thought nobody noticed me watching her, but RaShawn did.

"I been your best friend for like a thousand years. I know you think she cute."

He wasn't wrong — and during lunch, he decided to give me two options.

"D, you can talk to her, or we gotta play a game," he said.

"What kinda game?"

"If you don't go talk, we gotta play Letter B or Open Chest," he said.

Letter B and Open Chest were two games that were common in

my hood. Letter B made you pay attention to every word you said. If any of your words started with B, everybody playing got to hit you — until you said, "Letter B."

With Open Chest, you had to keep your arm over your chest like you were saying the Pledge of Allegiance, to protect yourself. If you forgot, your friends would hit you in the chest — hard — just to remind you to stay alert.Both games were a little too violent for eight- or nine-year-olds, but that's how we grew up.

As nervous as I was about talking to Kamaria, I knew the worst that could happen was getting embarrassed. That was way better than giving my boy a free shot to hit me in front of everybody.

"Hey, Kamaria, I'm Damian..."

"And you were staring at me in class when I had to talk, right?"

"Oh, you saw that?"

"My mama said, 'You won't know somebody's staring at you unless you're lookin' at them,' I guess she was right," she told me.

I figured she was saying she only knew I was staring because she was staring too. That thought had me Moonwalking inside my mind. Of course, I couldn't let her know that.

After school, I asked her if she wanted to walk to 6-12 with me and RaShawn. 6-12 was a convenience store close to Henderson. The name tells you it was trying to be like another numbered store, but we loved it anyway. So, as soon as that 3:00 bell rang, we took off running.

RaShawn and I went there so often, I already knew I wanted that lemon-lime salt that came in the green and yellow container. It probably wasn't even candy, but it was my thing. RaShawn loved that bootleg Kool-Aid powder that came with a candy stick you dipped in it.

"That's what y'all gonna eat?" Kamaria asked.

"Yeah," RaShawn said.

"I bet you don't even know what flavor that stuff is."

"I do too know what flavor this is," RaShawn shot back.

"What?" Kamaria wondered.

RaShawn looked down at the package, squinting like he was about to make a discovery.

"This is red," he said proudly.

"Red ain't a flavor," Kamaria told him.

"I don't know where you from, but red is the best flavor."

She tried to keep a straight face, but it didn't last. RaShawn was good at making people laugh. When she let out a little giggle, our friendship officially started. As the years passed, that friendship kept evolving, and when RaShawn was taken away, Kamaria was the first person to show up at my place to check on me.

I still didn't know how to express my pain, so when she tried to talk about it, I mostly stayed silent. Somehow, she was able to understand what I was going through. So, when school started again, she was the person I looked forward to seeing the most.

After she complimented me earlier in the day, I kept looking for her, but she was nowhere to be found. By the end of the day, I had given up on seeing her, but that's when I heard her voice again.

"Damian Roberts. What's up?"

"Hey, Kamaria. I've been looking for you," I said.

"How was the rest of your day?" She asked.

"I kept looking around for RaShawn. My bro didn't deserve to go out like that."

"You're right. He didn't deserve that... nobody does," she said, her voice softening.

I could feel the weight of everything hitting me. I knew it was only a matter of time before I broke down, and so did she. She knew other guys would clown me if they saw me crying, so she told me to give her a hug and put my head on her shoulder.

I don't know why my pain broke free then, but it did. It was bad enough I was crying, but doing it in front of Kamaria — in public — made it worse.

"My bad," I muttered, pulling away and wiping my face.

"Knowing you, that's probably one of the few times you've cried since RaShawn's been gone."

"Yeah, but I don't want people thinking I'm soft," I admitted.

"D, you're too smart to be acting like this. You're really letting other people's opinions control you so much you're afraid to mourn the loss of your best friend? You can't keep acting like everything's fine when we both know it's not."

"I don't know how to let it go," I told her.

"You don't need to let it go, you just have to keep moving," she said.

Kamaria grabbed my hands and looked me dead in my eyes.

"I know you had big plans for the Kimball takeover with RaShawn. Now, you have to make even bigger moves for him. And I know I ain't as hyped as RaShawn was, but I got your back, now and forever, D."

I always heard people talk about how important it was to be friends, but as a man, that ain't really something we want to deal with. When we find a girl we want to be with, friendship is one of the last things on our minds. Well, it's one of the last things—until you find someone whose friendship means the world to you, even if it's not what you ultimately want. Kamaria was that girl, and she always had a way of making me see things differently.

School was emotionally rough those first few weeks, but she helped me make it. I'd sometimes find myself in class staring at a nearby desk, expecting to see RaShawn trying to "compare answers" on our assignments or cracking jokes about somebody's outfit.

"Bro, my T-Jones would've cussed me smooth out if I tried to step out the door with all them wrinkles." I imagined him saying.

Most of the time, I'd laugh out loud before catching myself. Usually, I'd apologize for the disruption, and they would keep teaching, but one day, I couldn't hold the laughter in. RaShawn's spirit took over my imagination—it felt like he was right there next to me.

"Dude must think them wrinkles are Pokémon, and he 'gotta catch 'em all' ..."

By that point, I was laughing so hard, tears rolled down my face.

"I know something must be going on inside your head, Damian," my teacher, Mr. Murphy, said.

"A'ye, he pro'ly just trippin' 'cause his homeboy died this summer.

Look at him—looks like he about to cry right now," one of my classmates said.

"Is that true, Damian?" Mr. Murphy asked.

"Nah, I ain't about to cry! They lyin' on me!" I blurted out.

"That's not what I was asking," Mr. Murphy said. "Did you recently lose your friend?"

I wanted to tell him even though I lost my homie, I was good, but I was tired of lying.

"Yes, sir," I said, lowering my head in shame.

"Class, we're gonna take a break from today's reading because an opportunity for a life lesson is in front of us."

The class groaned in disappointment, but Mr. Murphy didn't pay it any mind as he continued.

"It's sad how accustomed to death we are around here. Damian, what was your friend's name, and how old was he?"

"His name is... my bad, his name was RaShawn, and he had just turned 16."

"I'm sorry for your loss, I really am. What did your friend want to be?"

I instantly started to smile again.

"He was all over the place. One day he wanted to be a rapper, then he'd just flip the script and talk about how much he wished we had some money so we could start investing in the stock market, and I don't even know what that is."

"Your friend sounded like he was an intriguing and intelligent individual."

"Yeah, he was. He said he wanted to go to Paul Quinn or Prairie View 'cause his family went there, then, he acted like he hated school."

"I can guarantee he didn't hate school. More than likely, he was just bored because no teacher was challenging him and showing him they believed in his abilities. None of you will have that problem in my class, I promise you.

Mr. Murphy was a real one. After he finished talking to me, he used the rest of the time to ask if anyone else had experienced anything similar to what I had. All but a few people raised their hands.

"Do you all understand how sad it is that we've all had to deal with that?" Mr. Murphy asked.

"We?" Someone asked.

"Yeah, we. Unfortunately, we have early loss in common. When I was seven, I watched my cousin die from a stray bullet while we were playing outside. That day changed my life. And believe it or not, that's what this class is all about. Everyone who made history reached a day that changed them. See, we're not in this class, or in this world, to just learn about history. We are all here to make history."

And just like that, as if our lives were part of some kind of movie, the bell rang right when he finished speaking. I was about to step out of the classroom when Mr. Murphy motioned for me to stay back for a minute.

"Again, I want to say how sorry I am for the loss of your friend. I recommend you and your family seek a professional to talk to."

"I hear ya, but talkin' to folks ain't really what we do around here."

"That's true, but let me say something. What we've seen has caused us to have PTSD. We have nightmares, we're nervous, and we carry guilt about not being able to save those we care about. Don't let your view of 'being a man' cause you to sacrifice your own mental health."

I took what Mr. Murphy said to me and I held it closely as I silently left the room. I probably would have never compared what I had seen and gone through to someone who had been in an actual war, but what we dealt with was a war of its own. We all tried our best to dodge bullets while avoiding the landmine-like obstacles scattered all over our streets. Admittedly, I did have post-traumatic stress disorder, but I wasn't sure if I'd ever be brave enough to do anything about it.

After Mr. Murphy's class, I eventually told my parents I wanted to go to therapy. They both questioned how we could afford something extra when they could barely take care of our necessities. Because of that, I tried to get some extra hours at Minyards to not only help with household expenses, but also so I could seek some emotional help.

When I went to my next shift, I was feeling good, but the vibes of my co-workers in the store didn't match mine. At first, I wasn't worried about a few folks ignoring me, but when half of my shift went by and nobody had anyone spoken, I had to say something.

"What's up?" I asked one of my co-workers.

"You didn't hear? Cordae died last night," she replied.

I shook my head in disbelief. I had just worked a shift with him the week before. It didn't make any sense, but death doesn't ask our permission, nor does it ask about our desired preferences.

When my shift was over, I stayed outside for a minute. I was supposed to get on the DART bus that passed in front of the store, but I didn't feel like it. When I saw that yellow and white bus pass by, I couldn't do anything but look inside and focus on the people. My mind started imagining what each one of their lives was like.

A lot of times, people in the hood aren't bad, we're just put in bad situations. I didn't recognize anybody on that bus. I didn't know what they had gone through, or why their lives were the way they were. All I knew was, they were in Oak Cliff, and that was enough to make me feel connected to all of them.

I left the store parking lot and for some reason, I found myself walking down the street to Kiest Park. Kiest Park was a bunch of parks, fields, courts, and playgrounds all together in one area. I didn't know where I wanted to go, but I had plenty of options. I stopped and sat on one of the swings.

"Man, it just don't stop," a voice said.

I didn't see anyone. I figured I was tripping, but then I heard it again. I looked up and saw Rashawn standing right in front of me.

"I had to check on you. I know you've been down since you heard about Cordae. It's wild out here," he told me.

"Why does it keep happening?" I asked.

"You know how it is, you either gettin' somebody, or you the one gettin' got. You gotta be on your toes at all times."

Within seconds, it started getting harder to breathe, and I felt lightheaded. My vision blurred, and I thought I was about to pass out.

"Say, what up wit' you?" A stranger asked.

"I just ain't feeling good," I replied, moving slowly.

"You can have this, if you want," he said, holding a bottle of water.

It's not the smartest idea to take drinks from strangers, but I was desperate. I nodded silently as a way to say "thank you."

"You good? You got a way to get back to your crib?" He asked.

"Yeah. The buses still run for a little, so I'm good," I said.

That was all he needed to hear before he walked off. As soon as he left, RaShawn came back to finish our conversation.

"It ain't all bad, is it?" He asked.

"That's the crazy thing. You just as likely to see a random person try to help, as you are to see somebody trippin' 'cause they think you looked at them wrong," I said, shaking my head.

"It's the dichotomy of the hood, my boy," RaShwan told me.

I just started laughing.

"I know you weren't dumb, but I ain't ever heard you say dichotomy."

"You use words based on the conversation you havin'. We weren't having no conversations worthy of four-syllable words. I had to save that kinda stuff for when I was tryin' to impress a girl."

"Already."

That moment of joy faded and RaShawn left me alone in the park. I soon headed to another bus stop, knowing without a phone, my parents would be worried. By the time I made it home, I was worn out.

My mom stepped into the room when I did.

"Where have you been?" She asked.

"I was just at the park. Had to clear my head."

"That should've been easy 'cause ain't nothin' in there," Lexi yelled from the couch.

We had our fun, but then, my parents sent my brother and sister to another room.

"Why'd you go, Damian?" Mama asked, her voice serious.

That's when I finally started to explain what happened to Cordae. Mama was already on edge because of RaShawn, but hearing about Cordae pushed her to another level. She said she wanted me to start going to school and come straight home. She even wanted me to quit work, even though the recent losses had anything to do with my job.

"I know you want what's best for him, but he ain't do nothin' wrong, He can't live if you keep him locked up," Pops said.

"I'm not trying to lock him up, I just don't want anything to happen to him," Mama continued.

"I don't, either, but he's not a baby anymore. D is almost grown. He got a job, he probably talkin' to some girl we don't know about, and...he's living, babe. We can't shelter the boy 'cause we scared."

They were arguing over me, but it almost felt like I needed to "stay out of grown folks business." Then, they pulled me in.

"Damian, what's really going on in your head?" Mama asked.

I questioned if I wanted to say anything. I saw my father clown his friends when they showed emotions. I wasn't ready to deal with that, but I closed my eyes and decided to let my words go free.

"I love and hate this place. When it's good, ain't nothin' like it. When it's bad, it makes me wish I wasn't here. When folks ask me where I'm from, that Cliff pride comes out, though. I stick out my chest and tell 'em I'm from O'Cliff. If they're not from here, they be like, 'I heard about that place,' and I can tell by their face what they mean. They think it's dangerous, and everyone here is a dumb thug. I'm tired of that. Plus, if we all love our hood so much, how come we don't love the people who live in it?"

My words were really affecting my parents, especially my dad. Mama didn't grow up in Oak Cliff, but Pops grew up in the same house we were living in. So, the neighborhood meant more to him.

As far back as I could remember, he used to tell me stories about him shopping at Red Bird and Wynnewood, or how he went to Carter, Kimball, and South Oak Cliff (SOC) football games with his friends. His stories taught me the names of streets like Illinois, Hampton, Singleton, and Zang before I had an idea of where any of them were. Me questioning the people in his hood hit him differently.

"You think we don't love each other?" He asked.

"We can't say we love each other when we're killing each other every day. If that's love, I don't need no love in my life," I replied.

My mom walked over to me and put her arms around me. She started crying, and when I saw that, I followed suit.

"Boy, stop all that crying. Ain't nothing happened to you. You ain't gotta be out on these streets working like I had to when I was your age. You too soft, that's the problem. You couldn't make it back in my day," Pops told me as he pulled me away from my mom.

I knew the same thing he was doing to me had been done to him by my granddad. He was just passing on what he learned.

"D, can you go to the kitchen and get something to drink, or something to snack on?" My mother asked.

She wasn't worried if I actually wanted anything, she just wanted to reset the energy. It was her way of controlling the environment without having to confront my dad and have him feel emasculated.

I went into the kitchen and started thinking about what it had to be like for Pops growing up. He grew up during the civil rights era. So, he had to deal with segregation, as well as forced integration. Being forced into an environment where people don't like you would be hard for an adult, so navigating it as a child had to be impossible.

At some point, he had to get so tired of being hurt, he wanted to cry, but his father didn't give him that option. At the same time, he probably created a safe where he stored all of the emotions he, or his father, deemed as being too soft to release into the world. Eventually, he probably forgot how to retrieve those emotions from the safe, and later, he no longer knew they existed. At least, that's how it seemed.

When I went to my room that night, Elijah knocked on my door with a serious look on his face before he walked over.

"Why was Pops acting like that?"

For a second, I didn't want to say anything that would make him view Pops differently. Then, I realized he would need to know how Pops was because he'd soon be getting the same treatment as me.

"He was actin' like that 'cause I was crying," I told him.

"I know, but why?"

"As you get older, you'll see how unfair the world can be. I'm 16 years old. This ain't supposed to be how life is. I'm hurt, Elijah. I was crying because I'm hurt, and sometimes folks just get tired of being hurt."

"I'm sorry you lost those people. I know RaShawn was like a brother to you, and I know if I lost you…"

He stopped himself right there.

"Don't worry, I'm gonna do my best to be around to annoy you for a long time," I told him.

"You better," he said as he ran out of my room.

As the night passed, I was hoping Pops would talk to me about what happened, but he didn't seem to think that was necessary. That ego of his was something I hoped wasn't passed down to me, nor was it something I would allow to be passed down to any future kids of mine.

"Damian, are you ok?" Mama asked before she went to bed.

"I'm kinda hurt about the losses and Pops, but I'll be a'ight."

"Your dad is stubborn, but you're actually breaking him down."

"It don't seem like it."

"That's because you don't know where he started. Your father grew up in a different time, so he doesn't deal with emotions well. We discussed that after you left, so I hope you can forgive him. Be patient. I know he'll be able to open up to you one day," she said.

"Okay."

"And I know losing friends is hard. RaShawn was basically one of my kids. He was over here just as much as you, eating all of our food."

"Yeah, he told me he always felt safe over here."

"That's so sweet. I really love and miss that kid."

Mama had the power to make you feel like it was all good, even when it wasn't. I was still in pain, but I was able to get a decent night's rest thanks to the little talks I had with her and Elijah.

When I got up the next morning, everybody was already eating.

"Hey Pops, can I speak to you in the living room?" I asked.

We all have moments when we have to confront our parents. This conversation was the first of many.

"This ol' school way of thinking ain't it. I know you want me and Elijah to be the best men we can be, but our generation ain't like yours. My closest friend was killed in front of me, and I just lost a co-worker who was younger than me. I'm a teenager, and that stuff hurts. So, yeah I cried yesterday, and I'm pro'ly gonna have more tears if this stuff keeps happening. I'm gonna need a hug from Mama to let me know I'm not alone, and I'm gonna need hugs from you, too. I know your dad ain't hug you, or tell you he loved you, but we need to be different. And it ain't just about me—you should be able to cry when stuff hurts you, too."

It took a few seconds before he responded.

"I would've never said anything like that to my father, but I should have. Y'all are smarter and more in touch with your emotions than we were. I admire you for that, but if you want me to grow, I need patience. Now, I have to say something else I wish my father would have said to me. I'm sorry."

His apology was a pleasant surprise.

"There are times when I'm dealing with stuff, and a hug from your mom is what keeps me sane, so I knew what you were dealing with. I didn't know how I was gonna bring it up to you today, but I had all intentions of doin' it. I'm glad you were man enough to do what I wasn't able to," he continued.

Pops was smart, so I know he phrased his last sentence that way on purpose. It was his way of acknowledging he heard everything I had to say and understood that "being a man" wasn't gonna be exactly the same for me as it was for him.

"Thank you, Pops," I said as I tried to shake his hand.

He pushed my hand away and pulled me in for a hug. All I could do was smile. My father didn't know how much his words and that hug meant to me—or maybe he did, and that's exactly why he did it.

3

———————

My mindset was a little different after spending time with my dad that morning. I left the house feeling like something had changed, even though I didn't know if it actually had. When I got to school, I headed to the cafeteria to grab some breakfast. I had already eaten at home, but I was just extra hungry. I guess serious parental conversations boost your metabolism in the morning or something. I think that's how science works.

One of the first faces I saw after I got my food was Kamaria.

"So, why are you here so early? Out of all the years I've known you, your mama ain't never let you come to school without eating. Mrs. Roberts don't play that."

"Naw, she shol' don't. And you right, I ate before I left the house. I just needed a lil' more before class started. Anyway, how are you?"

"I'm good, I was just up late last night studying for this test I got later on today," she told me.

"I know you got it, so don't trip."

"Thanks. I hope you're right, 'cause I can't have nothin' bring my grades down. I gotta make sure every college I apply to is begging me to go there."

"You know they will. Anyway, guess what happened."

"What?" She asked, leaning in.

I told her about how bad I felt after finding out about Cordae, and how I saw RaShawn at the park. Then, I told her about how my dad stopped me from hugging my mom.

"Dang! I'm sorry about your friend. And I'm also sorry about how your dad acted."

"Thank you, but I can't leave out what else he did."

"What did he do?"

"Yo... he actually apologized to me."

She was just as shocked to hear about him apologizing as I was to receive it. Back in those days, parents didn't really admit to messing up. I guess they wanted us to believe they had everything together, even though we knew they didn't.

We went on to give my dad his props for doing something so unusual. By that time, the bell for first period rang and we both started heading to class. We were at opposite ends of the hallway when Kamaria suddenly ran back over to me.

"You're already making a difference in your family, Damian. Who knows how much that talk y'all had will impact your dad? I just wanted to let you know I'm proud of you for not being scared to speak your mind."

When she spoke, she looked me directly in my eyes, so I knew she meant it. It could've just been wishful thinking, but it felt like she had more to say to me than she actually did. I had absolutely no proof of that—it was just a feeling.

She didn't even give me a chance to say anything back before she ran off. So, I spent the first few minutes of class trying to convince myself I wasn't tripping.

"What was that about? That wasn't just a regular compliment, right?" I asked myself.

I could've spent all of first period trying to figure out what just happened, but my mind wouldn't let me. Instead, I focused on the lesson my teacher was trying to bestow upon us. It almost felt like a switch inside my brain was flipped and I was able to see it was time to live up to my potential.

Actually, a better description would be—it was like I heard the voice of God telling me to straighten up. That was something I couldn't ignore, even if I wanted to. Don't get it twisted, though—just because I heard it was time to straighten up didn't mean I magically knew the answers to every question on my tests or assignments, nor did it make my dyslexia disappear. I still had to work; I was just finally willing to actually do it.

Over the next few weeks, I went from barely getting C's on my tests and assignments to expecting nothing less than A's. A lot of my teachers noticed the difference and started asking me what changed. I just told them I was finally starting to see life differently. I was changing for me, but deep down, I hoped Kamaria would notice, too.

One day, she let me know she did.

"D, I see you gettin' all A's and stuff. You really doin' your thing!"

"Man, I 'preciate it, Kamaria."

"What made you start focusing on your work? I been trying to get you to do that for years."

"True, you have. The change started 'cause it finally clicked in my head. I can't really make things better for everyone around me if I ain't doin' better, you feel me? Plus, I been tellin' you—school ain't even that hard, I just hadn't really been tryin' like I know I'm supposed to."

The exact look she gave me when we had our conversation about my father apologizing came back again. This time, though, my heart started beating fast like it did when I first saw her. Something was going on, and I had to find out what.

"We're friends, right?" I asked.

"You already know we are, ain't no need to even ask me that."

"So, check this out. Do you still think we can't be more than that?"

Real talk, I was scared to hear what she was about to say, but this was one of those moments where I had to speak my mind.

"We've talked about this before. You know—"

"My bad for cuttin' you off, but you used to tell me you wouldn't talk to me like that 'cause I wasn't serious, 'cause I wasn't focused. But you said yourself—you see I'm different."

"Yeah, you've changed a little, but I don't know."

"Kamaria, I care about you, for real. But if you don't think I'm good enough for you, just let me know."

"D, don't do that. It ain't like that at all. You're like the best dude I know, and any girl would be lucky to be with you."

"Any girl but you, huh?"

"Damian. Please don't be like that."

"I ain't trying to be like nothin'. I just don't get how you say you lookin' for certain things in a dude, but you keep passin' me by. I'm right here, and ain't nobody gonna treat you like I will. You deserve everything, Kamaria. I just want you to give me a chance to be the guy who tries to give it all to you."

I regretted everything I said as soon as it came out. Not 'cause I didn't mean it, because I did, but because I didn't know if I should've put myself out there like that again.

"Damian, can I be honest with you?"

"Yeah," I said, my head dropping a little.

I already thought I knew what she was about to say, 'cause she'd said it so many times before. I was just trying to prepare myself to have my heart broken again.

She put her hand on my chin and gently lifted my head up.

"I want you to really hear what I'm about to say, Damian. Are you listening?"

"Yeah, you know I'm listening."

"Damian Tyrell Roberts, I love you, and I have for a long time. Me saying you're just my friend hasn't been true since... well, for a while."

I let out a huge sigh of relief. Then, my mind processed what she said.

"Did you just say you love me?"

"Yeah, I did. And if we're being real, I know you love me, too."

"I mean... I ain't gonna front, I do."

"Good!"

What did we really know about love at sixteen? Neither of us had lived long enough to truly understand it, but we knew the feelings we had for each other were real. So, we just assumed that had to be love.

"So, hol' up. If you love me, how come you shot me down every time I tried to holla at you?"

"That's exactly why," she said.

"What? You know that don't make no sense, right?"

She laughed the cutest laugh I ever heard. Well, maybe it had always been that cute, but it just sounded different since I knew she loved me.

"Yeah, I know it don't really make sense, but it's the truth."

"So, you shot me down 'cause you love me, but you talked to them other dudes 'cause you didn't love them?"

When I said it out loud, even she looked confused for a second, but then she continued explaining.

"Damian, if something happened when I was with somebody else —relationship wise—I would've been surprised. Since I didn't really care if it worked out or not, I could just move on. But with you, I forced myself to turn you down every time because I was scared if anything ever went wrong, I would lose you forever. And I don't want that," she told me.

"You mean that?"

"Yeah, I do."

"So, what's different now?"

"I told you—you're different. Plus, I can't hold onto that fear forever."

"What if...."

"I don't wanna worry about the 'what if' anymore, Damian. I just wanna see what happens. I mean, you're already my best friend. I've been around you long enough to know what kind of person you are, and I know you already love me. I really don't think you'll do anything to hurt me, so I'm gonna trust you with my heart."

When she said that, the time to pretend I wasn't hyped was over with. After all the years I'd been hoping she'd give me a chance, out of nowhere, she finally did.

"So, does that mean we're together-together?" I asked.

I felt dumb asking it, but I didn't care. I just needed to know if

Kamaria was really saying after all those years, she was finally ready to be my girlfriend.

"I mean… if that's what you want, then that's what it is," she said.

It was funny how she acted like she had given me the power to make the decision about our relationship status when she knew I had been waiting on her for years.

"Well, I guess I can tell all those other girls to back up off me 'cause I'm taken."

"Yeah, let 'em know," she said with a smile.

"A'ight, babe, I'll tell 'em."

I don't even know why I felt the urge to call her "babe," but I did. I almost thought she'd get mad, but she didn't.

"Dang, you got comfortable real quick, huh?" She asked, grabbing my hand.

"Kamaria, I don't think you get it. I've been waiting since we were kids for you to say you'd be with me, so yeah, I'm comfortable."

"Well, that's good. I like it—and it feels good to hear you call me that. Just promise me something, Damian."

"What's up?"

"Promise you're always gonna keep it 100 with me, and that we'll always be friends."

"I got you, for real," I told her.

"And I know we just said we're gonna be together, but I gotta tell you something that might change how you think about being in a relationship with me."

She had me nervous, but whatever she had to tell me, I was ready.

"You know how everybody talkin' 'bout how they're doing all this stuff with whoever they're with?"

"I think I know what you're talkin' about."

"Well, that ain't me. I ain't never been with nobody like that, and I ain't tryin' to do that right now."

"That ain't no problem."

"No, Damian, I need to make sure you understand what I'm sayin'. We can hold hands, hug, and kiss and stuff, but that's it. I can't be out here doin' things like that with anybody without knowing if they're the one I'm gonna be with for real. Even with you, you get me?"

"I hear you."

"So, now that you know where I stand, and what I'm looking for, do you still wanna be with me?" She asked.

Kamaria asked me like she really thought there was a chance I was going to change my mind. Don't get it twisted—I definitely was not expecting her to say what she said, especially so soon after we had just agreed to officially be a couple. Hearing it didn't exactly feel great, either. I had been waiting forever to get into a relationship with her, and as soon as I finally moved past that hurdle, she told me I would have to keep waiting, this time, until she decided if I was "the one," before we could do anything.

She was waiting for my answer—waiting to see if I still wanted to be with her after getting that crucial piece of info. Part of me was like, "Nah, we ain't doin' that. There's too many females out there." The other part was like, "Bro, is you crazy? You been waitin' on this girl since you were a kid and now you ready to throw it all away? Were you waiting on her, or just trying to add to your body count? You can't hold off a little while to prove yourself to her?"

She needed to hear confirmation that I'd do right by her—so that's what I had to give.

"Look at you, Kamaria. You fine than a mug, I've always told you that. It shol' ain't gon' be easy, but if I gotta wait, then I gotta wait. I wanna be with you forever, and I want you to know for sure I'm the right one for you before you do anything you may regret later on."

Kamaria had always been more than just a cute girl I wanted to try and get so I could brag to my friends. I know it sounds wild, but even before she said I would have to wait on her, I had already pictured us being together—having a family like my folks did. Teenagers probably don't normally think like that, but I always felt different about her. When she said she'd be my girlfriend, it felt like I grew up a little.

4

———————

Being in a relationship with Kamaria helped me cope with some of life's difficulties. She didn't make bad things stop happening around me, but she always made sure I knew I could talk to her about whatever I was dealing with. In turn, I tried my best to be there for her, too. I wanted to protect her and make sure I did my part to keep her happy. I also had to step out of my comfort zone and start going places because she liked to go out way more than I did.

"You wanna go to Bronco Bowl this weekend?" I asked.

Bronco Bowl was an entertainment center, bowling alley, and arcade that would host all sorts of events.

"Didn't they close it down?" Kamaria wondered.

"I don't know if the bowling part is open, but they still have concerts and stuff there all the time."

"Last time I checked, they only had rock concerts. No offense if that's what you like, but that's not me."

"I ain't trying to see nothin' crazy. I just wanna spend some time with you."

"Aww, babe, that's sweet. Who's gonna be there?"

"I think Korn and Limp Bizkit," I told her.

If looks could kill, I would have been dead that day.

"Damian, I just said I don't wanna hear no rock. That stuff is too loud, and I can't ever understand what they're saying. That mess gives me a headache."

"True, but I ain't trying to go see them, either."

"So why you trying to go when they're performing?"

"Because Pharcyde gonna be there, too."

"I heard that name before, but I can't think of their songs."

"Yeah, I gotta take you out more. Pharcyde is one of the dopest groups out there. They sing that song that says, 'Can't keep running awaaaaaay...' You know that one. They play it everywhere."

"Oh, yeah. I don't know all the words, but I love that song. They play that all the time on 100.3, especially whenever I listen to Russ Parr."

"You ain't gotta know all the words to have fun," I told her.

"Cool. Wait... is your mom gonna let you stay out that late? And what day is the concert on?"

"Good questions. The concert is on Saturday, and I was gonna beg my mama to let me stay out."

"Oh, okay. I see you thinking ahead. I'll ask my mom if it's cool for me to go out, and I'll let you know. Don't trip if she tells me no, okay? You already know how she is."

"Yeah, I do. If she says you can't, I ain't trippin'. If I don't get to do nothin' but talk to you on the phone until we both get sleepy, I'll be happy with that. I ain't gonna be as happy as I would be if we can go to the concert, but I'll be happy."

What I said was sappy and corny, but I meant it. Kamaria always had that kind of impact on me, and when she said she'd be my girlfriend, I didn't have to hold anything back anymore. The thing about being myself is, not everybody liked me. For some reason, Kamaria's mom was one of those people.

I hadn't done anything for her to dislike me, but Kamaria always made it clear I wasn't one of her favorite people. As the weekend got closer, Kamaria told me when her mom found out she was trying to go somewhere with me, she told her she couldn't go.

"Why yo' mama don't like me?" I asked.

"She don't know the more mature you. She only knows about the D who wasn't serious about school."

"How can I change that?"

"You can start by talking to her on the phone."

"Yeah, but I don't know if she's really gonna know how for real I am over the phone."

"So that means you wanna meet her in person, right?" Kamaria asked.

Over the years, I'd seen Kamaria's mom plenty of times, but I never met her. I'd spoken to her in passing, but that was it. Kamaria never forced a conversation between us, and I wasn't pressing the issue, either. Since we were dating, things were different. I wanted to be with Kamaria for the long run, so even though the thought of meeting her mama scared me, it was something that had to be done.

"Yeah, set it up. I need to get in good with my future mother-in-law."

I must have been trippin' to say something like that, but it made Kamaria happy. I let her know I wanted to take them out to dinner, so we would all have a chance to talk. Plus, I've always liked to eat.

"Hey, I just thought of something," I said.

"Yeah, what's up?" Kamaria asked.

"Does your mom even know we're together?" I asked, even though I was scared to hear the answer.

When Kamaria stopped smiling, I already had an idea of what she was about to say.

"No, but..."

"You ain't gotta explain. I get it..."

No lie, I was in my feelings. I was ready to tune her out, but I told myself not to. If I wanted her to trust me, I had to trust her. If I wanted her to be real with me, I had to be man enough to at least hear her out.

"Chill out, Damian. Let me say what I was gonna say."

"My bad. Go 'head."

"All I was saying was that she doesn't know, but it ain't because of you. I just don't want her trying to convince me not to talk to you. Me and Mama get along most of the time, but I'd be ready to fight for my boo."

My defense dropped real quick. How could I be mad at her when she said things like that?

"Yeah, that makes sense," I told her.

We parted ways, and that evening, I had to do a little convincing for my parents to let me go. I was trying not to tell them I was going to meet Ms. Anderson because I knew they'd want to meet Kamaria, too. But in order for them to say yes, they had to know where I was going, and why.

"Oh, you goin' to meet your girl's mom?" My dad asked.

"Yes, sir."

"You ready for that?"

"I think so."

"Boy, it can't be no thinking. Either you are, or you're not."

"I am," I said confidently.

"Your dad's just giving you a hard time," my mom said. "If you and this little girl call yourselves going together, we need to meet her, too."

"Yeah, we gotta meet your lil' girlfriend, Damian," Lexi said joyfully.

Pops was ready to let me take the car, but Ma shut that down real quick.

"You only have a learner's permit, and you can't drive by yourself. We don't wanna give DPD no reasons to stop you. We need you to get back here safely. It might be best if we drove you," Mama said.

"Mom, I can't have y'all drive me over there. I'm sixteen, and that would be embarrassing. I'll just catch the bus like I planned on doing."

With that, I called Kamaria and let her know I was about to catch the bus to her house. Then, I finally headed out the door. It only took me a few minutes to make it to the bus stop, but it felt like it took forever for the DART bus to show up.

When the doors opened, the driver looked at me like he already knew I was on a mission. I paid my fare and nodded before taking a seat. The only open spot was next to a man who looked to be in his fifties or sixties. As soon as I sat down, he turned towards me and started talking.

"How you doin', young man?"

"I'm good, sir. How are you?"

"I'm okay, just makin' it back home after visiting my grandkids," he said.

"That's cool. I bet they enjoyed spending time with you."

"Yeah, they did, but I got more out of it than they did. My son and his wife got them all kinds of coloring books and games, so we just played and had fun. They told me I could've spent the night, but I didn't wanna be a burden."

"It sounds like they all love you. That's really good."

"Yeah, I have a good family. God is good."

"All the time," I said.

"Oh, you know about God? That's a good surprise."

"Yes, sir, I know about God. Why's that a surprise?" I wondered.

"Well, with all these killings and robberies and stuff y'all young folks be doing, sometimes I don't know if y'all even believe in Him."

He was right, and sometimes I would question if my peers believed in a higher power, too. For a moment, I thought about RaShawn again, and how all that time had passed since his life was taken. I never heard anything about a police report, and I was never questioned about anything, so I knew nothing ever happened to the people who committed the crime.

It was as though nothing ever happened. It reminded me of that scene at the end of "Boyz N The Hood" after Ricky's life was taken and Doughboy said, "Either they don't know, don't show, or don't care about what's going on in the hood." Thinking about that was bringing sadness to my heart, and I didn't want to bring that energy to Kamaria's house. So, I had to quickly get back into the conversation I was having with the gentleman sitting next to me.

"Yes, sir. I couldn't make it without God. I deal with too much not to be able to go to Him with my issues."

I had just met the man, but he looked at me like he felt proud.

"You remind me of my youngest boy," he said.

"Well, that's good, right?"

"Oh yeah, it is. My youngest graduated from South Oak Cliff and went off to school at Texas Southern University down in Houston. He's real smart and he's always loved going to church. We're all proud of him. You got mannerisms just like him. In this world, even if we're not connected by blood, we're still supposed to treat each other like family—especially us Black folks."

"Thank you, sir."

"You're welcome. Hey, if you don't mind me asking, where you headed this time of evening?"

Some people might've taken offense or thought he was being nosey, but I didn't take it that way. To me, it just felt like he was an older relative who wanted to check on me.

"Believe it or not, I'm going to meet my girlfriend's mother."

"Oooh, that's a big deal. But you seem kinda young for that."

"I'm sixteen, but I've been knowing this girl since I was about eight. I've been one of her closest friends all these years, but she finally agreed to be my girl."

"I see you, young buck. You better make sure you treat her right, okay? I don't want you to be one of these boys who gets with a girl just to see if you can, then try to get another one while you're still talking to the first. There's enough of that going on, and we need to get back to respecting our women. They go through enough as it is without us adding extra problems. We gotta treat them like the queens they are, you hear me?"

"Yes, sir."

"Hey, do you have a gift for them?"

I patted my pockets like I was looking for something, knowing there was nothing there.

"No, sir, I don't."

"Okay, my stop is next, and there's always this man selling flowers right by the bench. If you want some, I'll buy them for your lady and her mother."

"You would really do that for me?" I asked.

"I shol' will. I told you, you remind me of my son, so I gotta make sure you make a good first impression."

"Well, I appreciate it."

We sat in silence for a few seconds before the bus started slowing down at the next stop.

"Walk up to the front with me and just wait there. I know the driver, so I'll ask him to wait a minute or two."

I followed behind him, and before I knew it, he was handing me two bouquets of flowers. I thanked him, not just for the flowers, but for his kindness and conversation. He smiled and wished me well as the bus doors closed, and I headed back to my seat.

I sat down, closed my eyes, and tried to plan out everything I was gonna say when I met Ms. Anderson. The funny thing about making a plan is, life generally doesn't even recognize your plans exist. I'm pretty sure that's by God's design.

By the time I got off the bus and started walking to Kamaria's house, every word I thought I was gonna say decided to rebel against me. It's like they all lined up to leave my brain in a single file line. When I made it to Kamaria's door, I had no idea what I was gonna say.

My nerves started taking over. The anxiety hit so hard, I was almost shaking. All of my confidence disappeared, but I kept trying to convince myself it was gonna be a good night. I rang the doorbell and waited, praying Kamaria would answer before her mom did. Unfortunately, that ain't what happened.

"So, you must be Damian. Kamaria told me y'all datin' now."

She didn't even try to fake like she was happy to meet me. She didn't shake my hand or anything. As a matter of fact, she didn't even say hello. Still, I was determined to make a good impression.

"Yes, ma'am. It's nice to meet you. I got these for you and Kamaria," I said, handing her one of the bouquets.

"That's actually nice of you. I guess you can come in," she told me.

I had been friends with Kamaria most of my life, and I had never set foot inside her house. In fact, I didn't even know where she stayed until that day. Since it was my first time there, I tried to look around without seeming nosey.

They had pictures of who I guessed were family and friends all over. I also noticed the "Footprints in the Sand" poem hanging up. Everybody in the hood had that in their house back then. The message was how God never leaves us—even when we have convinced ourselves He has. It was a reminder I wasn't alone, and seeing it also made me compare their home to mine.

Their place was different from ours. At home, we only had a few family pictures. Our walls were mostly covered in posters, books, and random stuff my parents picked up from Black Images Bookstore in Wynnewood. One wasn't better than the other—we just had different vibes. Our homes had a lot in common, too.

Both homes needed work. That was normal in the hood. I noticed a small leak in their ceiling, and a faint brown water stain spreading around it. We had one just like it at our house. Their popcorn ceilings were fighting to hold up fans that had seen better days—same as ours. But like my folks, I figured Ms. Anderson was just thankful to have a roof over her head.

"Hey, D," Kamaria said, walking into the room.

"Hey. These are for," I said, handing her the other bouquet.

We wanted to hug, but we didn't.

"Thank you! They're beautiful, right, Mama?"

"Yeah, they are. Y'all can hug each other—it's alright. Ain't no telling what y'all be doing when I'm not around. We haven't had a real conversation, but I know how mannish you are," she said, looking right at me.

I almost laughed. Kamaria and I had joked before about her mom calling me mannish, so hearing it in real life was wild.

"I still don't know what that means," I whispered to Kamaria.

Kamaria couldn't hold back her laughter as well as I could, which earned us the side-eye from her mom.

"Ms. Anderson, can I use your phone to let my folks know I made it?"

"Yeah, the phone's hanging up on the wall in the kitchen."

Back then, we didn't have cell phones. Most houses had a landline phone—usually a corded green or yellow one hanging in the kitchen. I spent a few minutes talking to my mom on theirs before heading back to Kamaria and Ms. Anderson.

"Why are you here?" She asked, bluntly.

"Mom, why are you being like that?" Kamaria jumped in.

Her mom didn't answer—she just gave her that look. The one every Black kid knows not to argue with. I had to save my girl, so I jumped in quickly.

"Ms. Anderson, I'm here because me and Kamaria started talking. When I heard Kamaria introduce herself to the class back in the day, I knew she was special. I respect her, and I gotta respect you from jump—'cause she wouldn't be here without you. I want you to get to know me, so you can see I'm good for her."

I was pouring my heart out, but she wasn't buying it. She clicked her teeth, rolled her eyes, and sighed deeply before saying—

"That sounds good, but do you mean any of that, or you just saying something 'cause you think it'll sound good to me?"

"Yes, ma'am. I mean all of it," I said.

Kamaria had been quiet for most of the conversation, but she finally jumped in.

"And he's been my friend all these years, Mama. He's always made sure I was okay, no matter what I was going through," she said.

"Ms. Anderson, I can say a lot about your daughter, but more than anything, I just wanna keep being there for her, no matter what."

I did most of the talking. Ms. Anderson would ask a question here and there, but she wanted to see how I interacted with Kamaria— how we looked at each other, how we moved. She was seemingly reading our body language more than listening to our words.

After about an hour, I asked Ms. Anderson if I could take them both out to dinner—maybe Bronco Bowl.

"It's always some stuff happening at the Bronco Bowl. Y'all can go out, but I don't want you going over there. Come up with something else and ask me again when you figure it out," she said.

It sounded harsher than it really was.

"And what about him taking all of us out?" Kamaria asked.

"I ain't into all that fancy dinner stuff. You ain't gotta impress me, just take care of her. I don't wanna do dinner, but I'll get some lunch with y'all," she said.

"Okay, that'll work. Where you wanna go?" I asked.

"I'm down for Wingfield's. You know about them?" She asked.

"C'mon, Ms. Anderson, what kinda dude you think I am? How can I be from Oak Cliff and not know about Wingfield's? I go there all the time. Them burgers'll have you full all day, won't they?"

As crazy as it sounds, I think me showing love for Wingfield's won her over a little bit. Kamaria smiled at me and slowly reached for my hand. Ms. Anderson looked us both up and down when it happened, but she didn't say a word. That alone felt like progress.

I had to take the win and leave, so after confirming our lunch date at Wingfield's, I talked to Kamaria and her mom for a little while longer before heading back home. I was expecting things to be way worse than they were, but honestly, it all went well. My goal wasn't necessarily for Ms. Anderson to like me—it was just for her to be open to giving me a fair chance with Kamaria without trying to destroy what we had. And in my mind, that's exactly what happened —whether it was actually true or not.

5

————————

After meeting Ms. Anderson, I felt like hope wasn't trying to run and hide. In some ways, it was like I was starting to experience life for the first time. I was still in the same neighborhood, but I was able to focus less on what could go wrong, and more on the good I was seeing.

The negativity was still there, but it wasn't consuming me like it was before. Kamaria was helping to adjust my mindset, even when she wasn't trying to. She was a phenomenal person who didn't try to change me, but seeing how she was maneuvering through life made me want to be better.

She was always a top-tier student, and I admired that, but for a long time, I wasn't willing to put in the work to see if I could be like that, too. This was especially true when the forces of dyslexia were attacking my progress. Then, I started doing better—not because she told me to, but because I knew she had standards I had to meet if I wanted to have a chance with her, and I knew she wasn't going to accept any excuses from me. It takes a special person to demand change without ever having to say a word.

Even though I thought everything was good, one day Kamaria randomly asked me where I thought our relationship was going, and what I thought of her. Evidently, some of her friends were starting to put thoughts in her head.

"I wanted to be with you because you're my friend, you're smart, and you always want the best for me. The fact that you're fine, just makes it better. I want to be with you forever. This ain't just no high school thing, Kamaria. I really love you."

She wanted to say something, but she just hugged me. She buried her head into my chest for a few seconds, and when she looked at me, she had tears in her eyes.

"No other guy has ever genuinely expressed that to me. My father—from the first memory I have of him to the day he left us—never told me he loved me. My brother..."

"You have a brother? Out of all these years, how have I never known that?"

"You never knew because I never mentioned him to you. He got locked up before we moved because of some drug stuff. That's why my mom made us come out here. She wanted us to start over."

Then, as she continued with what she was saying, she asked me something that almost destroyed me.

"Why didn't they love me, Damian?"

I always thought about the pain I was holding onto, but that was the first time I felt the pain my girl was carrying. I talked to her about what I was going through, not knowing everything she was dealing with. She smiled through it all and kept her head held high, even when she was feeling low.

"All I know is, anybody who leaves you is missing out on a great person. Look at everything you've already accomplished at sixteen. Imagine what you'll do in the future. I know it hurts, but it's their loss. And you're gonna hear 'I love you' so much from me, you might get sick of it."

Right then, I had a much better understanding of what it meant to protect someone you care about. A big part of it is actually protecting their hearts and emotions. I tried my best to keep that thought at the forefront of my mind as our relationship grew.

While I thought about our relationship, and what we'd be able to do together, her focus was on making sure we were preparing for our separate futures, not just what we were doing as a couple.

"God puts greatness inside all of us, and we aren't gonna waste that. I want to get the best out of you, and I want you to get the best out of me. That can't happen if we don't take care of ourselves."

I remember telling my dad about our talk when I got home.

"Your girlfriend is making you better, and it's hard to find somebody that does that—especially at your age."

Pops was right, and his statement made me think about him and mom.

"How did y'all know you were supposed to be together?" I asked.

"I wish I could say she fell in love as soon as she saw me, but she just friend zoned me. My boys clowned me, and that peer pressure made me act like I didn't care about her. That's when I went through my 'dog phase.' You know what I mean?"

"Yeah, you was out there like Tupac," I said.

"Boy, I don't know nothin' 'bout no Tu-pac—or no one pac, either."

"Pops, you old, for real! Tupac is a rapper."

"You know I don't listen to that stuff. I'm into The Temptations and Anita Baker. Anyway, what you mean I was out there like Tupac?"

"Tupac had a song called, 'I get around.' That was you, huh?"

My father got quiet, so I didn't know if I had gone too far. The longer we sat in silence, the more I knew I had messed up. Then he looked me in my eyes and responded.

"I said my boys were clowning me about your mom, but they were talking bad because of how few chicks I had been with. Don't be stupid like I was and try to sleep with girls because you can. Don't treat her like you ain't worried about her leaving—because if that's how you act, you can't be upset if she does. Trust me, that's how I almost lost your mother."

"How did that make you feel?" I asked.

"Like the stupidest man on earth. She was fine, smart and she had no problem telling folks she was with me. With all of that, I acted like

I had to prove to my boys I wasn't in love with her. But the thing that almost made her leave me for good was the one time I stepped out on her."

"For real, Pops? Why?"

"I was stupid, that's the only reason. There will always be fine women, but ain't no amount of fine in the world worth givin' up who God got for you. I got with a girl while I was dating your mom, and she found out about it."

"Did she yell at you, or hit you or something?" I wondered.

"Nah. When I told her what I did, she didn't yell, hit me, she didn't even get mad. She asked, 'So, you were really willing to give up the rest of your life for a few minutes?' Then she said, 'I hope it was worth it, because when the love I have for a person leaves my heart, I change the lock and never let it back in.' Then, she walked away."

"How did y'all end up staying together?" I asked.

"I begged yo' mama like a Keith Sweat song. She wasn't tryin' to hear it, so I had to show her with my actions."

I learned why, even when having a major disagreement, Pops really listened to what Mama had to say. Even though the infidelity thing happened early on, he was making sure she knew he'd never be the person he was back then. He learned how valuable she was to him, and he learned from his mistake. My issue was nothing like his, but it helped me understand I needed to hear what Kamaria was telling me, instead of trying to interpret what I thought she meant.

After thinking about the conversation I had with Kamaria for about a week, I started to consider going to college a lot more. When I told my parents, they were extremely happy, but like most of the people in our area, my family didn't have a lot of money. Subconsciously, maybe that was one of the reasons I didn't really consider going to school before.

"Should we tell him?" My father asked my mom when I told them how I was feeling.

I couldn't hide the confusion on my face.

"We've been saving for the day you told us you wanted to go to school. We may not have enough to take you through all four years, but we have enough to give you a good start," Pops explained.

My folks had the ability to make miracles seem commonplace. Hearing they started a college savings account for me was surprising and it helped ease my mind. It actually got me more excited about possibly going to school. For some reason, it also made me think it was a good time to consider therapy again.

My parents were doing the best they could with me and my siblings, but at some point, we all had to do some things on our own. So, with no extra money in my pocket, I started calling around to see if I could find some kind of cheap therapy.

Fortunately, I found assistance within the community college system. When I told them I had no money, they told me their sessions were free because their students needed experience for their classes. They made sure to tell me I'd be speaking to a student—not a licensed therapist—but I needed the help, so I agreed.

Without getting permission from my parents, I set up my appointment with one of the students. I was nervous, but once I actually got into the room and started talking, I realized my healing was on the other side of that nervousness.

"What's going on?" The student asked.

The student was only a few years older than me, and I didn't know if he could actually help, but I continued.

"I'm here because sometimes, I just don't know how I'm gonna make it."

He wrote some things down in his little notebook before continuing.

"What do you mean by that?" He asked.

"Are you from here?"

"Not sure why you're asking, but yes, I'm from Dallas," he told me.

"I don't mean Dallas. I mean from here—from Oak Cliff."

"Oh, no, no, no. I'm from North Dallas," he said quickly.

The way he responded let me know exactly what he thought about my hood.

"How you said that shows me you think Oak Cliff is beneath you. You said it like it was an insult for me to even ask you that."

"I'm sorry, I didn't mean it like that."

"But the thing is, you did mean it like that. Some of y'all from other parts of Dallas really think you better than us."

I was getting mad, but I had to think about why I was there. I wasn't there to have a turf war. I was there because I needed help—and I couldn't let the pride of my hood block my healing.

"For real, why you think like that about my hood?" I asked.

"Growing up, I always heard things about Oak Cliff. I was told I had to be extra careful when I crossed certain parts of I-35 or I-20 because it was dangerous."

"I've been living in O'Cliff my whole life, and I've been to more funerals than weddings. Before my sophomore year, my best friend got killed. Not too long ago, my co-worker had his life taken at a football game. You scared 'cause of what you heard. Imagine if you had to see and live through the same stuff you saw on tv?"

He didn't answer my question, but he decided to ask me if I would be willing to write a letter to RaShawn, but I didn't understand why.

"That's dumb," I said, not caring how he took it.

"That may be true," he said calmly, "but are you willing to do it?"

I finally agreed. When I made it back home, I went to my room and started writing the letter.

"What up? I know things are better where you are. You ain't missing much on this side. I was able to stop all of the craziness we talked about before you were taken, but folks still be trippin' over lil' stuff. I'm glad you ain't gotta worry about none of that. I know you got that fresh white 'fit lookin' clean, don't you? You probably get a new pair of white Forces every day, huh? Knowing you, you done brushed your angel wings so much they got waves. You crazy, bruh."

I started crying, but I decided to keep writing.

"Just because you're not here, don't mean we don't think about you. Me and Kamaria talk about you a lot, for real. I hope Heaven treating you right, and when God tells me it's time to go, I hope I'll see you again.

A'ight, peace!"

When I finished, I put the pen down and read over what I had just written. I read it once, then I read it again. I just let my tears fall, moving only slightly to make sure they didn't wash away the words.

"What are you doing?" Elijah asked as he burst into my room.

"I just finished writing a letter for therapy," I blurted out.

"Bro, therapy ain't for us," he told me.

"Well, what we supposed to do when we have issues?" I asked.

My brother looked at me like he was disappointed, and ran out of the room. When he left, I folded up my letter and put it inside an envelope. Feeling better, I stood up and stretched. As I did, Elijah walked back into the room and handed me $20.

"I don't know how much therapy cost, but could you ask the doctor if he could talk to me, too?" He asked.

I could tell he had a lot on his mind, but I didn't know exactly what was bothering him.

"It's free, so you can take this back. And he's not a doctor—he's a student. What's going on with you, though?" I asked, not knowing if my brother would open up to me.

"I kinda be gettin' bullied and sometimes, I don't know if I wanna live anymore."

I didn't expect to hear my little brother say anything like that, so my heart sank. I never would've known Elijah felt like that—he always seemed so happy. I grabbed him and hugged him.

"I love you, bro. I hate you feel like you don't wanna be here."

In the 90s, we weren't emotionally expressive, so that was the first time I remember ever telling my brother I loved him. I could tell it made him feel awkward, but it also seemed like he needed to hear it.

"Tell me more about what's going on with you," I said.

"I don't think I'm smart. I don't like not feeling like I belong, and I'm tired! I think it'd be easier for everybody if I wasn't here."

"Bro, we're your family. We need to know when you're hurting so we can help. And since I'm sayin' that, let's go tell Ma and Pops about us both going to therapy," I continued.

With no hesitation, we interrupted our parents' evening routines.

While Elijah stood quietly behind me, I told them how we both were feeling. They knew about my situation, but I stressed the severity of what Elijah was dealing with. I told them about therapy, and I expected my father to give me a hard time about it again.

"If I haven't made you understand how important you are to this family, and to this world, then I've failed you as a father," Pops said.

"And I've failed you as a mother. There's no way in the world you should feel like that. If you need to talk to someone, other than us, I think we need to find a way to make that happen."

Mom stopped what she was saying and called Lexi into the room with us. She didn't continue until Lexi was standing right next to us.

"Let me be clear when I say this: I love all of you. I love each one of you differently, but equally. You all have changed our lives, and we're blessed you're here. We value you. We love you."

"That's cool, and I love you, too, but where is all this coming from?" Lexi asked.

Elijah could've let Mom explain why she was giving a speech about love, but he didn't.

"I feel like trash. People be dealing with a lot, and they get so stressed they don't think things will get better."

"Yeah, but we ain't really got nothing to be stressed about."

"You don't have nothing to be stressed about. We live in the same house, but my life ain't like yours. I don't wanna be here sometimes," Elijah said.

Lexi went over to Elijah and started crying. Soon after, we all started telling Elijah why we loved him, and what he meant to the family. He said we didn't have to go on about our love and adoration for him, but we did it anyway.

We always heard prayer was the only answer. I guess that's why so many people thought if they couldn't directly see God doing something for them, it wasn't supposed to happen.

"I'm kinda surprised to hear you say it's okay for us to get help, Mom. I thought you'd say we should just pray about it," I told her.

"God is in charge, but He will only help those who help themselves. You can ask God to help you, but you have to work for results, too. Prayer is the first step, but it's not the only one," she said.

The family's therapy conversation ended after that. I was happy knowing I wouldn't have to sneak around to try and get better. It also felt good knowing I'd be able to get some help for my brother. My sister—well, she just seemed happy we were happy.

"Thanks, Damian," my brother told me as he went to his room.

When he left, the phone rang, so I went to the kitchen and answered it. Kamaria was calling to invite me to a family get together her cousin was having that Saturday. I was nervous, but I agreed to go. Before I knew it, I went from talking to Kamaria on the phone to getting ready to meet up with her after my early shift on Saturday.

Her mom let me ride to the party with them, and every mile she drove, made me think I made a mistake. When we passed by K-Mart, Ms. Anderson told me we were almost there.

"Who's this?" People asked as soon as we made it.

"This is my boyfriend, Damian," Kamaria said, with no hesitation in her voice, as we went inside..

I was trying to figure out how to escape the awkwardness I was feeling when I noticed a few of Kamaria's family members playing Spades, which is more than just a game for a lot of us. When you tell somebody you're good at it, you better be ready to prove it—or be prepared for folks to clown you nonstop.

"I see you lookin', new guy. Game's almost over and they gonna need somebody to go against. You got a partner?" Someone asked.

"Yeah, me and Kamaria gon' run it," I said.

In all the years I'd known Kamaria, we never talked about Spades. I didn't even know if she'd ever seen anybody play, let alone played herself. When it was our turn, I just hoped for the best.

We were told the house rules as we sat down.

"Around here, we don't do that deuces-high stuff. We play straight Big Joker, Lil' Joker, you can only bid blind if you at least a hundred behind, and y'all can't bid less than four."

"We got it, Uncle Donald," Kamaria replied as the cards got shuffled, cut, and dealt.

When I looked at my hand, I couldn't hide my excitement. I had both Jokers, the Ace, King, Queen, nine, and ten of spades.

"How many books you got?" Kamaria's uncle asked.

I already had a number in mind, but I didn't wanna seem too eager, so I counted again.

"I got five," I said, being very conservative.

"Boy, you ain't got no five. You startin' wrong by biddin' more than you got. Don't be tryin' to show off for Kamaria," he said, laughing.

He was trying to get in my head, but nothing could've stopped me that hand. Kamaria and I ended up getting ten books, which meant we "set" our opponents. Starting off with negative points definitely wasn't how they thought it'd go.

By the end, they couldn't do anything but laugh at how bad they'd been beaten.

"Mar-Mar, you didn't have to bring no Spades hustler with you. You wrong for that," her uncle joked.

After the game, I was embraced like I was part of the family. I could tell Kamaria was happy, which made me feel even better. I even caught Ms. Anderson smiling like she was glad they accepted me.

"Say, Damian, we got some ribs, burgers, and potato salad in the kitchen. Go on and get you and Mar-Mar somethin' to eat. I know she'll 'preciate that," someone told me.

I told Kamaria I'd be right back before heading to the kitchen like I was told. There was so much food in there. I grabbed our two plates, and with the plates in hand, I stepped out looking for Kamaria. I didn't see her, though.

"Get that worry off your face. She in the backyard with the rest of the family," another relative told me.

I made my way to the backyard. Almost everybody outside was either stuffing their face or dancing like they were auditioning for Showtime at the Apollo.

"Hey, D, put the food down and come dance with me," Kamaria said as soon as she saw me.

As soon as I grabbed Kamaria's hand, a member of the family

turned on Method Man and Mary J. Blige's "You're All I Need." Kamaria and I started dancing like we were the only ones there.

"This means we now have a song," I whispered to her.

She pulled me close and kissed me. Everyone outside made some kind of comment or noise to let us know they saw what happened.

"Y'all look cute and e'rything, but me and your daddy used to like the original song Meth and Mary got that from," Ms. Anderson said.

"What you mean, original song?" I asked.

"You ain't know they got that from Marvin Gaye and Tammi Terrell?"

"I ain't never heard no song from them together," I said honestly.

"I know he didn't say he ain't heard the original song," a lady yelled out.

The next 30 minutes became a lesson in music history. We talked about R&B, jazz, gospel, and rap. One of the elders suggested we listen to each other's stations on the radio, so that's what we did. They put it on K104 and 100.3 Jamz so we could listen to the music me, Kamaria, and the other young folks liked. Then, out of nowhere, one of the older women at the party went to the radio.

"Alright, now it's time for me to get my groove on," she said as she started searching for her station.

"That's my great aunt, Brenda. She's a trip. I can only imagine what she 'bout to put on," Kamaria said.

As soon as she found her station—Soul 73, the one that played old-school gospel on Sundays—we heard a man start singing:

"I wanna ta-ta ya baby..."

"What does that even mean?" I wondered aloud.

"See, I don't know if you ready for Johnny "Guitar" Watson. You too young to know what this song is talkin' 'bout, but when you get some life in your rearview mirror, it'll all make sense," she told me.

After we all danced a little longer, the sun decided it had worked enough the day. The stars started to fill the sky, and as the moon clocked in, we couldn't help but look up and take it all in.

"It's so pretty, isn't it, D?" Kamaria asked.

"Yeah, babe, it is. With all that goes on around here, it's good when God forces you to look up. Back in the day, I used to spend a lot of time at my cousin's house. When it got dark, my aunt and uncle would come out on the porch so we could keep playing. They'd have us look up at the stars and tell us, whenever we missed our loved ones, we could imagine the stars were all the people who weren't with us anymore."

"That's beautiful. When you look up, do you still imagine stuff like that?" Kamaria asked.

"When they passed after the car accident, I did it a lot, just hoping I'd see them. Now, I don't do it as much, but I've looked at the sky a few times since RaShawn passed. Every once in a while, I'll see a star blinking, then it shoots across the sky. I always tell myself that's RaShawn, 'cause even with all the other stars, my boy gotta find a way to stand out."

Kamaria squeezed my hand tightly as we switched our attention between the night sky and everyone still out at the party. Right then, Ms. Anderson told us it was time to go. I grabbed the plates I made earlier, covered 'em with foil, and we got ready to leave.

When they dropped me back at home, it felt like Kamaria and I had reached a milestone. Somehow, my father must have sensed that feeling, so he asked me about my future with Kamaria. I didn't think I was ready for marriage or anything like that, but I started to think more about the concept of it.

I asked myself what it would take for me and Kamaria to be together for the long run, and what I would have to do ensure she felt the same way I did. Yeah, those questions would be the ones I would have to work hard to find the answers to.

6

When I went back to school, I was still asking myself the same questions I was the night before. I don't know why, but I was. As I made it through my classes, I felt almost like I wasn't supposed to be there. It was as though my mind was forcing me to feel bad when I had no reason to.

That day was one of the few days where I didn't have any homework, which meant I was able to drop all my books in my locker before I left. As soon as I put my combination into the lock, Kamaria walked over to me. She just stared at me without saying anything.

"Hey, babe, how are you?"

She still didn't respond. She just wrapped her arms around me. I didn't know what was going on, but I'd learned I never had to force a conversation with Kamaria. She'd talk when she was ready, but right then, she just needed me to hold her. We stood in silence for the longest minute of my life before she finally said something.

"This can't be real," she said, still holding on to me.

I had no idea what she was talking about as she began to cry.

"My great auntie Brenda is gone."

It took a minute for the name to register, but when it did, I was in total disbelief.

"What? Brenda from the party? The one who got hyped up about that Johnny "Guitar" dude?"

"Yeah... I... she... I-I..."

When she got overly excited, Kamaria would sometimes have trouble breathing. I tried my best to get her to breathe.

"Take it easy, babe," I said.

It took her a couple of minutes, but she finally managed to calm down. Then, a smile suddenly crept across her face.

"She was eighty-five, and the one time you met her, I know you could see how happy she was with the life she was living. That was her all the time. And can't nobody say she didn't live her life. And if she lived her life to the fullest, why do I need to be sad? I mean, it hurts, but Great Auntie lived, Damian. She lived, for real."

Her tears came back, but they were different the second time around. They were tears of mourning, but also of joy. She was sad about Brenda's passing, but happy that she lived. I would've never been able to look at death like that, but Kamaria was different. She was feeling better, but sill needed some companionship. So, she asked me to catch the bus with her. About thirty minutes later, we were making our way toward her house.

We spent most of the bus ride talking more about Kamaria's great aunt. She told me Brenda always talked about how hard it was growing up for her and her family. She was born in a time that was much worse than what we were used to, so being Black, poor, and in the south was very different for her than it was for us.

Kamaria said Brenda told them there were a lot of people who tried to break her spirit and steal her joy, but she made a promise to herself that she'd never let anyone do that.

"Keeping joy was her thing, no matter what was happening, and she did that until her last day," Kamaria told me.

A week later, we paid our final respects at Brenda's home going service. As soon as we stepped into the church, we were handed programs with pictures of Brenda from when she was a little girl, all the way up to the family party where I met her. One of the most obviously consistent things in all those pictures was Brenda's smile.

The pastor gave an amazing eulogy and told stories about how Brenda was famous for running around the church, giving no regard to the hat that looked ready to fly off her head at any moment. All of the chosen songs were ones the choir said were Brenda's favorites.

Brenda seemed like she was always the life of the party, so it was only fitting the celebration of her life seemed like a party, too. The spirit of Great Auntie Brenda didn't allow any bad vibes or foolishness at her service. There was nothing but togetherness, laughter, and love spread throughout the entire two-hour ceremony.

Everyone in attendance let it be known how much they'd miss Brenda, but so many people were just smiling because of how she touched their lives. When people celebrate you the way everyone did for Brenda, you know you lived life right. When it's your time, that's really all you can ask for.

After Brenda's funeral, Kamaria and I made a conscious effort to minimize everything that was unimportant and maximize the gratitude we showed for everything positive that was happening. And since we were still building our relationship, we finally decided it was time for our families to get to know each other. Kamaria's mom told me from day one that she liked to go to normal places around her, so Kamaria and I decided we should all go get snow cones.

There was only one place around our way we would ever go, and that was Aunt Stelle's — which, for some reason, most of us called Aunt Stella's. Since we called it that, I honestly don't know what the real name was. It was a little spot that had been around as far back as I could remember, and everybody who lived in Oak Cliff knew about it. When we pulled up and I saw that sign with the snow cone on it, I got just as excited as I did when I was a kid.

Stella's had a menu full of unique flavors, and I stared at it every time, even though I always got the same thing.

"Let me get a large pink lady with tiger's blood and banana," I said as everyone else finally walked up beside me in line.

I didn't care what everybody else was ordering because I was ready for mine. When they called my name, I immediately dove right in, not waiting on anybody else.

When everyone else had their snow cones in hand, I went ahead and started to introduce them.

"Y'all, this is my girl, Kamaria, and her mom, Ms. Anderson."

"So, you're the young lady my son has been going on and on about," my mother replied.

"Girl, she talks about your son all the time, too," Ms. Anderson joked as she shook my mom's hand.

That was all it took for our mothers to get cool with each other. Shortly after that, my siblings got so comfortable with Kamaria they started asking her every ridiculous question they could think of — and she answered every single one of them.

I had high hopes for everyone's first meeting, but it went far better than I imagined. When the opportunity presented itself, I pulled Kamaria over to the side.

"This is pretty cool, ain't it?" I asked.

"It's more than cool, D — this is what I've always dreamed of."

"What do you mean?"

"It's one thing to find a person you mesh with, it's another for the families to get along. I have relatives who hate their in-laws, and I prayed to never have that issue. I told you about my brother and my father not being in my life, so if we become one family, then your father and siblings may help fill the void I've had most of my life."

I was ecstatic the meeting went well, but it reminded me that, in order for us to maximize the gratitude we had for our lives like we said we wanted to do, we would have to keep making sure we were healing. With that being something I wanted to accomplish, I continued going to therapy — and I made sure Elijah did the same. Every once in a while, I would even ask Kamaria if she'd be willing to seek help. Sometimes she seemed okay with the idea, but other times, she just wanted me to change the conversation.

The process of healing is different for us all, so I never tried to press her, or anyone else, to do anything. I had my hands full trying to make sure I stayed on the right track. I stayed focused on what I wanted to accomplish in all aspects of my life, and by my senior year, I had been promoted to assistant manager at Minyards.

The promotion meant I had some extra money in my pocket, which allowed me to save up and buy my first car — a 1989 Oldsmobile Delta 88. It may not have been my first choice, but I was happy to have the independence she gave me. And yes, I called my car a she. I also named her Ebony, even though she was white.

She didn't have a sound system or tinted windows, and she'd been around the block a few times. Every time I turned the key, some kind of light would turn on. If I got in the car and didn't see the check engine light, I'd think she was mad at me. She had issues, but she was mine, and you couldn't tell me she wasn't clean. Some people called her a hooptie — I called those folks haters.

Ebony made me cooler than I was, regardless of her condition. I had a few growth spurts over the years and I had reached a good 6'1 (or 6'2 with the right shoes on), but I used to push the bench seat in the car so far back, I could barely see where I was going. I would whip the steering wheel so hard my arm was hurting every day. That's just how I rolled — well, except when I was taking my brother and sister somewhere, or when Kamaria and I were going out.

"Bro, what are you doing?" Elijah asked me the first time he was formally introduced to Ebony as we were about to go somewhere.

"Man, this is how all the players do it. You ain't know?"

"The players, huh?"

"Yeah," I said.

"So, why did you push *your* seat so far back?" He asked again.

"Oh, so you think you funny?"

"Nope, but you do," he said, laughing obnoxiously.

During this time, I was feeling better about my life. Therapy was going well and Kamaria's mom was still getting along well with my family. Without pushing me, Kamaria even had me going to church more often. For a long time, I thought going on Sunday was enough, but I got to a point where I needed more. So, I started going to Bible class on Wednesday nights. It really helped me connect to God, and that connection was instrumental in my healing journey.

That connection was tested around October. It was one of those rare days when everyone in the family was free. Nobody had to work, nobody had any games to play in or attend, nothing. So, we had to take advantage of the opportunity. Lexi suggested that we all go to the movies together. Mind you, at this time, I'm 18, so having a family movie night wasn't something I would normally want to do.

Getting older makes us want to spend less time with our families, but at that point, I also realized we may not have many more chances to go out and have fun together. So, I threw out that initial feeling of not wanting to be with my loved ones and agreed to go out with them.

I told everyone I wanted to drive them in the 88.

"Hol' up! Are you volunteering to drive us?" My father asked.

"Yes, sir. I think it'll be cool," I said.

"We better hurry up before he changes his mind," my mom joked.

I don't know what movie we saw that night, but I know for a fact we went to Astro Drive-In. A lot of folks never got to experience a drive-in movie theater, but they were actually cool. Astro was one of —if not the only—remaining drive-ins around Dallas when I was growing up. It was off of Duncanville Road and Ledbetter, close to the community college where I started my therapy sessions.

Admittedly, we were crowded in my car, but we had a great time. Strangely enough, after a long history in Oak Cliff, Astro ended up closing down not too long after we went. I heard it was because of a fire in the concession stand, but for some reason, they decided not to open back up. We never would've thought our last time going would actually be the last time we'd ever have the chance to go.

After the movie, we went to Pancho's Mexican Buffet. As the name indicates, Pancho's was a Mexican food buffet—but it was unlike other buffets. They had all my favorites: enchiladas, burritos, tacos, rice, beans, and those sopapillas with honey that everybody liked, but that's not what made them different. At Pancho's, you'd get your first plate just like you would at every other buffet. Once you finished your plate, you didn't even have to get back up and go through the line. Oh no, that ain't how they did it at Pancho's.

All you had to do was raise the little flag they had at each table. When you did, someone came over, took your order, and brought back whatever you wanted. Back in the day, it didn't get much greater than that. As some of the elders around the way used to say, that would make you feel like you were living "high on the hog."

After dinner, we were all feeling good. We had the itis—so we were all ready to get home and go to sleep. We all held our overly stuffed bellies as we got into the car and made our way back home. Whenever we stopped at a light, I'd sneak a quick look at my family, hoping they didn't see me staring at them.

I silently thanked God for us being together. The smiles on everyone's faces meant everything to me. I didn't want the moment to end, so I drove a little slower than I normally would have.

"You okay?" Mom asked, waking up from her power nap.

"Yeah, Mom, it's all good."

That's all she needed to hear. She turned around and went back to sleep without missing a beat. I ended up taking a few detours, instead of going directly to the house, just so I could spend as much time with them as possible. When I finally pulled into our driveway, everyone stretched and got out immediately.

I stayed in the car for a few seconds because sometimes, older cars just need a moment to wind down. I always had to make sure Ebony was okay before I left her for the night. So, we had our own little private conversation until she told me she was okay.

I was smiling as I made my way out of the car. I felt like the joy I was feeling inside was bright enough to light up the night sky. As soon as I got out, that light disappeared when I heard Lexi scream.

"What's up, little sis?" I asked as I ran toward the house.

Nobody said anything, but I soon found out while we were out, somebody broke into our house and took almost everything my parents worked so hard for. Surprisingly, they didn't bother my parents' car in the driveway, which is one reason we never suspected anything unusual had happened. Inside, we found they had taken our tv, entertainment center, couch, and even some of my parents' books. They stole our Nintendo 64, the few pairs of Js I'd gotten since sophomore year, and some of our clothes, too.

Looking at our home and thinking about everything that had

been stolen, had us all feeling empty, but when my mother saw our family pictures thrown all over the place, she broke down.

"They saw our pictures! They looked at our family—our memories, who we are—and they still decided to steal from us. I feel so violated," she said as she slumped down to the floor.

My brother and sister hugged her while I walked over to my dad. He was silent. His face was almost blank, giving no indication of what he was thinking. He looked around and then just stared into space.

"We gon' be okay. This ain't gon' stop us," I told everyone.

I don't know why I said it, and I don't even know if I believed it—but it felt like something we all needed to hear.

"Yeah, they think stealing our stuff is gonna do something to us? They don't know who we are!" Lexi exclaimed.

"For real! Plus, the idiots left the most valuable stuff," Elijah said.

"What do you mean?" Mom asked, fighting tears.

"They took a whole lot of stuff we all really liked, but they messed up and left the pictures. We can get more stuff. It might take a while 'cause we ain't got no money, but we can get that back," Elijah joked.

"Yeah, Mom. Look at this. You remember when y'all saved up and took us all to Six Flags? Elijah kept begging for lemonade and soda and kept having to go to the bathroom, and Pops was getting mad at him. And Pops and Damian were scared to ride any of the roller coasters, but then you said you would get on The Texas Giant with us. This is the picture they took when we were at the very top, right before we dropped down that big ol' hill with that sign of Wile E. Coyote and Roadrunner on it. Man, that made my stomach feel like it left my body—stayed in the air—and fell down to me when we made it to the bottom," Lexi said as she showed Mom one of the framed pictures that had been thrown off the mantle.

"Yeah, and remember when we all went to that haunted house for Halloween? Look, this is the picture of Lexi and Elijah in their Power Rangers outfits. They really believed they could save the world if they had to," I said.

"And they told us they weren't scared of any monsters. They even said if any of them got close to us, they were gonna beat 'em up. As soon as the first ghost said, 'Boo!' they both were outta there so fast, we had to run out to catch them," Pops added.

"We looked like fools runnin' after them, too. We gaspin' for air, and they actin' like they got an unlimited energy supply," Mama joked.

"Mom, we only did that 'cause we didn't want to hurt nobody that night. We had promised Zordon we were gonna remain peaceful," Elijah joked.

"I don't even know who Zordon is. And why did you make a promise to him to remain peaceful when we had monsters runnin' around town?" Pops wondered.

"C'mon, Dad, Zordon is the one who gave us our morphin' powers. We made the promise because we knew all of the lil' kids would be out, so we didn't wanna accidentally hurt nobody. Plus, I didn't wanna break a nail," Lexi added.

The way my mama laughed as she heard everyone talking and looking at those pictures made us all forget what happened—at least temporarily. The distraction of looking through the scattered pictures was nice, but when reality set back in, we were upset and sad, yet thankful. Who knows how things would've turned out if we hadn't all left the house together?

I didn't want to think about how things could've gone, so I let those thoughts go without speaking them aloud.

"Let me go ahead and call 9-1-1, even though I know the police ain't gonna do nothin' for us," Pops said.

The police didn't have the best track record in neighborhoods like ours. What my dad said was pessimistic, but he was speaking the truth. Even with that being the case, I wasn't going to let whoever broke into our house break our spirits, too.

When Pops went to make the call, I started putting the pictures back where they belonged. It didn't take long before the rest of the family joined me. Our house was still messed up, but putting the pictures back served as a symbolic victory. It showed us that we had the ability to stand strong in the face of adversity—and how much value we found in things we initially might have thought didn't have any. God has a way of making you change your perspective, and how we responded after the robbery was an example of that.

"Well, they said they'll be here as soon as they can," Pops told us soon after calling the police.

"I'm sorry, y'all. I should've been able to protect y'all. I should've been able to protect our home," Pops said.

Our father always took the responsibility of protecting us seriously, and even though we weren't at home, he honestly felt like what happened was his fault. It was similar to me feeling like I could've done something to protect RaShawn, when in reality, there really was nothing I could've done. I guess my desire to protect was in my DNA.

"You know this ain't got nothin' to do with you, right?" I asked.

In his heart, he knew what happened wasn't because of anything he did—or didn't do—but he'd convinced himself otherwise. As we talked and waited for the police to show up, he actually tried to list out all of the reasons why he was to blame for the night's events.

After a while, I gave up trying to convince him to stop taking responsibility for the robbery. As the man of the house, he just didn't want to see his family deal with any unnecessary negativity, and when we did, he just wanted to do all he could for us to move past it, even if it included making himself a reason it occurred.

I walked to my room and handed the situation over to God—'cause I heard that's what you're supposed to do.

"Father God, please look over my family. My father is telling a lie as if it's the truth. He's made himself believe it's his fault we were robbed tonight. Right now, he's still a little too scared to be as vulnerable as he needs to be. I ask that You keep working on him. Show him love, so he knows he's loved. Show him strength so he knows he's strong. And show him the truth so he can recognize a lie, even when he's the one telling it. Please, God, allow him to put his pride to the side and let him know this situation is not about him. And even though what happened was bad, this too shall pass. In the name of Jesus I pray, amen."

When I finished praying, I went back to my family. We ended up waiting about forty-five minutes before we saw sirens flashing outside our window. Then, we heard the doorbell ring.

"Who is it?" Pops asked, even though we already knew.

"DPD," they responded.

He knew we needed to talk to them, but it almost seemed like he didn't want to. His movements showed defeat, though he tried his best to hide it.

"Y'all come on in," he finally said.

By that point in my life, I had a strong disdain for the police. I was old enough to have watched the news when they showed what happened to Rodney King in Los Angeles. I remember hearing how the cops involved got away with it—and how confused I was by it all. I also learned at a young age that the cases of police officers abusing their power weren't limited to other states. Oh no—the crooked Dallas police officers wanted to show they could do anything they saw anyone else do.

There were countless examples of utterly chaotic actions by the police right here at home. Cops had taken the lives of people all around the city. They used excessive force and falsified reports on people who looked like me. They planted drugs on folks who had no priors and ruined their lives. They created false descriptions of people who committed crimes just so they could match them with the Black and Brown people they had issues with.

They didn't care about gender, nor did they care about age. They targeted teenagers, young women, elderly men, and everybody in between. Even with all that, I never wished any ill will on any of them because I knew how dangerous their job was. I knew the good cops in the city—the ones who genuinely wanted to protect and serve— usually outweighed the ones who were racist, small-minded narcis- sists only looking to protect their overly inflated egos. Still, I just wanted to avoid dealing with them as much as I possibly could because I couldn't predict what type of cop I might be dealing with.

That night, there were two cops in uniform, and another person who was dressed in a suit. I thought they'd take the time to introduce themselves to us, if for no other reason than to make us feel comfortable, but they didn't seem to think making victims of a robbery feel comfortable was necessary.

"So, what happened?" One of the two cops asked.

"We went out for a few hours, and when we came back, this is what we found," Mom explained, pointing at our home.

"I'm sorry that happened," the same cop said.

"Yeah, it's unfortunate, but what do you think you did to make someone want to target your house?" The other cop asked with a smug look on his face.

"What? Hey, yo, I know you can't be serious with that question," Pops said angrily.

I could see the atmosphere changing quickly, so I asked Elijah and Lexi to go with me to my room. While we were in there, I tried to distract them from what was going on, but it didn't work.

"Why do you think this happened to us? Do you think we actually did something, like that cop said?" Lexi asked me.

I wanted to say something deep, philosophical, and inspiring, but I figured trying to come up with something would've been disingenuous, so I just kept it real with them.

"Lexi, we ain't do nothing to get robbed. Sometimes stuff just happens, and there's not always a reason for it," I said.

"Look at all the houses on this street. Out of everybody, they just had to pick us, huh?" Elijah asked.

"Are you saying you wish they would've robbed somebody else?" I asked my siblings.

They paused and looked at me, almost like my question confused them.

"Nah, I didn't want them to rob anybody else, but I didn't want them to come here."

"I ain't trying to justify what they did, but you gotta realize how hard it is out here. Even with all of us working, it's still a struggle. Sometimes folks get tired of barely making it, and they want to feel what it's like to have what other people have."

"I get it, I guess. I'm really glad we still have our pictures, but that don't make me feel no better about my stuff being gone," Elijah told me.

"I'm mad they got us, but being mad ain't bringing our stuff back."

"It's not even just about the stuff they took, Damian," Lexi said.

"What you mean?" I asked.

"They took the ability to feel safe at home away from me and left me with a fear I've never had before."

How was I supposed to respond to that? How was I supposed to comfort my siblings and make them believe they'd be safe when someone had just broken into our home?

"Hey, kids, could y'all come back in here?" Pops yelled out.

Without properly concluding our conversation, we went back in the room with our parents. By that time, the cops were gone.

"What happened? What did they say?" Elijah asked.

"Well, they asked us to provide all the information we could..." Mom started.

"Then, they told us there's been a string of robberies within a few miles of us. They were pretty sure all them were connected, but they had no leads. Nobody has seen anything, which means they don't know who to search for. They looked for clues and evidence—at least that's what they pretended to do. They said they dusted for fingerprints, but I doubt they actually did," Pops said hopelessly.

"So, what does that mean for us?" Lexi asked.

"It means we have to keep going like we been doin', 'cause ain't nobody gonna do anything to protect us," I said.

I regretted my words. Moments before, I was trying to be positive for Lexi and Elijah, and then, I just flipped and gave them the exact energy I was trying to keep away from them.

"My bad, y'all. I just got frustrated. I'm sorry," I told them.

"You ain't the only one frustrated, so you don't need to apologize for nothing. You know what I just realized?" My father pondered.

"What?" Elijah asked.

"I realize I owe y'all an apology, too."

"For what, babe?" Mom asked him.

"I got all caught up in what I was told being a man is supposed to look like. Y'all know I try my best to provide for, and protect y'all, but this really didn't have nothing to do with me. I couldn't predict this was gonna happen. So, I apologize for that anger you saw when the cops got here and tried to act like it was our fault."

It took a lot for my father to say what he did. Again, in those days, parents weren't known for apologizing for anything they did or didn't do. That night, my father showed another glimpse of his emotional growth. Without speaking, we all walked over and hugged him.

"Dad, we'll be okay. Haters can't stop us," Lexi told him.

Right then, Pops started crying and laughing at the same time. It was one of, if not the first times, I actually saw him do that.

"Are you alright?" Mom asked.

"Yeah, y'all just got me...how you kids say it? 'In my feelings.' I can't even be mad at the thieves no more 'cause I can't let that anger get more attention than the love I got for y'all. They got us for a few things, but we still here! God got us!"

We were still shocked Pops was crying, but also inspired by what he said. We ended up briefly leaving the house again that night just to get some wood for the broken windows, and new locks for the doors. He asked us if we wanted to stay at a hotel for the night while he made sure things were fine at home. We could have done that, but nobody wanted to leave him. Plus, we all felt like if we left our house for the night, we would've let the robbers win. There was no way we were going to give them that satisfaction.

"This is gonna sound crazy, but do y'all wanna have a sleepover?" Lexi asked.

"What do you mean?" I asked.

"If them thieves didn't take our blankets and pillows, we can spread them on the floor. Even though they didn't take our beds, I think it'll be fun," Lexi said.

"Well, let me gon' call Pizza Inn and put in an order," Pops said.

We just had Pancho's, but we couldn't turn down pizza, especially from Pizza Inn. We went and got the stuff we needed for the house, and a few minutes after we made it back home, the delivery person was ringing the doorbell with our food.

That pepperoni lovers pizza with extra cheese hit the spot for all of us. We were all dancing around, holding plates, and smiling. As crazy as it sounds, eating pizza and preparing to sleep on covers spread over the floor together, was enough to make us look beyond the boarded windows. We almost forgot we were robbed hours before.

As we wound down for the night, I was more thankful than I had been in a while. It's ironic how losing things you think are important can make you more grateful for still having the things that really are. My eyes began to get heavy, and as they did, I looked over at my family and watched each one of them have their own separate conversation with God.

Although I will never know for sure what they were saying to God, nor should I, I know whatever it was, the enemy was mad at them. I know the devil didn't want any of us to have a conversation because he didn't want us to still have faith. So, that in itself was a huge victory. That night showed me how strong we really were. Lexi said the haters couldn't stop us, and she didn't know how right she was.

7

———————

When I woke up that Saturday morning, I realized I hadn't told Kamaria what happened. I hesitated while dialing her number because I didn't want her to worry.

She knew I was a creature of habit, and if I didn't have to get up early, I normally didn't. She already knew everything wasn't okay.

"We all went to Astro and saw a movie last night, then we went to Pancho's. When we got back, we found out we had been robbed."

She asked about everyone with genuine concern, just as she always did. I let her know we were shaken up, but okay. She offered to help, but I told her we were fine. I also told her I needed to spend the day with my family, and she completely understood.

We didn't want to leave the house because, subconsciously, I think we feared someone would break in again. We also didn't want to stay home because everywhere we looked, we saw reminders of what happened the night before. It was strange how different we were feeling than the night before.

Mom eventually suggested we take a walk, and we all agreed. Crazy enough, as we were getting ready, Elijah ended up finding out the robber, or at least one person responsible for the robbery, had dropped their license in his closet. He quickly handed the license over to Pops.

As my father looked at the person's picture, I could see him getting angry. He was staring at the person who caused my mom to say she felt vulnerable in our home. He had the person's address, and I could sense a part of him wanted to seek revenge.

"Vengeance is mine, I will repay, says the Lord," I told him.

"You're right, Damian. Thank you, because you already know..."

He stopped mid-sentence.

"Let's just call the police and let them know we have some info," Mama said.

Regardless of the hood saying, "snitches get stitches," we called the police and provided the info on the license. Later, we were visited by the police again. The second time around, we dealt with officers who cared about our well-being. This was evident from the fact that they greeted us, asked how we were, and apologized for what happened.

"I grew up on Hampton, so I know how it is. Ninety percent of the time, this feels like the greatest place on earth. Your friends live close to you and 'mama-nem' live down the street. Then, that other ten percent..."

The first officer paused, and the second officer jumped right in.

"And that other ten percent makes you wonder why you're here. I was on Kiest until I fought a convenience store employee who accused me of stealing. My mom partially blamed my actions on who I was around, so she made the decision to move. I hated it, but I needed the change. Once I got grown, I had to move back. My heart has always been in Oak Cliff."

What they said showed they cared and they were from the same neighborhood they were trying to protect. Their words didn't make me forgive all cops for what I had seen and heard about, but it did help me to not hate all of them. When they left, we felt better about the situation, even though we didn't know if anything would actually happen.

Although we planned to walk around the neighborhood that day, we never did. Kamaria called and asked if she and her mom could come by. There were no plans for what they wanted to do, other than just visit with us and make sure we were okay.

At first, my mom had concerns about having someone at our house when it was still a mess, but despite acting like she was fine, every once in a while, I'd catch a glimpse of sadness in her eyes. We were all hurt that someone had broken into our house, but it hit her a little differently.

At that time, I just thought of our house as where we lived. For Mom, it was the home where she and my dad watched our family grow to include three kids. She had a lot invested in it and she wanted to protect its sanctity. That's where the sadness came from. Eventually, she agreed to have Kamaria and Ms. Anderson over because if nothing else, she needed someone to talk to about the experience.

When they came over, they spoke to all of us, but Mom quickly took them (and Lexi) into the living room to talk. That left me, Pops, and Elijah to talk amongst ourselves to see how we were handling things. I expressed my disappointment in whoever broke into our home, not just because they stole from us, but because they were probably from our neighborhood. That meant, they knew how much we were all struggling and decided to add to the problems of their own neighbors.

If the person was ever caught and ended up doing time, that meant we helped him become a statistic, even though it was because of his own actions.

"Damian, I think we're about to head out," Kamaria said from the other room.

When the conversation with my brother and father reached a good stopping point, we joined everyone else. My mom and Ms. Anderson were wiping away tears, but they were both smiling, which was a good sign. Kamaria hugged Lexi and told her things would get better. She was talking to Lexi, but I received the message, too.

Once our visitors were gone, we were all silent for a little bit. We were once again in the reality of what happened.

"A'ight, let's go ahead and get this place cleaned up. We're not gonna let the spirit of defeat hang in this house any more," Pops said suddenly and seriously.

Without explanation, everyone understood that cleaning up was a simple, yet symbolic gesture. Getting our place back to normal—or as close as we could—would make us feel victorious, in spite of what happened. Normally, when we cleaned up, Mom would turn on some music, but since all of our radios had been stolen, we couldn't do that.

Instead, Lexi decided to take it upon herself to become the music. Lexi is not, and I repeat, is not a good singer. That didn't stop her from clearing her throat before she started throwing out notes as if she was the best in the world, though. She was so confident, you couldn't tell her she wasn't Michael Jackson, Sade, Prince, Aretha Franklin, and Mariah Carey all rolled into one.

In reality, the voice cracking sounded terrible, but it made us all laugh, and it put us in a better mood as we cleaned. Sure, our house had a lot more empty space than before, but after a couple of hours, it felt like our home again.

"Welcome back home, everybody," Elijah said.

Removing the remnants of the break-in set everyone's mind at ease, and a few weeks later, we got a call from DPD telling us they caught the people responsible for not only robbing our house, but several in the area. My parents felt good about how things turned out, and they were happy because all of the repairs to our home had been taken care of. It was a good thing because my mom was not going to be happy if we couldn't have our traditional Thanksgiving dinner at home.

Mama went all out for Thanksgiving. She cooked enough food for an army because she liked to help the less fortunate. Before we ate, we served others around the neighborhood and at a shelter. It felt good to serve, and what we did that day made me think more about what I could do in the future to keep that feeling present in my life. Then, it hit me. I needed to do more to change the hood I claimed to love so much, but how?

Out of the blue, I started thinking more about the colleges I had applied to. Other than going to an HBCU, I wasn't sure where I wanted to go. I had already applied to schools in Florida, Alabama, Mississippi, Georgia, DC, and, of course, in Texas.

I was born and raised in Texas, but I was primarily considering going somewhere outside of home. It may have been because whenever I thought about the next phase of my life, I kept hearing RaShawn's voice from the dream when he told me I wouldn't be doing what I was purposed to do if I never experienced life outside of Oak Cliff.

I agreed with the statement, but I may have been looking at it wrong. Initially, I was thinking I needed to leave Oak Cliff as soon as possible, but the closer I got to the end of the school year, I started to think my adulthood needed to start where my childhood was ending. I asked everyone's opinions on where I should go, and they all told me I had to do what was best for me. They didn't provide a direct answer, but what they told me made me think more for myself.

I ended up thinking more about Texas schools. I dwindled my choices down to Texas Southern, Huston-Tillotson, Prairie View, and Paul Quinn, which was in Oak Cliff. These schools were all close to my heart because I had family members who had attended them.

I ended up focusing all of my energy on Paul Quinn. Thankfully, I had already been accepted to the school, and even though they didn't think it would be, the money my parents saved for me was enough to take care of my tuition for all four years.

"Hey, y'all. I made my final decision on which school I'm going to," I told my family one day.

That's when my dad hilariously started acting "extra" and being more dramatic than I had seen him act in a while.

"Do I need to get the camcorder so I can record you telling us?" Pops asked.

I felt picking a college was a step towards my future, but I didn't think it was that big of a deal until I saw how my parents were acting. Pops talked about getting the camcorder jokingly, but as I prepared to tell them which school I was going to, he actually went and got it from the garage. Fortunately, when our house was robbed, the thieves didn't check in there, so we got to keep a few of the things we had forgotten we even had.

I inhaled and exhaled before I started speaking.

"I'm going to The Paul Quinn College," I nervously told them.

The energy in the room was high for a while, but then I noticed my mom started to look a little tired. Not knowing what she needed, I just went and got her some water.

"Here you go, Mom. You okay?"

"Yeah, I'm good. Maybe I just got a little too excited for you. I'm too old to be jumping around like your brother and sister," she said.

She was acting like it was all good, but I knew better than that. I couldn't tell what was bothering her, and she didn't want to tell me, so I didn't push the issue. Instead, I went to call Kamaria to let her know about my decision.

When I told her, she was shocked. I was the same person who didn't even want to college, here I was telling her where I was going. She was excited for me, but she also sounded sad. With my news out of the way, I asked her if she made a final decision, and what else was on her mind.

"The main ones still in the running are in DC and Florida, but nothing for sure," she told me.

"Florida and DC? So, nothing at home?"

"Not really. I love Texas, but sometimes I feel like it's just time for me to get away for a minute."

When we met, Kamaria said she was going to be the smartest kid in class. She worked and became the smartest person in school. So, she deserved to go wherever she wanted to, regardless of what I had to say about it.

I needed to spend some time with her, so I asked if I could take her to a movie. Thankfully, she agreed to go with me. A little over an hour later, I had gassed up the '88 and I was ringing on the doorbell at her house.

"I know we were supposed to be going to the movies, but do you mind if we go to Big T."

Big T Bazaar, or Big T Plaza as it later became known, is an indoor flea market that has everything you could ever look for. If you want electronics, clothes, jewelry, shoes, or anything else, you can find it at Big T. I can't vouch for the authenticity of said products, though.

When we went in, nothing stuck out. We saw music I already had, and clothes I didn't want, except for those hood Bugs and Taz shirts where they were dressed like Kriss Kross. I had to get me and Kamaria one, even though she said that wasn't her thing.

We saw a lot of stuff I could do without, and I started to think we were wasting time until we saw a jewelry kiosk. As soon as I stopped, Kamaria looked at me as if she thought I was trying to get her a ring. I told her I would get her one at some point, but when I did, it wouldn't be from there.

"We need grills," I unexpectedly told the guy at the kiosk.

"That's what we're doing? I don't think I can pull off a grill," she said.

"I'm just sayin', if both of y'all wearin' grills together, it'll look like y'all got... I don't know... intellectual street cred or something," the jeweler said.

I never heard "intellectual street cred" before. The term was so contradictory, it was funny. Plus, the way the salesperson said it made me feel like I had to buy something from him. It took some convincing, but I finally got Kamaria to agree to get a grill, too. After getting the mold done, we ended up agreeing on getting rose gold.

The salesman told me what I needed to pay to get started and how long everything took. I paid the deposit, and then we left. We ended up going to UA 8, even though it wasn't really close to Big T. We laughed our way through whatever movie we watched and had a good time.

We continued to enjoy each other's company at dinner, and that's when the conversation about school and our relationship started back up.

"How will we make it in different states? You'll be seeing all kinds of women when I'm not around," she said.

"There will always be women around, but they ain't you. And you'll be around a lot of guys," I replied.

"D, you have my heart. Trust me, I'm not worried about other guys. When I get to school, I'll just be worried about making sure my grades are on point."

Plenty of my classmates told me she was going to find somebody new and throw away our relationship. I had pushed those thoughts to the back of my mind, but when she reminded me we would be in different states, I started thinking about them again.

Regardless of how I was feeling before she started speaking, her assurance calmed me down, like they normally did. We went on with the rest of our night without speaking about separation again. By the time I dropped her off back home, I was still concerned, but I was feeling a little better about our future.

8

————————

I remember being excited when I got the call from the jeweler at Big T a few weeks after we placed the order for the grills.

"Boy, y'all showed out with these mugs," I told the jeweler when I made it to Big T, took my first look at the finished grills, and made my final payments.

Being happy with how they turned out, I went right to Kamaria's house so she could see them. When I got there, she pulled me inside her crib as she ran to the restroom to try on her new jewelry. In less than a minute, she was smiling with her mouth open so I could see how she looked as Mar Mar The MC, her rapper alter ego.

After seeing how we looked with our grills, we went to Braum's and got some combo meals and freshly baked peanut butter cookies. I realized how much the conversations and companionship would be missed when she went away, so, for the rest of the school year, I tried to spend as much time with her as I could without interfering with all the other things she needed to take care of.

Before I was ready, they started talking about prom at school. Kamaria hadn't said anything, but I prepared to go anyway. One day, without speaking to her about it, I brought some gifts I bought for her, including a necklace, with me to school. I had to get there early to avoid a bunch people seeing me put everything in my locker.

Kamaria had gotten so far ahead in school, she only had to be there for the second half of the day, so I usually saw her for the first time at lunch. I didn't know if I was even going to give her all the gifts until I heard her voice that day. She said she had gotten into an argument with her mom, so she wasn't feeling her best. I had to cheer her up, so I asked her to follow me to my locker.

I wasted no time handing the gifts to her, but I waited to give her the necklace until I actually asked if she would be my date.

"I'm glad you're my girl, and I'm tryin' to go to the prom with you." The words were nowhere near as eloquent as they were in my head, but Kamaria didn't care. She hugged me as she agreed to be my date and asked me to put the necklace on for her.

A few days later, after I had gotten everything I needed to be fly on prom night, I called Kamaria, but her mom told me she was getting her hair done. It was a good idea and it made me look in the mirror to see if I needed to get mine cut.

"That ain't it," Elijah said, as I looked at myself in the mirror.

Before I looked in the mirror, I thought I would be okay to go to the prom without a haircut, but I was wrong.

"I love you, Ma. I gotta get to Ced B's before they close," I told her as I quickly made my way out of the house.

She smiled, but something seemed off. She looked a little out of it, like she didn't have much energy, but I didn't think too much of it. I just ran out and went straight to the barbershop. When I got there, they didn't waste any time calling me out.

"Where you been?" They asked.

"I've been around," I said.

"Wit' yo' head looking like that, it's obvious you ain't been around here," Cedric joked.

While he was cutting my hair, Ced got a little emotional when I told him I was about to graduate.

"I've been cuttin' this boy's hair since he was nine. His daddy used to bring him and his homeboy in here for cuts. What's his name?"

"RaShawn."

"I ain't seen him in a minute. Did he find a new barber or something?" He asked.

I realized the passing of time just gives you the chance to keep living without being overwhelmed by sadness, but it doesn't take the sadness away.

"The hood got him a few years ago," I told him.

"Man, I'm sorry. I had no idea..."

The vibe changed immediately. When you're a Black man, you don't always feel like you can express what you're dealing with, but the barbershop always felt like a safe spot. Right then, everyone gave me the freedom to speak more about RaShawn and what happened.

The talk started with my situation, then it morphed into a conversation about the bigger problems in our neighborhood.

"It's sad. Sometimes we're the cancer that's killin' us," Ced said.

Cedric's choice of words, once again, took me back to that street preacher who'd said the same thing years before.

"If we're the cancer, how can we be cured?" I asked.

"Young brother, ain't no cure for cancer," someone said.

The "cure" seed was planted in my mind as I left. I wouldn't see the harvest of those seeds until much later in life, but I could feel another shift in my thinking.

By about 2:30 on prom day, I realized I hadn't even talked to Kamaria and didn't even know what car I was driving to the prom. Yeah, I had my Delta 88 in the driveway, but I didn't think taking Ebony would be appropriate for the evening. I asked my mom if I could use the car, but she actually rejected me. I was disappointed, but there was nothing I could do. I couldn't force anyone to let me use their car, so I just had to use what I had.

I went into my room and started laying my suit out on the bed. Out of nowhere, even though I was disappointed, I felt the unyielding urge to get on my knees and pray.

"God, I don't know why you've blessed me. I don't know why you've spared me. I don't even know why you find me worthy, but here I am. I ain't grown, but I'm no longer a child. I don't know where

I'm going, but I know where I've been. Nobody but You, God, could have brought me through. Nobody but You could've brought my family through. I am grateful. As I go out tonight, I ask that You keep me on the path of righteousness. I ask that You help me fight the weakness of my own flesh with Your strength. Help me like only You can, God. I thank You in the name of Jesus. Amen."

I didn't immediately get up. Instead, I got off my knees and just sat on the floor. I prayed all the time, but I couldn't understand why my spirit felt the urge to pray at that moment. Then, Lexi knocked on my door. She had a concerned look on her face as she began to speak.

"Do you respect Kamaria?" She asked.

"No doubt."

"Tonight's your prom, and I know what happens after prom. I just wanna know if my brother is respectful to women."

"Lexi, I love Kamaria, and there's nothing I would intentionally do to disrespect her, or any other woman."

Right then, I understood why I prayed for power over my flesh. I knew the desires of things I wanted to happen with Kamaria, while real, weren't as important as showing some restraint.

After I finished talking with Lexi, I heard Pops come home. For some reason, his co-worker, KG, was with him.

"Hey, y'all. I just came over to drop off the keys for D's rental."

"What are you talking about?" I asked.

"Yeah, your mom and I saw you were dealing with a lot, so we decided to take care of your car situation," Pops told me.

"That's why I said you couldn't use my car," Mom chimed in.

When I saw the car they got me, I was too hyped up to play it cool. They got me a bubble-eyed Lexus, the same color as my suit. After seeing the car, I felt like I was obligated to start getting ready.

My folks started taking pictures as soon as I walked out of the room with my suit on. Before I left, my brother and dad dapped me up, my mom gave me a hug, and Lexi looked at me and nodded, as if to silently remind me of what we talked about.

I felt different almost as soon as I got in the car and turned it on. Everything felt better than it did in my car. Even the air felt, not just cooler, but more...air-y than than I had experienced before. And I know that doesn't even make sense.

Before I drove off, I had to make sure the sound was right. I turned on the radio, and it was already on K104. They were jammin', but I wanted to listen to my own music. I got out and ran to get my CD book out of my room. A few minutes later, I was waving to everyone as I got back into the car.

Even though I had my music, I ended up turning the radio to 107.5, The Oasis, the smooth jazz station at the time. They played some Najee and Gerald Albright and I was nodding my head like I was listening to the hardest of 808s, but when they played "Smooth Operator" by Sade, I lost my mind.

As the song ended, I made it to Kamaria's place. I got out and grabbed the corsage I had for her. I rang the doorbell, and as I waited for someone to answer, I just started singing Sade again.

"Smooooooooooooth operator."

I was really into it. I had my closed eyes and everything. At that moment, I believed I was on par with D'Angelo.

"Sing it, D," Ms. Anderson said as she opened the door with a huge smile on her face.

"My bad, Ms. Anderson. I was trying to keep these vocals a secret," I joked.

"Boy, get in this house," she said as she gave me a hug.

Me and Ms. Anderson had come a long way. When I first met her, I never thought we would be getting along as well as we were. She was a kind and caring person, and her tough exterior was just there to protect her and Kamaria.

"How do I look?" Kamaria asked as she finally made her appearance.

My grin said everything I wanted to say. My eyes almost had trouble focusing because of her aura. Ms. Anderson quickly pulled me to the side because she said she needed to talk to me. She told me she had grown to like me and she appreciated how I treated Kamaria. She wanted to make sure I treated her daughter with respect and reminded me Kamaria trusted me with her heart.

I winked to let her know she could trust me. Then, I walked back over to Kamaria.

"Are you ready?" I asked, finally putting the corsage on her.

Tears of joy started to fall. I took out my pocket square, dabbed her eyes, and I held her hand as I opened their front door. Ms. Anderson, and the family members who were helping Kamaria get ready, took pictures as we made our way outside. When we drove away, I quickly noticed how quiet she was.

"What's up? You okay?" I asked.

"Yeah, but did you ever think we would get here? Can you believe we're really gonna graduate soon?" She asked as she looked at me.

"When you said you were gonna give us a chance, I almost didn't know what to do. I was kinda scared, for real. That's how it is with gettin' outta school. We've been asking for this for a while, and now we're here. We may be scared, but this is what we wanted," I said.

We continued our conversation as we navigated around the frustrating streets of downtown Dallas towards our destination. When we made it, it was almost as if she didn't want to be there.

"Hey, we can go if you want to," I said.

"I appreciate it, but we went through too much trouble to get dressed, so we're not about to leave before they see how fly we are."

"True story! I'm lookin' dapper than a mug," I told her.

Her smile was returning, and when she was ready to go inside, I got out and opened the door for her. As her heels touched the ground, I noticed some of her dress was still in the car, so I reached down to help her out.

"There you go, Queen," I said, sounding like an extra from Love Jones.

As we walked inside, whatever song was playing just faded out. The room was quiet, and people just happened to look towards the door.

"You see that? People are staring at the queen," I told her.

"Hey, y'all lookin' good," Nadia, one of Kamaria's friends, told us as we got settled in.

I went to the prom not knowing what to expect, but I had a really good time. I started off thinking we would dance for one or two songs and possibly leave early, but we ended up being the life of the party, and we were on the floor about 90% of the time... okay, maybe it was 70%, but math was never my strongest subject.

"Okay, it's time to announce the King and Queen of this year's prom," the principal announced after one of the songs went off.

"...and your homecoming queen is... Kamaria Anderson."

The announcement had both of us shook. We started jumping up and down like little kids getting ready for recess. A few minutes later, they were surprisingly announcing me as the king. I thought it was a joke at first, but I went and joined my girlfriend on stage anyway. Admittedly, we both thought it was cool to be elected by our peers.

We celebrated our victory with our classmates for a little bit, but before we knew it, the prom started to wind down. We took pictures and had conversations with people we hadn't talked to all year, After we won our tiles, I expected that to happen. What I didn't expect, was the talk I had with Kamaria.

"D, did you plan anything for after the prom?"

"I just thought we'd go find something to eat and hang out."

"That sounds good, but do you think you could walk me upstairs to our room, first?"

"Yeah, I can. I... what?"

I was caught off guard by her question, and when my brain finally processed what she asked, I didn't know how to respond. I looked at her to make sure I heard her right. She had a coy little smile on her face as she grabbed my hand and walked us over to the elevator.

"Press five, please," she said while we stood alone in the elevator.

I had a lot running through my mind, but I couldn't say any of it. When we reached the fifth floor, she pulled out a key card I didn't even know she had, and opened the door to room 512. We stepped inside, and I could feel her pulse racing as quickly as my heart was beating. For a moment, we were both silent.

Soon, she sat down on the edge of the bed and motioned for me to sit next to her.

"I've always told you I didn't want to go there unless I felt like the person I was with was going to be there for me. Nobody's been there for me like you, so..."

She told me when we started dating I needed to be careful with her heart, and I didn't take that responsibility lightly. So, as much as I wanted certain things to happen, I knew I couldn't do anything with her that night. It wasn't because I didn't want to, it was because she deserved more than being a stereotypical prom story.

"Babe, when the time is right, we'll both know it. But now ain't it. Don't get me wrong, as good as you lookin', I... girl, you... well, you feel me, but..."

"I get it, and thank you for loving and respecting me."

That moment helped me understand why I felt the urge to pray before I left the house, and why Lexi asked me if I respected women. My spirit won over my flesh, but I didn't know how long the victory would last, so Kamaria and I just talked about our futures.

She ended up telling me she decided to go to Howard. I was a little shocked, but not completely. I knew it was on her list, I just hoped it wouldn't be her final choice. A lot of our peers probably spent their nights doing other things, but the conversation we had that night helped me understand how life was about to change for us —whether I liked it or not.

The next morning, we got up, and had breakfast. I was still forcing myself to pretend I was happy about Kamaria's decision, but I was actually heartbroken. I was gonna find somewhere for us to hang out a little longer, but Kamaria asked if I could just take her home because she was tired. So, that's what I did.

When I dropped her off, I expected to see her mom. I was sure she would ask a million questions about the night, but surprisingly, she wasn't there. I congratulated my girl again on being named Queen before giving her a kiss and heading back to the crib.

As I pulled back into my driveway a little later, I thought about everything that happened that night. As soon as I opened the door, I saw everyone sitting together in the living room, looking dejected.

"Don't be sad. I know y'all missed me, but I'm back," I said, trying to bring some life into the room.

Nobody responded, so I knew something was wrong. My father was holding my mom's hand as he told me to sit down. I started to get nervous, even though I had no idea what was going on.

"Damian, we got a call from the doctor today," Pops said.

"On a Sunday? That ain't normal, is it?"

"No, it's not. They usually only do that when it's something that can't wait."

"Okay, so what was so important they had to call? " I asked.

"I have cancer," Mama admitted.

She said it so calmly—so matter-of-factly—it took a few seconds to process what I heard. I sat there motionless until the weight of those three words finally made me move.

"So that's why you've been so tired. I'm sorry, Mom."

She stood up and motioned for all of us to move closer to her. When we did, she wrapped her arms around us.

"I don't believe in giving up," she said, "but I'm in stage 4, and we've already been told, no matter what I do, I don't have very long."

"What you mean, you haven't been given very long?" I snapped.

"I may have a month, but that's being optimistic," she told us.

Mom wanted us to keep her illness in the family, and we respected that. She said she would need help, but she didn't want us to stop living our own lives. We wanted to drop everything for her, but she wouldn't allow it.

As she wished, I helped her when I was home, but I still had to handle my own stuff. With everything on my mind, that final week of school was hectic, but it went by fast. On the last day, I just went to get my yearbook signed, and see some folks I probably wouldn't see again after graduation.

Flipping through the pages of the yearbook, I got stuck in the senior section. It had pictures from throughout the entire year—even one of Kamaria and me being crowned King and Queen. Then, I saw something I didn't expect: a whole page dedicated to students we'd lost, who would've been seniors that year.

I saw people I had forgotten about. Then, I saw a picture of RaShawn from freshman orientation. Seeing that goofy grin on his face reminded me of the good times, but it also reminded me how early he was taken away. My mood changed instantly.

Normally, seeing Kamaria made everything better, but not that day. She grabbed my hand and we sat down on the floor near the lockers because she knew I was upset.

"What up? Y'all alright?"Another senior asked as he was passing by.

Many times, when someone asks if you're alright, you just say "yeah" to be polite. But not that time.

"Nah, I ain't good. Seeing e'rybody who ain't make it got me in my feelings," I said as we slowly stood up.

I'd been clowned so many times for showing emotions, I expected it again, but I didn't care.

"Yeah, I knew you and RaShawn were close. He used to be on my basketball team when we were like eight, but he got embarrassed one day when a kid crossed him over and he touched urf, not earth—urf, u-r-f. He quit the team that day and ain't never come back. Man, it ain't been the same since he been gone. I'm sorry, bro. I know we all gotta go, but we ain't gotta set each other's expiration date."

I didn't expect the conversation to go the way it did, but it was a pleasant surprise. There were no jokes about my sadness—just real concern and empathy.

"It was nice to see two Black men talk about loss and emotions. You two remembered RaShawn, you expressed how you felt, and nobody got made fun of," Kamaria said.

When she and I went our separate ways for the rest of the day, I made myself stay in the moment and enjoy what little time I had left in high school. I talked to people I hadn't spoken to in a while, told some juniors to hold it down since they'd be running the school, and made sure to speak to a few teachers before I left.

A lot of teachers impacted me, but none like Mr. Murphy. I couldn't let the last day pass without hollering at him.

"What up, Mr. Murphy?" I said when I saw him.

"Damian Roberts—do my eyes deceive me? Are you actually stopping by to visit your old teacher?"

"I couldn't leave this place without stopping by here; you're my favorite teacher."

"That's a title I hold with pride. So, are you ready for your next chapter?"

"I don't know, but time gon' keep goin' whether I'm ready or not," I told him.

"I believe in you, Mr. Roberts. You have greatness attached to you. I know your family, Kamaria, and even the spirit of your friend won't let you do anything less than live up to your potential."

"You remember me talking about RaShawn?"

"I do. And I also remember meeting your family, and seeing how happy you were when you finally started dating the girl you'd been friends with most of your life. Just because I'm no longer your teacher doesn't mean I don't keep up with you and my other students. Y'all are like my children, and I want the best for you. I truly mean that."

"You a real one, Mr. Murphy. I appreciate you, and I promise, I won't let you down."

Mr. Murphy was always dropping jewels, and I appreciated every word. There was always intent behind what he said. I never once had a conversation with him that didn't feel genuine—including that one.

I left and went to the cafeteria to sit at the same table I tried to claim every day. It was in the center, so I could see everything going on. While I was looking around, I started making a random beat on the table, something we all used to do.

Suddenly, this girl came over and started to freestyle. Then, a dude joined in. Before I knew it, we had a full ten-person cypher where people were taking turns showing off their skills. When I switched up the beat, the rappers switched up their flows.

Everyone did their thing, but the one who shut it down was Kamaria. She just happened to walk into the cafeteria and saw the crowd. When she noticed me in the center of everything, she had to join in. When she spit her freestyle, she called herself Lil Mar-Mar. I guess she no longer wanted to rap under the moniker of Mar-Mar The MC, like she said before.

She rapped about AP Calculus, being top of the class, and a

bunch of other stuff she called "Nerd Swag." She ended her verse saying, "You can't go where I go, you ain't seen what I seen. Don't act like you don't know, you gotta bow down to the queen."

I gotta admit, it was cute seeing my girl show a side I didn't know she had. Once the songs ended and the crowd broke up, Kamaria and I were left sitting by ourselves at the table.

"That was crazy," she said with a huge smile still on her face.

"The cypher was cool, but it was wild seeing you rap. I ain't know you had that in you."

"D, I've been in Oak Cliff most of my life. In my heart, I've always been a rapper."

"Well, you did that! I almost got off beat when you started rapping 'cause I was so hyped. I was thinking, 'It ain't nothing my baby can't do.' I was proud of you."

She put her head down a little and smiled. Us melanated people don't really blush, but she was close. We held hands and walked out of the school. She asked if I could take her home so we could talk. As we got in the car, she ended up telling me about being selected as valedictorian and how she was getting nervous about making her graduation speech.

"You been workin' toward this your whole life—you got it. Just don't overthink it. Tell the people who you are, and how you made it. Give 'em some words of encouragement and keep it moving."

"I guess you're right. I just don't want me stumbling through my words to be the last memory some people have of me."

After talking about her speech, we discussed her college decision. During the convo, she wondered if she was making a mistake by leaving, and how I was able to make the decision to stay at home.

"You said you made up your mind to leave. If you stay, eventually you might start looking at your mom different. You'll start looking at me different. Oak Cliff probably won't even feel the same," I told her.

"But how is me staying any different than you? You don't think you'll regret the city and everybody, too?"

"Nah, it ain't like that for me. I wanna get out when the time's right—but that ain't now. With my mom's health the way it is, it wouldn't be right for me to go, anyway."

As soon as I said it, I remembered I hadn't told her about my mom's diagnosis because Mom wanted us to keep it in the family. I tried to keep the conversation going, but Kamaria wasn't having it.

"Yeah, I ain't trying to go nowhere right now..."

"No, don't keep talking like I didn't hear you. What you mean, 'your mom's health'? What's going on?"

"She got stage 4 cancer. They told us she ain't got long," I blurted.

I heard myself say it, but it felt unreal. I sat in silence, waiting for Kamaria to respond, but for a while, she didn't say anything.

"Your mom... she's such a good person. Why her?"

"I don't know, but I guess it's part of the plan," I said.

I talked like I was enlightened, but truthfully, I probably had less faith in God than I ever had before. When I should've been talking to Him more, I foolishly thought He couldn't help me. So, I hardly talked to Him at all.

"Is she doing chemo and stuff?" Kamaria asked.

"Yeah! Mom's a soldier. She gonna do everything she can to be around as long as possible."

Then, I felt Kamaria's hand reach for mine. She felt my pain, and I felt hers. That small touch was the comfort we both needed. It gave me permission to stop trying to be strong, and just let myself feel whatever I felt.

"Hey... can I be real with you?" I asked.

"Of course," she said, wiping the tears from her face.

"I'm scared, babe. That's my mama, and they said she ain't got long. How we supposed to handle that? How we supposed to start thinking about life without her?"

I leaned forward and buried my face into the steering wheel. I can't say for sure if that was the first time the thought of losing my mom really hit me, but it's a moment that stands out.

"Don't go there, D," Kamaria said softly. "We gotta cherish every moment we have 'cause we don't know when we won't have any more."

She was right, but realizing that didn't make me feel any better. My therapy sessions had taught me that sometimes you have to be okay with not being okay — and that was one of those times.

I pulled myself together just enough to get back on the road while we kept talking.

"Do you think your mom's at home?" Kamaria asked.

"Yeah. Why, what's up?"

"Do you think I could stop by for a minute?"

I agreed, and when we got to the house, I felt my energy drop as soon as I walked in. It wasn't because of anything anyone did — it was just the atmosphere. Mom saw us walk through the door and tried to smile, but I could tell it took effort. Same for Kamaria. Mom was disappointed when she found out I told someone outside the family about her health, though.

"Mrs. Roberts, I love you," Kamaria said, holding her hand. "Since I've been dating Damian, you've been my second mother. You've been there for me when my mom wasn't, or didn't know how to be. So now, I'm gonna be there for you any way I can. And please don't ever think people will see you as weak — that's impossible. Your strength will never be in question."

"I appreciate that, Kamaria. I love you, too," Mom said with a small smile. "Did you ever figure out where you're going to school?" She asked, trying to change the subject.

"Yes, ma'am... well, I think."

"What do you mean?" Mom asked.

"I thought I was set to go to D.C., but I've been second-guessing myself. What do you call it when you feel bad for making it out of a situation and somebody else doesn't?"

"You're talking about survivor's remorse," Mom said.

I wanted to jump into the conversation, but I stayed quiet — just listening to my mom's wisdom.

"As a mother," Mom said gently, "what we want more than anything, is to see our kids live a better life than us. Over the years, I've built a genuine friendship with your mom, and I know for a fact that's what she wants for you."

"Then, why is she acting so sad, Mrs. Roberts?"

"Pride doesn't negate sadness, Kamaria. Your mom isn't acting like she's sad—she is. But I doubt she'd want you to forgo your dreams for her."

"You got a point, but what am I supposed to do?" Kamaria asked.

"You're supposed to go live the life your mom sacrificed so much for you to have. She wants you to be great, whether that's here or somewhere else."

Kamaria was really paying attention to every word my mother said. By the end of their conversation, Mom had put her at ease. It was amazing that, in the midst of what had to be excruciating pain, my mom was still able to make someone else feel better. I walked over and gave her a gentle hug. I wanted to say something, but at that moment, holding her said everything words couldn't.

Kamaria wanted to talk a little more before I took her home. As she and my mom continued to converse, Pops came in with the rest of the family.

"Hey, Miss Kamaria. How are you?"

"I'm good, Mr. Roberts. How are you?"

My dad wanted to be the pillar of strength he normally was, but when he looked over at the weakened version of my mother, he couldn't. Instead, he politely asked us to give him a minute. He pulled up a chair, sat next to Mom, and held her hand. They looked into each other's eyes before my father closed his. He started to whisper, and even though I couldn't hear everything he was saying, I could tell he was praying. My mother soon followed his lead and closed her eyes, too.

We figured they needed time alone, so we went into the living room, where my brother and sister soon joined us.

"Look at her. We just found out about her having cancer, and everything's already different. It's like we gotta watch her waste away, and there ain't nothin' we can do about it."

"Yeah, she shouldn't have to deal with this," Lexi added.

"Who should?" I asked, looking at everyone in the room.

The question left my mouth before I even processed it. I don't know what made me ask it, but it was similar to when I asked who deserved to get robbed, after it happened to us. My question pushed the conversation down a path we probably wouldn't have reached otherwise.

"Lexi said Ma shouldn't have to deal with this. It ain't like I disagree, but cancer don't care who you are. What makes us think we're special?"

"You know what she was saying," Elijah told me.

"I know exactly what she's saying—but like I said, we ain't special."

I was getting upset, but it wasn't because of anything anyone said or did. I knew my tone and delivery were harsh, especially under the circumstances, but I was saying it so everyone—including myself—could hear the truth clearly. I was honest, but the way I said it was wrong. Elijah looked like he wanted to fight, Lexi had her head buried in her hands, and Kamaria just shook her head in disappointment.

"I'm sorry, y'all. I shouldn't have talked to y'all like that," I told them.

"Why did you even feel like it was necessary to talk to them like that?" Kamaria asked.

"I don't know. I guess it's just 'hurt people, hurt people.' My bad."

I didn't get the instant forgiveness I expected. Lexi and Elijah both went to their rooms without saying another word. And Kamaria was looking at me like she didn't wanna be around, either.

"I'm gonna drop Kamaria off," I told my folks as I opened the door.

"Could you come here?" My mom asked Kamaria before we left.

"Yes, ma'am," she said, walking over to my parents.

Mom smiled and used all her strength to stand up.

"I know I wasn't supposed to, but I heard what y'all were talking about in there. My boy might've been too blunt with what he said, but he's not a liar. Nobody deserves cancer, but we can't question God's plan. And I have to accept the sickness as part of my journey."

"Yes, ma'am, but—"

"No buts, Kamaria. Hear me out, 'cause I don't know how much strength I got left. I just need you to see his heart. D is our firstborn, and he's always felt like it's his job to help us with any problem we have. For the first time in his life, there ain't much he can do. Knowing him, he probably thinks he's letting me down 'cause he can't fix me. So please...forgive him. Life's too short to let love leave your heart," Mom said.

"Plus, you know, no matter how smart the dude is, we all do some dumb stuff. D ain't no exception," my dad added.

After that, there was a seismic energy shift. Mom gave Kamaria a hug, and then we left. I remember feeling okay the rest of the night, but stress started creeping in soon after. By graduation day, the only thing on my mind was my mom. There was no way she was supposed to leave the house that day, but there wasn't anything any of us could say to convince her to stay home, so we stopped trying.

I had to leave earlier than the rest of the family to get in line at the graduation site, but when I looked at my mom, I felt guilty. I hadn't done anything wrong, but I almost convinced myself that having her come out when she was in pain was selfish. Then, as I started driving to pick up Kamaria and head to the venue, I started seeing things differently.

Denying my mom the chance to see me walk across that stage would've taken joy and fulfillment away from her. The truth was, as much as we didn't wanna think about it, we could all see Mom fading away. My graduation could've been one of the last moments she'd get to forget her pain and just feel proud. That's when I realized—letting her come wasn't selfish, but stopping her would've been.

When Kamaria got in the car, we talked happily about finishing high school. She let go of the last bit of anxiety she had about her valedictorian speech, and overall, we were feeling good. We had finally reached the moment we had been waiting for.

As the ceremony got started, it seemed like all of the staff had something to say. They watched a lot of us go from insecure freshmen, to overly confident seniors. They were the ones who cared for us when a lot of us didn't have anyone else. So, when I thought about it like that, I understood why I saw just as many tears as I saw smiles.

"Look at ya girl," somebody sitting in front of me said when it was time for Kamaria to speak.

I couldn't hide the smile on my face, even if I wanted to.

"Boy, you lame," the same person said.

"Man, ain't nobody—"

"Don't trip, I'm just playing."

When he turned back around, I was finally able to focus on what Kamaria was saying.

"...and the crazy thing is, God has something in store for all of us. Folks wanna tell us what we can't do because of where we're from, but I don't believe 'em. We're here for a reason, and now, it's time to start figuring out what our reasons are. We left our marks on Kimball, now it's time to start leaving our marks on the world."

Man, you couldn't tell me her speech wasn't one of the greatest ever. Her words brought me a joy that stayed with me until later that evening when her, her mom, and my family all met up for dinner. My dad tried to pick a place to go, but he was trying to show out and be fancy, but as usual, none of us wanted that.

"I don't know 'bout y'all, but I really just want something from Sweet Georgia Brown," I said.

SGB was a soul food spot on Ledbetter that would always get you right.

"Well, it looks like Sweet Georgia Brown it is, then," my mom said.

She tried to smile, but I could tell she was in pain. I didn't wanna say anything 'cause I knew she was trying her best to be happy for me and Kamaria.

"Say bro, can we ride with you?" Elijah asked suddenly.

His question was enough to distract me from what I was thinking about.

"They just wanna give you a break," I told my dad, as we headed to the car.

"Yeah, right. Let that be the reason," Pops said with a big smile.

Eventually, Lexi, Elijah, and Kamaria got in the '88, and everyone else followed behind us to SGB. I had my CD book and Sony Discman in the glove compartment. I asked Kamaria to grab them so I could connect everything to the cassette player and get the vibes right in the car.

"Damian, please don't play no old folks music," Lexi said.

"Yeah, that's why we didn't wanna ride with Pops and Mama," Elijah said.

"I got you," I told them.

I went through my CDs and put one in without telling them what it was.

"What you 'bout to have us listen to?" Kamaria asked.

"I'm really on my Texas stuff right now. I promise y'all gon' like this."

With that, I let my lil' ol' mix CD play. It took me a minute to get everything on it 'cause it wasn't as easy to get music back then as it is now, but I had tracks from Lucci, Mr. Pookie, UGK, Big Pokey, S.U.C.—everybody who was poppin' in Texas at the time. I had everybody in the car jammin'. By the time we made it to Sweet Georgia Brown, they were actin' like they were stuck to their seats.

Once we finally got inside, I looked around the restaurant like I was seeing it for the first time. The smell hit me like it was brand new, too. When our group sat down, we wasted no time putting in our order. We asked for everything on the menu.

"Okay, your food'll be out in a lil'," the waitress told us.

We were enjoying each other's company, but when the food came out, all that talking stopped real quick. Everything made us just sit there and eat. That silence continued when they brought out the pound cake, banana pudding, and peach cobbler. It was some of the best food we ever had.

I looked up from my plate and saw everybody had almost finished everything—except my mom. She had barely touched her food. I expected her to eat slowly, but it was worse than I thought.

"What y'all 'bout to get into?" My dad asked.

A question like that, in our community, was code—it meant it was time to go.

"We got some family comin' to the house a lil' later to celebrate Kamaria. You know you family, so y'all welcome to swing by if you want," Ms. Anderson said.

"Thank you, but I don't know if I have it in me to go anywhere else. I may just go home and take a nap," Mom told her faintly.

"Girl, I understand. Get your rest."

When we all got home, Mom took a nap, just like she said she was going to. At that time, Pops told us he needed to have a talk.

"I just wanted to let y'all know some things you may not already know. Your mom keeps telling me she's heard from God, and she knows it's almost time for her to go home."

My emotions had a stranglehold on me, and I couldn't say anything. My siblings, on the other hand, had plenty to say.

"What? Mom ain't goin' nowhere. I don't wanna hear that," Lexi exclaimed.

"Yeah, y'all actin' like you already gave up," Elijah yelled.

"You know ain't no quit in us," Pops replied.

"So why you talkin' like that?" Elijah shot back.

Dad walked over and kinda huddled us together.

"I'm saying it because it's true. She didn't want y'all to be caught off guard, but she couldn't tell y'all she feels like she's almost out of time," Pops told us.

I heard everything being said around me, and I had my thoughts about it, but I still couldn't say a word. Our father wrapped his arms around us and hugged us. He said all he needed to say, no matter how hard it was for us to hear. Deep down, I think we all knew he was right, but none of us wanted to accept the thought of losing our mother.

"I'm gonna go in the room with her for a minute," Pops said before leaving the room to join Mama.

Even though the day had been full of celebration, that night was a heavy one. I tossed and turned, hearing the cries of my sister and brother drift throughout the house. I prayed over and over for my mom to get better. Then, around two in the morning, I heard God talk to me.

"You seek healing for your mother, but your request is selfish. Do you want her to be better for her, or for you?"

The question was hard to answer. I wanted her to be better because we needed her, but I didn't want her to be in pain anymore.

"I don't want my mom to suffer," I said just loud enough for God to hear me.

"Is there any pain amongst the angels? Is there any suffering when you're in My home?"

I didn't need to answer. I knew what He was saying. I let out a heavy sigh before finally closing my eyes. My tears escaped captivity, and I couldn't stop them. Eventually, my mind quieted enough for me to get a little sleep.

9

I woke up around 6:30 the next morning. I sat up and held the covers like I used to when I was younger. I stared into the darkness and listened to the silence. Then, my father walked into my room.

He normally slept late when he didn't have to work, so I already knew what was going on. Within seconds, he dropped to his knees before burying his face in the carpet right inside my room.

"Get up, Pops," I whispered, trying to pull him up.

I couldn't move him, so after a while, I quit trying. I just stayed on the floor with him until he was ready to get up.

"She's gone, D," he said so faintly I could barely hear him.

Eventually, we both stood up and quietly walked to his room. As soon as we hit the threshold, my father pointed to my mother, who was still in her usual sleeping position.

He stepped aside to let me know I had permission to go to her. I started to tremble, unsure if I wanted to move closer, but I knew I had to. The first step felt like I was learning to walk again. Each one got harder, and by the time I made it to her, I wanted to turn around and leave.

I didn't think I'd have the nerve to touch her, but I had no reason to fear my own mother. I grabbed her hand, and when I did, I could feel the last bit of heat slipping away. I kept holding it as I closed my eyes and prayed that she'd have a safe transition. After my prayer, I kissed her on her forehead, just like I had done almost every morning.

"I love you, Mom. Thank you for e'rything."

"Are you okay?" I asked as I looked at my dad.

"My best friend's gone. When she was gonna leave me back in the day, I begged her to stay. I can't beg her no more, D. She gone, and ain't nothin' I can do to get her back."

I put my head down and closed my eyes again. I imagined my mother wasn't gone—just sleeping. I opened my eyes when I heard my dad let out an agonizing yell that took me back to when I saw RaShawn's parents in the hospital. The scream he let out woke up Lexi and Elijah. Soon, both of them were running into the room.

"What's going on?" Elijah asked, still wiping the sleep from his eyes.

We couldn't say anything. My dad just took a step back. It took a few seconds for them to look at Mom. When they did, the looks on their faces made my heart sink. Pops moved in between them. He put his arm around Elijah and held Lexi's hand.

"She fought as hard as she could, but God said she ain't have to fight no more," Pops said, his voice trembling.

Her skin tone was starting to change, which made my brother and sister too scared to touch her. They just stared at her as the tears from their eyes fell onto our mother's face. For a brief moment, it looked like she was the one crying. Even in death, it was like she was still hurting whenever any of us were.

We stayed in that room praying, crying, and looking at my mother until the coroner showed up. He talked to my dad for a little bit—gathering information, giving some back to us—and soon after, he was taking the matriarch of our family out of our home, covered in a body bag. Nothing could've prepared me for that moment.

My dad and mom were together since they were young, so I couldn't begin to imagine how he was feeling. I was still outside with him, watching the space where the coroner was a few moments before. He told me to go inside and check on my siblings because he needed some time to himself.

Inside, we all talked about how we were feeling, and some of the things Mama said that we would always remember.

"You remember how she'd be like, 'You don't believe fat meat's greasy, do you?' That confused me for a long time," Elijah said.

"Yeah, that confused me, too," Lexi added.

"Then, she explained it, 'You have the choice to partake in whatever you want, but you can't be surprised if your decision ends up bringing consequences you don't want to deal with.' I used to think there was no way that phrase meant all that," I said.

"She could let you know how bad you disappointed her and turn around and lift you up," Lexi said softly.

When Pops came back inside the house, he kept apologizing as if Mama's death was his fault. Our parents were superheroes to us, and at that moment, it was like someone had taken the Vibranium away from the Black Panther. It was heartbreaking.

We ended up staying to ourselves the first day after Mama's passing because we needed to. We had to have time to process the fact that God called Mama to leave our home and go to His. The next day, we slowly started to tell people. Of course, I told Kamaria.

She immediately said she was on her way. I wanted to tell her she didn't need to come, but I couldn't. I had been trying my best to stay strong around my family, but I was in so much pain, I didn't know how I was gonna make it. When she rang the doorbell, I ran outside and hugged her. It was at that moment I could no longer contain how I was really feeling.

When she got to our house, she didn't say anything. She just held onto me tightly and let me express myself without judgment, like she had so many other times before. I told her we didn't even know how we were going to pay for Mama's service because whenever my parents would talk about life insurance or retirement, extra bills would always show up.

I kept reminding Pops he could use the money they'd saved for me to go to school, but he wasn't having it. He told me Mama's spirit would cuss him out if he even thought about touching any of our "school money." So, I had to respect it and help him figure out another way to take care of things.

"My dad tries not to talk to me about it too much, but I know he stressin' 'cause I see it in his eyes every time I look at him. Usually, when the family had to find a way to pay for something, he and my mom get it taken care of, but now…"

I remember feeling helpless. My dad lost the love of his life, didn't know how he was gonna pay her final expenses, and there I was, a so-called grown man living at home, and couldn't contribute. My senior fees and activities had been chewing up my money all year, and with college applications and other random stuff that had to be paid, I didn't have anything extra.

I was feeling bad about my lack of money, but unlike me, Kamaria didn't hang her head in defeat. She just immediately leapt into action and asked me if I had prayed about it. God was crucial in my life, but sometimes I lacked that mustard seed faith you're supposed to have.

"No, I was just trying to find ways to make something happen."

"That's the problem. You focus too much on what you can do, but you can't do anything right now."

I thought she was trying to clown me, so my face changed while my mind got ready to say something defensive. She noticed the change and said something that stopped me.

"Whatever you thinkin' right now, that's not where my heart is. I'm just saying, you don't have a lot of extra money, and I don't either. We can't do anything right now, but God can do everything."

Her words stuck with me, and they convinced me prayer was the first step that needed to be taken. So, that's what we did. When we were done, I still didn't know what we were gonna do, but I felt more confident something would get done.

"Damian, could you come here for a minute?" Pops asked.

"Should I stay here?" Kamaria asked.

"Nah, babe. Let's see what he talkin' 'bout," I said as we went to the living room, where he sounded like he was.

"What's up, Pops?" I asked.

"Oh, hey Kamaria. I didn't know you were here," he said when we walked in.

"Yes, sir. I'm so sorry about Mrs. Roberts. She was like my second mama."

"I appreciate it."

There were a few seconds of awkward silence. I could sense Pops wanted to talk about Mama's service, but he was too embarrassed because Kamaria was there. We assured him it was all good because we were talking about the same thing.

I knew my father was too prideful to admit he needed help, but a sense of relief briefly showed on his face when Kamaria offered help.

"We gonna be alright, Pops, I promise," I told him.

That statement was one of faith, proof that prayer was already working. I still had no idea how we'd come up with the money for my mom's final expenses, especially after my dad told me how much everything would be, but I knew God would make a way.

I could've talked myself into doubting my own words, but that wouldn't have done any good. I also could've let stress stop me in my tracks, but my mother deserved the best, and my family was gonna do all we could to make sure she got it. God soon gave me the idea to start asking people in the neighborhood if they could help in any way. The thought alone made me uncomfortable, but comfort wasn't a requirement for doing what needed to be done.

Before crowdsourcing was a thing, and before cell phones were in everybody's hands, the best way to ask for help was face-to-face. So, after letting Kamaria and my dad know what I was gonna do, I went outside and started knocking on doors. Without hesitation, Kamaria joined me.

My heart was pounding heavily as I walked up to the first house. I was incredibly nervous, and I didn't like to bother people, especially unannounced, but I knocked anyway. The kindness of the gentleman I spoke with set my mind at ease and calmed me down enough to keep going. I was truly surprised at how helpful people were.

Not everyone could donate money, which we understood, but

everyone was willing to do something. Some people had connections at funeral homes and told us we could possibly get discounts. Others knew folks who did floral arrangements, and someone who worked at Foley's said they'd ask their manager if they could use their discount to make sure everyone in the family was dressed right for Mom's service. The hood had our backs, for real.

"Damian, most of these people don't even know y'all like that, but they still love you. God said, 'Love thy neighbor,' so this is exactly how things are supposed to be. When someone in the neighborhood is in trouble, the neighbors are supposed to work together to make sure they're okay."

"Yeah, my mom has always said most of the people around here ain't nowhere close to what the news tries to make us out to be, and as usual, she was right."

The more people I talked to, the better I felt. The elders kept reminding me Mom was in a better place because of how she lived. The young folks told me to keep my head up. And all the while, Kamaria was right by my side, letting me know I wasn't alone.

After a few days, we put together the donations with what we already had and were able to pay for Mom's service. All that work was just to make sure my mom was sent out with honor and respect. The crazy thing is, when we realized we'd met the goal, we almost forgot the funeral was the next step.

Before we knew it, we had gone from fundraising, to sitting down in the church on the day of my mother's service.

"As we get on with the proceedings, I wanna see if any of the family members, or friends, have any words to say for our beloved Katherine Roberts," the preacher said once the service started.

People were still taking their seats while soft music played in the background, and we all looked at each other. I wanted to say something, but I didn't know if I could. Before I made up my mind, Lexi and Elijah — walking hand-in-hand — made their way to the front. They slowly looked around the room and, almost in unison, took a deep breath before Lexi started speaking.

"You know how sometimes stuff happens and you wonder why?

Well, that's how I been feelin' since we found out Mama had cancer. Then, when she passed, I started asking what we did that was so wrong for her to be taken away from us. I know that ain't the right way to think, but that's the truth. You know what, though? I always heard people say, 'God don't make no mistakes,' so as much as I don't understand this, and as much as it hurts not to have Mama anymore, I know there's a purpose for it."

As she paused, Elijah let go of her hand just long enough to put his arm around her. While she gathered herself, he stepped closer to the microphone. Ever since he was little, Elijah had always been more of an introvert, but when he needed to speak, he could do it with humor and humility.

"Like my sister said, there has to be a reason Mom got called away from us so soon. I don't think none of us know what that reason is, but there is one. I know..."

His strength and stability suddenly left him. He stopped speaking. As tears began to build in his eyes, he looked at Lexi, then at everyone else in the church. I could tell he needed me up there, so I went on stage to be with him and Lexi. Just like he'd done for our little sister, I put my arm around him and leaned in close.

"You got it, bro," I whispered to him, hoping the microphone didn't pick me up.

He inhaled deeply a few times before finally continuing.

"Look, I'm hurt right now. My T-lady... my bad, I mean, my mama... is gone. That lady is the greatest woman I've ever known. I've learned so much from her. I just hate that the moments she used to drop gems on us are over. She'd say stuff that had me so throwed off at first 'cause I didn't get it, but then, when I wasn't even thinkin' about it no more, her words came back around. Then, the same stuff I didn't get would end up makin' all the sense in the world.

It's like when you listen to rap music... well, y'all might not listen to rap... but sometimes they'll say one thing and you be like, 'That sound good,' but you don't really get what they talkin' 'bout. Later on, you'll be like, 'Oh, dude was snappin', for real, for real, with that verse!' So, I already know she might not be here to drop no new gems for us, but her greatest hits gon' be playin' in our heads for the rest of our lives."

He was doing so well, I thought I might have just stepped on stage for moral support—which was fine. But then, he glanced at Mom's open casket. That's when he lost it all over again.

"Dang. I don't know why I just looked over at her. She really ain't here no more, huh? My mama gone for real, ain't she? Dang, bruh. I thought I was good, but I ain't. My bad, y'all. Mama didn't want us up here crying. She smiled even when she was getting ready to see God, and I know she wouldn't want me to be like this. I'm sorry, Mama, but I ain't as strong as you. It's gonna take me a minute to really be able to deal with all of this, but..."

"But he knows he's not gonna have to deal with this alone. None of us are." I took a deep breath, steadying myself before I was able to continue. "My mom and dad have always told us that as a family, we have to have an unbreakable bond with one another. They told us, no matter what, we can't ever let any member of our family feel like they're alone, even when they need some time to be by themselves.

Every day leading up to... well, until the day Mama passed, like my brother said, she had a smile on her face. If you didn't know any better, you would have thought Mama was feeling better. See, Mama was a soldier, for real. If God gave anybody a direct flight to Heaven, with no layovers, it had to be Mama. That's why she was good with going, even though we obviously still ain't. She was good because she was prepared, and she did her best to make sure we were prepared, too. Actually, when you think about it, if you know you are going to meet God, you would smile, too, even if it meant leaving some people behind. Well, even though Mama wasn't with us for a long time, I have to thank God for sharing her with us. Mama, we love you, and I promise, we will never forget you."

There was loud, but scattered applause throughout the sanctuary. I looked at my father to see if he was going to join us on stage, but he silently assured me he wasn't. We all had to pass by Mama's open casket to get onto the stage, so I figured that was something he just wasn't able to do. We didn't even have to talk about it because it was something we all understood.

After all the songs had been sung, and all the friends, family, neighbors, and co-workers said what they needed to say, the preacher gave an altar call.

"Sister Roberts is going to be with God because she lived her life according to His Word. She was an obedient servant of the Lord. Her kids even told us as she was spiritually getting ready to transition to the next level, she was smiling. She was only able to do that because she wasn't afraid of what was going to happen. The preparation her eldest son talked about was giving her life to Christ. If you want to have eternal life, you have to be born again," he said.

Unsurprisingly, one of Mama's last acts of service was bringing people to God. She lived her life trying to show people His love, so it was only right that her celebration of life did the exact same thing. The Kingdom grew by at least seven or eight people that day, including Ms. Anderson. I was incredibly happy to see her give her life to Christ, and I could tell Kamaria was, too. Unfortunately, I wasn't in as much of a celebratory mood for them as I should have been.

Honestly, I didn't even know Kamaria and her mom were there, but I should have known they would be. The relationship they had established with my mom had organically grown to one of genuine love. And so they both told me it was their honor to pay their respects to my mother. I tried to thank them, but I know my energy was lacking. I hoped they understood my heart was heavy, so I was unable to interact with them the way I normally would have.

After the Prayer of Salvation had been completed, the preacher gave the benediction. We all stood in front of our seats, watching as they closed the casket on Mama. Once it was sealed, Pops grabbed his chest because his heart was gone. That's when it hit me, we had just seen our mother's face, in the physical form, for the last time. Unfortunately, I'd been around death all my life, but that one hit different.

I remember moving after that, but I don't remember controlling any of my movements. It felt like I was having an out-of-body experience. The world moved around me, but I couldn't focus on any of it. Everything was happening fast, yet somehow in slow motion at the same time. That feeling only intensified when my mother's casket was lowered into the ground.

"Ashes to ashes…"

When I heard those famous three words, I completely lost control. I don't actually know why those were the words that set me off, but they did. I'm not even sure anyone finished the sentence after that because I started yelling loudly enough for my mother's spirit to hear me in Heaven.

Eventually, I fell to the ground. In that moment, I felt like I was drowning in sadness. I couldn't wipe the tears away, couldn't be brave for my family. Right then, I had no choice but to grieve. I cried like a baby, and the person who would normally comfort me in times like that was the reason I was crying in the first place

I felt hands patting my back, trying to lift me up physically and emotionally, but nothing worked. People tried to encourage me with their words, but as much as the meant what they were saying, the words were just empty syllables, meant more to make them feel like they'd done their part to help. Everybody told us they loved us and were praying for us, but I didn't believe them. If they loved us so much, why did they let our mom die? Why didn't all those praying people talk to God with us and ask Him to give us just a little more time with Mama?

Eventually, I stopped asking myself rhetorical questions and got up. Kamaria, Ms. Anderson, and my family were all standing right there, but none of them said anything until they knew I was ready for a conversation.

"My bad, y'all. I…"

I was truly embarrassed, but I also felt more liberated than I had been in a long time.

"You miss your mom. You ain't gotta apologize for that, 'cause if you do, we'd all be apologizing," Pops said with a slight grin.

Those were the most words he had said all day, so I figured he was finally a little more open to talking, especially since he'd seen me break down in front of everybody.

I looked at everyone as I started to brush the dirt off my clothes.

"Has it really sunk in for you?" I asked my father.

He shook his head. "I don't know how to answer that. Sometimes I know she's gone, but other times I tell myself whatever I need to hear to make myself believe she's still around. You know the crazy thing, D?"

"What's up, Pops?"

"You go through so much of your life looking for the one. You hope you'll find that woman you can trust with your heart, but I ain't never think that if she passed before me... I wouldn't get my heart back. You know what I'm saying? I ain't got a hole in my heart I'm missin' a whole part of me."

I had never heard my dad talk like that before, but Mama always made him act differently than he would have on his own. Whether it was emotions or boxing, he always believed in keeping your guard up. But when something hits you hard enough, you forget all about defense because you're too busy trying to recover. I could tell that's what was happening with him.

We all spent a little while longer standing around Mom's new resting place. After the dirt was placed on top of her casket, we circled around the headstone that was already in place. When everyone else had gone back to their lives, we stayed, talking about how we'd move forward. It was awkward. It was hard to talk about moving on when the person who kept the family moving was no longer there.

People always say time heals all wounds, but I don't really agree. I think time just makes your wounds and scars less visible—but I can't say everything gets healed. My mom's absence spoke volumes, but the memory of her voice and messages kept us from being stuck in our sadness.

A few days after we laid my mother to rest, I heard her voice speaking out to me.

"What are you doing, Damian? What's going on with my family?" I heard her ask.

I couldn't see her, but her voice was as clear as if she was sitting in the same room with me.

"We all miss you, Mom. It's kinda hard to act like ain't nothin' changed when my whole life is different," I told her.

"I get it, Damian, but you can't let me halt your progress. I never want to be someone who holds you back."

"No, it's not like that at all, it's..."

"But it is exactly like that. If you are not doing what you're supposed to do, and it's because of me, how am I not the one who's holding you back? I thought your father and I raised a man who wouldn't let anything or anyone stop him from doing what he needed to do to accomplish his goals."

I couldn't tell if my mother was speaking to me, if I was speaking to myself, or if God was using my mom's spirit to get a point across, but whatever it was, it worked. I turned on the radio, and the first song that came on was Sam Cooke's, "A Change Is Gonna Come." It was just about to go off, so all I heard was Mr. Cooke sing, "It's been a long, a long time coming, but I know a change gon' come. Oh yes, it will."

"Yes, sir, Mr. Cooke you're right. A change is gonna come," I whispered into the night air as I turned the radio back off.

I heard all I needed to hear. From that moment on, I told myself I was going to move differently. If there was going to be a change, my actions had to be more intentional than before. I had to regain the faith I once had and do my best to spread that same energy to my family.

10

———

Time grew wings after my mother passed. It seemed like I was graduating from Kimball one day, and the next, everyone was getting ready for school again. My siblings told my dad they needed a fresh start, so they wanted to transfer to Townview.

The school was a new high school with a bunch of magnet schools in it. I have no idea how my siblings managed to get their applications accepted so close to the first day of school, but they did. I guess it was one of those moments that proved when the favor of the Lord is with you, abnormal things may happen.

With all of the changes happening in our lives, I volunteered to take them to school. I figured it'd be good for us to spend some time together each morning, just in case they needed to vent. On the first day of school, it felt good to see them laugh. Moments like that had been few and far between after Mom died. Things almost seemed normal until we pulled up to Townview.

The school itself was nice, and you could tell it was one of the newest ones in DISD. It looked modern and almost artistic. I joked that I could practically feel the nerd vibes coming off of it. Then, I looked across the street and saw an old, run-down hotel. Let's just say, you could tell some unscrupulous things probably went on over there —but who was I to judge?

I drove up a little more to drop Lexi and Elijah off.

"No justice, no peace! No justice, no peace!"

I was thrown off when I saw a group of people yelling about justice. They were led by a dude in biker shorts shouting through a megaphone.

"Yo, what is goin' on at y'all's school? I asked.

"I heard folks talkin' 'bout this, but I thought they were jokin'. Dude with the megaphone is John Wiley Price. He's some kinda politician, but I don't know why him and his people are out here," Elijah said.

I asked Lexi and Elijah if they thought everything was good, and they said they were okay. Just as I was getting emotional about seeing them start something new, Elijah got out and slammed my door. It squeaked louder than it ever had, and all of the fuzzy feelings jumped out of the car right along with them.

Ebony wasn't the newest car on the block, so she made noises. Normally, it didn't bother me when it happened, but when Elijah slammed the door that day, and it yelled out like it was in agony, I couldn't help but feel embarrassed. I don't know why my car wanted to show out that day, but the door popped so loudly, everybody started ducking. Elijah just laughed and kept walking towards the school. Everyone else, including John Wiley Price and his people started staring at me.

After getting over Ebony embarrassing me in public, I stopped at the gas station on the corner. I went in and got me some Chili Cheese Fritos, which I did fairly often, in memory of my homie, and a strawberry Clearly Canadian. I paid for my gas and snacks and was walking out when I bumped into this slightly older dude with one of the ugliest shags I ever saw. Not only was it uneven, it looked like he had some bootleg S-Curl or something in it. He couldn't have been from The Cliff, 'cause that ain't something we did.

He accused me of wanting to fight, and I wasn't one for confrontations, but I wasn't going to necessarily shy away from one if I needed to protect myself. He was bigger than me, but I figured I would take a swing before he did. This fool caught my fist like my punch was nothing.

He shook his head and told me he saw me dropping my people off at Townview. He also said it looked like I should be going to somebody's school, too.

"Yeah, it's my first day at Paul Quinn," I told him.

"And you ready to squab, for what?"

"I done lost too many people to go out without fighting," I said, feeling like my emotions were about to get the best of me.

"Everybody ain't tryin' to fight, homie. Even if they were, every fight ain't for you."

He was right. As he finally released my still-clenched fist, I still thought he was trying to get me to let my guard down.

"Calm down before I calm you down," he told me in a stern tone.

He suddenly reached into his pocket and pulled out a few loose bills.

"It's yo' first day of school, and you seem like you got some other stuff on your mind. This ain't a lot, but hopefully it can get your mind back on track."

"Why you givin' me this? I was just tryin' to fight you," I said.

He thought about it for a second, then a confused smile showed up.

"Bruh, I can't even call it. Somethin' told me to just shoot some change yo' way, so that's what I'm doin'. I just need for you to do right in school and look out for your people, you feel me?"

I nodded, put the money in my pocket, and walked out. I put the gas in my car, then I got in, and sat there for a minute. I pulled out the money he gave me and found it was close to a hundred dollars.

"D, why you tryin' to block yo' blessings, huh?" I heard someone ask.

It was yet another time I looked around the car and didn't see anyone. I thought I was just trippin', but I should have known who I was hearing, and what was happening.

"We gotta get beyond doin' stupid stuff for no reason. People are countin' on you, so you can't let them, or yourself down."

When I made it to school, I put my head down when I accepted I was hearing RaShawn again. I sat in the parking lot, crying. It was about fifteen minutes before my first class was about to start, but I stayed in the car to see if he had anything else to say.

"This ain't the final step, it's just the next one, remember that," he said.

I thought I was ready to take the next step he talked about, but what if I wasn't? That was the question I asked myself, but I heard the voice of God speak to me shortly after.

"It doesn't matter if you think you're not ready because I've prepared you. The next step should be of no concern because your family walks in faith. And I promise you don't have to worry about letting anyone down, because I know who I raised up."

When God talks to you like that, any doubt you have in yourself is removed. I moved with confidence towards my my first class, which was "Intro to Public Speaking." I hated the idea of speaking in front of people, so the class was chosen because I had to take it, but I also figured I'd eventually have to get comfortable speaking in front of crowds, even though I didn't know why.

I got into class a few minutes late, and the professor called me out for it. I tried to apologize, but he wasn't having it. So, I just sat down and listened as he delivered a very dry lesson. The class my not have been entertaining, but I wasn't there to be entertained. I also couldn't waste any of the money my parents worked so hard to save for me.

"Each one of you has a copy of the syllabus, so I expect you to get your books and take care of your first assignment. If you have any questions, set up an appointment during my office hours, or see me before or after class. If none of these things are done, you're telling me you understand what has been discussed. I will see you on Wednesday," he said as he dismissed us.

When everyone left the classroom, I walked over to him.

"Again, my bad on being late," I told the professor.

"Although this is a public speaking class, I find some students fail to reach their potential because they like to hear themselves talk more than they like to listen. Those who do that make noise, while making very little progress. Do you get what I'm saying?"

"Yes, sir."

"Good. I expect a lot out of all of my students, but now that we've had this brief little discussion, I'm expecting even more out of you."

With that, he started placing his papers into the vintage leather briefcase he had on the side of his desk. It had seen better days, but the rips and tears showed it had character. I glanced at the briefcase one more time before I walked out.

Since I didn't have another class until later, I walked around to get a feel for my new campus. As I did, a random patch of grass seemed to be begging me to sit down. So, I obliged. I was still using the same backpack I had during my last few years of high school, so like my professor's briefcase, it might've been a little past its prime, but it had character.

I put the backpack down and used it as my pillow. I went back and forth between staring at the cloudless blue sky and discreetly observing the people walking by. It was crazy I was still in Oak Cliff, but since I was in college, it felt like I had been transported some-where else.

"Hey," I heard someone say, interrupting my peace.

I couldn't tell if they were talking to me, so I went back to enjoying my alone time.

"Don't be rude. I know you hear me," they said, confirming they were talking to me.

I sat up and saw this girl standing in front of me with a smile on her face. Her hair was freshly twisted, and the diamond studs in her ears sparkled every time she moved. She was wearing a mostly red dress, and she had the nerve to be rockin' a nice pair of shoes, too, but I wasn't really looking at her like that.

"Hey, I'm Destiny."

When she gave me her name, I stood up and shook her hand.

"What up, Destiny? I'm Damian."

"You a freshman, huh?" She asked.

I wanted to lie, but I had to keep it honest.

"Yeah, how'd you know?"

"Because you were shook when I came over here. No disrespect, but you just look like a freshman."

I laughed at her calling me out. Then, she told me she saw me across campus. She introduced me to a new smile with every word she spoke. I knew she was flirting with me, but I had to pretend to be oblivious to it.

"I gotta girl," I blurted out.

"Since school just started, I take it y'all were high school sweethearts. Well, you ain't in high school no more, Damian. Life'll get different real quick. I ain't tryin' to ruin your relationship, though. I respect you for even mentioning it."

"Cool," I told her, not knowing how else I should reply.

"I'll be seeing you around, trust me," she told me.

Once I was alone again, I sat down feeling almost guilty. Not because I'd talked to her, but because when she left, I was thinking about when I'd be able to talk to her again. That made me nervous.

I dug into my backpack and pulled out my headphones and CD player. I wasn't sure what was in there, but I pressed play. I fully expected to hear some form of rap, but I was pleasantly surprised I didn't. Instead of 808s and lyrics the elders would've deemed questionable, I heard the sounds of the Dallas legend, Roy Hargrove.

Roy was a world-renowned trumpet player, and his music could always make me relax. Roy could make his trumpet sing a language that communicated messages better than words ever could. My eyes closed as I started creating visuals for every note I heard. I felt myself smiling as the sun reinvigorated me like medicine to my melanated skin.

Although I was sitting on a patch of grass, listening to music on a busy college campus, there was a strange sense of quietness that surrounded me. That was, until I heard my mother's voice speaking to me.

"Being away has given me a chance to see how much you, Elijah, and Lexi have grown. Your wisdom has reached out and grabbed ahold of knowledge from generations of ancestors you never had the privilege of meeting. And I know you've noticed a change in your father. Being the oldest, you have more of a responsibility to your family than everyone else. You have to remind your father of who he is, while making sure your siblings are on the right path. You also have to maintain your passion and drive to move toward your own goals. It's a lot, but you've got this, son. I know you do. I love you."

I didn't ask for extra responsibilities, so I didn't think having them was fair. Selfishly, I just wanted to live my life and do me. That's what I thought to myself.

"C'mon, bruh. You don't even believe dat," the spirit of RaShawn suddenly said to me.

"I ain't even say nothin', so what are you talking 'bout?" I asked.

"We connected, bro. You ain't gotta talk for me to know what you saying. You wanting to do you and not wanting responsibilities ain't even real. There's a million schools out there, and you chose to go to one in Oak Cliff. That ain't gettin' away."

He was right, and Lord knows I tried to stay focused in my next class, but I couldn't. I kept thinking about why I made the decision to stay at home for school. My girl moved, my mom was gone, and my brother and sister were going to a school I had no connection with. So why was I still there?

I didn't want to see the world I grew up in become something different, but it had. Nothing forced me to realize how quickly everything changed like going two weeks without hearing from Kamaria. I knew she'd be busy learning her new city, dealing with classes, and having fun, but I still expected her to make some time for me. That wasn't the case.

We were a few years away from cell phones being a part of everyone's lives, so most of us had to use calling cards to make long-distance calls. The amount of minutes you had depended on how much you spent, and being a broke college student didn't give me much to spend. The few minutes I had on my cards were mostly wasted trying to get ahold of Kamaria, but after weeks of trying, I finally reached her.

"Hey, what's up? How's school?" I asked.

I was nervous even before she said anything because it felt like the conversation wasn't gonna go the way I hoped. That feeling was right. She ended up telling me she didn't know if we were going to work out. There was no reasoning behind it, no explanation, or anything. She just told me, and ended the call.

I tried to shake off the feeling of that conversation throughout the day, but it never left. She didn't say she broke up with me, but it felt like she did. By the time I left campus for the day to pick up Lexi and Elijah, I already noticed a difference in myself. I didn't want to tell them what was going on, but I eventually did.

"We love Kamaria, but if she made a stupid decision to let you go, then we gon' let her go, too," Lexi said.

"You know we got your back like a snug backpack," Elijah added.

I took a moment to look each one of them in their eyes and thank them for encouraging me when they had the perfect opportunity to crack jokes.

"D, you know we won't clown you when you're down," Lexi said.

"Unless you literally trip and fall down. We clownin' you all day long if that happens. You hear me? All... day... long," Elijah joked.

Their words were exactly what I needed to lift me up, in spite of how I was feeling.

"Y'all want something from Williams?" I asked unexpectedly.

"Damian, is that even a question? You know we do," Lexi exclaimed.

With that, we went to the closest Williams Chicken and got a few boxes of chicken, some fries, corn on the cobs, peppers, corn fritters, gizzards, and apple pies. I was doing too much, I know—but I had to eat through my feelings. During dinner, I just enjoyed my family. I didn't talk about my situation with Kamaria at all. Instead, we talked about how Lexi and Elijah were enjoying school, and how Lexi suddenly decided she wanted to join the band.

"Yeah, so I think I wanna try to play drums in the band," she said.

"Baby girl, you never talked about playin' music before. You don't even listen to music like that. What changed?" Pops asked.

"True, but today when I was walkin' the halls, I heard music playing and it grabbed me. When school was over, I ran to the band room and talked to the director, Mr. Hill."

"Oh yeah, I know Mr. Hill. He was the band director at O.W. Holmes for the 'Boss Band.' They was always playin' in parades and getting invited places. I forgot he went to Townview," I said.

"Yep! He told me a lot of people from Holmes joined him at Townview, but he said he's always looking for more people to join the band," Lexi said excitedly.

"That's dope!" Elijah said as he patted Lexi on the back.

After discussing Lexi's new love for music, we talked about how we were dealing with not having Mom. Surprisingly, we were able to share a lot more laughs than I thought we would. We caught ourselves looking over at Mom's chair and doing our best impressions of the things she'd say whenever we were overindulging in a meal.

"She'd say, 'Damian, you actin' like we haven't ever fed you.' Man, she just didn't get how hongry, not hungry, I'd get." I said with a huge smile.

"Lexi, girl, you better slow down. Fool 'round and choke or something," Lexi added.

"Elijah, Elijah. I must need to formally introduce you to the fork and spoon, 'cause if someone saw you eat, they'd swear we never taught you 'bout 'em," Elijah said, holding his stomach in laughter.

"She did me like that, too. She'd be like, 'Babe, for real? Can you save me some food? Oh, I guess I just stayed in the kitchen to make my favorite meal for you?' That kinda stuff'll stick with us forever," Pops said.

We got up and surrounded our father briefly before Elijah and Lexi went to their rooms. When they left, Pops and I had the chance to speak alone while I cleaned up. I could see him battling with himself. After all we'd dealt with as a family, he still had trouble expressing how he was feeling, but it was easy to see how sad he was.

In comedies, when they got to certain points, one of the characters would stand up and motion for the other to give them a hug. That's what I did with my father. He hesitated, but he finally stood up and hugged me. To me, that confirmed we were still making progress on his emotional journey.

"I pray living without her is a nightmare that God's gonna wake me up from. D, her pillow's been washed, I don't know how many times since she passed, but it's still holding the shape of her head. She left such an impression on this world, even inanimate objects got memories of her."

I held onto my dad like I did the day Mama passed. I wanted to offer words of wisdom, but God's voice distinctly told me to be silent, to listen, and to let my father say everything he needed to say before I uttered a single word.

"Cryin' every night don't even make me feel like a man," he said.

"You're our hero, but heroes have faults. You still thinking crying equals weakness is one of yours."

Conversations like that usually made him mad at me because he'd take what I was saying as me questioning how he was raised, but it was never that. It was about him being allowed to be human, and not seen as weak just 'cause he let himself feel life's pain.

"You've always been a truth teller, my boy. Keeping it real with me lets me know you got my back."

"Pops, if I gotta choose between telling you the truth to help you get better and getting yelled at, or stayin' quiet while you hold on to fake happiness, I'mma take the yelling all day, e'ry day."

"Already," he said.

"Already," I replied, smiling.

That word said everything we needed to say.

"A'ight, I love you, Pops," I said, thinking he wouldn't say it back.

"Yeah, yeah, I love you, too," he whispered with a smile.

The talk I had with my father that night made me feel better about him being able to move on after Mom's passing. Coincidentally, it made me feel better about moving on, too. Not just about living without my mother, but about realizing that as bad as I felt about Kamaria, I'd be happy again one day, too.

11

———————

The next few weeks were a bit different for me. When Kamaria first told me she needed her space, I didn't know what that meant. So, I found myself still trying to talk to her every few days. It took me a while to finally accept things had changed, and by the time I heard from her again, I was the one who didn't feel like speaking.

"I know you've been trying to call me, and I know I haven't called you back. My bad. I'm still trying to get myself together 'cause being away isn't as easy as I thought it would be."

"I ain't even trippin'. It's cool, " I told her.

I tried my best to act like I was unbothered by our situation, but I've never been the best actor. Kamaria knew me. Even without speaking to me for weeks, she could still sense when I was telling the truth and when I was lying. I guess that's why she started trying to call me over and over the next few days—but like she was with me, I became too busy to answer her calls.

I also convinced myself I was an idiot for trying to stay loyal to someone who told me she needed space. So, I threw loyalty out the window and tried to start my "playa era." I found myself searching all over campus to see if I could find Destiny, the girl who introduced herself when I was sitting on the grass. It took a while, but eventually I saw her walking with some of her friends.

"Hey, what up, Destiny? I ain't seen you in a minute. You good?"

Her friends all laughed and pointed at me. I was so embarrassed I wanted to run away, but I didn't. Instead, I just rolled with it.

"That's crazy, right?"

"What are you talking about?" Destiny asked.

"I don't know. I just knew your homies weren't laughing at me, so I figured somebody told a wild story or something."

"Boy, you crazy."

"I've been told," I said.

"Hey, y'all, give me a few minutes," she told her friends.

Destiny looked me up and down a few times before she started speaking again.

"Okay, I see you talkin' and movin' different. I take it you and your lil' relationship ain't make it."

Referring to my situation with Kamaria as a "lil' relationship" was disrespectful, and she knew it. She wanted to see if I was gonna get upset, and even though I wanted to, I didn't.

"You said life gets real when you leave high school, and that's what happened," I told her.

"Yeah, I knew it was only a matter of time."

I don't know why, but my heart sank a little when she said that. I sighed heavily, then I tried to continue speaking with my newly manufactured bravado, but for a moment, I couldn't.

"I just... I..."

"Look, you don't have to front. You don't even know me like that, for real. Don't lie to yourself, or me, about how you're feeling 'cause that ain't a good way to start a friendship."

"Oh, so we're friends?" I asked, trying to cover my smile.

"We could be, if you act right. And next time you wanna talk, just call me," she said, laughing as she walked away.

She looked back to see if I was still watching. I should've looked away so she wouldn't think she had me hooked, but I couldn't. I asked myself, "What kind of "playa" get hyped over every female who gives him attention?." It's wild I was questioning myself about that sort of thing, but being hurt over Kamaria really had me trying to change who I was.

As the days passed, it felt like I was two separate people; the real me, and Dame, my created persona. While Damian was reserved, Dame wanted to be the center of attention. To grow more into that new persona, I started going to more parties, paid less attention to my schoolwork, and started being around my family less, even though I was still living at home.

Dame became more dominant, and I started building a relationship with Destiny. Eventually, we started dating, or "talking" as we called it back then. Before her, the only real experience I had with a woman was Kamaria. When I was with her, I only wanted to be with her. That was Damian, though. As Dame, I told Destiny we could go out, but I couldn't promise her I wouldn't talk to other females if I had the chance.

I remember seeing a look of disgust on her face when I said that, but she quickly started laughing, trying to play it off. I started laughing, too. She thought I was laughing with her, but really, I was laughing at her. It was sad, honestly. Not just my actions, but the fact Destiny was willing to go along with it. She had too much going for her to even consider what I said, but she did. Right then, I realized how much power we have over others when they choose to believe in us.

When I first started talking to Destiny, I did it to get over Kamaria. It was easy to mess with her because she was cute, but I didn't have feelings for her. The more we talked and hung around each other, the more that changed. When I realized I was catching feelings for her, I had to make sure Dame wouldn't allow me to get played again.

One day, we decided to go watch our basketball team's game. Our squad was pretty good, but we weren't winning that night. During halftime, I got up to get us some nachos. I was making my way back to my seat when this other girl caught my attention. She saw me looking at her, but since I didn't say anything, she said something to me.

"We gonna win, or what?" She asked.

"It ain't lookin' good, but we'll see what happens."

I headed back to where I was going—but she wasn't finished.

"So that's it? You don't have anything else to say?" She asked.

"Nah, I'm just trying to get back to my girl."

"Oh, you got a girl?"

"Yeah, I do."

"You sure?" She asked.

She stood still, and her eyes told me to look her up and down before confirming what I said. She was undeniably fine, but so was Destiny.

"Yeah, I'm sure," I told her.

"Well, here's my number, just in case y'all ever have issues," she said as she moved in closer.

Then, without asking, she slipped a piece of paper into my pocket. The women in college were bold, for real. After she gave me her number, she just walked away, leaving me stunned for a minute.

"It's like that, homie?" A random dude asked me.

That's when Dame made his presence known.

"Yeah, it's like that," I said, acting like I believed it.

"So, you just gonna let her walk off?" He asked.

I wondered if I wanted to go back to my seat and chill with Destiny, or if I was really about to play into this new character and chase after another girl while the one I was talking to was close by? I had a flashback to when I was on the bus, going to meet Kamaria's mother. The gentleman I was sitting next to talked about respecting women and not trying to chase after one girl when you already had one. I told him I wasn't like that, but there I was, doing things I said I wouldn't do.

I ran over to the new girl and asked her if she wanted to go out. She asked me about the girl I was talking to, and I responded by telling her we were all young, and nobody was serious about their relationships.

"Oh, okay. You a playa, huh?"

"People play games, I'm real about mine," I replied.

I don't know where that came from. All I know is, after I spoke, I felt terrible about myself. At first, I was playing a role, but talking to that girl made me realize I was battling who I was becoming.

I told her my name as Dame, and she introduced herself as Marie. Shortly after, she ate a few of the nachos I had for Destiny, and walked off. I knew what she was trying to do, but I didn't acknowledge it. I just headed back to my seat like nothing had happened.

When I got back, Destiny asked me if I was okay because it took so long. I wasn't sure if she saw me with Marie or not, but I went on as if she didn't. She just gave me a look that I can't explain. Then, she grabbed a few nachos and focused on the basketball court.

"You really gonna act like you didn't see me watching you?" She suddenly asked.

"Huh?"

"I saw you talking to that girl. You said you was gonna talk to other females, but I told myself that wasn't you. That's my bad, 'cause I don't even know you. All I know is, you're not the same person I first met. Whatever changed, I ain't 'bout that life," she told me, sharp and steady.

I thought that was the end of it, but when she grabbed the rest of the nachos from me, I knew it wasn't. She took her time, took a few more bites, then calmly stood up. Without warning, she backhanded me across the face and threw the container of nachos at me.

"If you wanna be together, you need to get it together, freshman," she said as she walked off.

I sat there, cheese sauce dripping off me, and my face tingling for a minute. Everybody around me was laughing, and I was embarrassed, but I deserved it. So, I started laughing at myself, too. I should've gotten up and left, but I wasn't in a rush to get home.

Even after the game, I stayed in my seat. I looked around the empty stands until my eyes made it back around. I stopped looking when I got back to where Destiny was sitting. As I sat there questioning my life choices, RaShawn paid me a visit.

"That playa life ain't workin' out for you, huh?"

I always responded when RaShawn talked to me, even though I

knew he wasn't really there. It made my spirit feel better to pretend I was having a real conversation, but right then, I didn't feel like talking.

"You ain't gotta talk to me, but I'm still gonna say what I gotta say. You been mopin' 'round campus 'cause Kamaria broke your heart, and I get it, trust me. You pro'ly don't remember, but this girl named Tika broke my heart when we was in eighth grade. The whole thing was on some Romeo and Juliet type stuff."

That's when I broke my silence.

"What you talkin' 'bout, RaShawn? You don't even know nothin' 'bout no Shakespore," I said.

"Shakespore? Bruh, who is that? I guess you mean Shakespeare, right? You're so uncultured. How you gonna tell me I don't know something when you don't even know dude's name?" He joked.

Even as a spirit, RaShawn was still clowning me like only a brother could. I laughed at what I was hearing because he was right. I'd almost forgotten how smart RaShawn really was.

"You right. My bad. How were y'all like Romeo and Juliet?"

"Like the Montagues and Capulets, our families were enemies, but it was because all my family went to O.W. Holmes, and her people went to Zumwalt. And I already know you wanna ask me how we met. Well, since you gotta be nosey, I met her when my family was at Luby's after church and I saw her in line. I asked for her number, and the rest is history."

"I don't ever remember you talkin' 'bout her."

"Why would I talk about a girl who broke my heart?" He asked.

"That makes sense."

"Best believe, if I said it, it's gon' make sense. Anyway, I thought she was the one, and couldn't nobody tell me nothing. Then, I saw her all hugged up with some ol' buck-toothed, messed up edge-up havin', He-Man-watchin' dude who thought he was everything just 'cause he was a bench-warming quarterback."

"That's crazy, but what does this have to do with my situation?"

"D, she broke my heart. That's what it has to do with your situation. You tryin' to be a playa 'cause Kamaria broke your heart, but you know that ain't you. Now 'cause you tryin' to be somebody else, you done hurt this Destiny chick. Folks said college changes you, but these the kinda changes you makin', D?"

Our talk ended without warning, leaving me thinking about what was said. RaShawn was right. I was heartbroken. I was changing into someone who wasn't me, but when he asked if that was the kind of change I wanted, I had no answer. Then, I thought about it. Being the old me had me without my best friend, my girl, and my mom. Why would I want to still be that person?

I got up and went to my car. When I got in, I just sat there. My chest hurt, my heart was literally aching. The night played back in my head again and again until the sadness got too heavy to fight. I knew my actions didn't reflect who I was, and that's why I was in such turmoil.

I tried to convince myself I wanted to be the guy who could date different girls all at once, but if I was dealing with that much emotion because one girl saw me talking to another, how could I really expect to juggle more than one? Nah. I wasn't a playa because I couldn't handle the game.

I turned on the radio. The music I had didn't fit my mood, so, like my father usually did on Sunday, I put it on Soul 73. They were right in the middle of a blues song. If was one from the homegrown legend, "Oak Cliff T-Bone," aka T-Bone Walker. I didn't know then that he influenced folks like B.B. King. All I knew was that he was from the same place I was, he was well-known, and his music helped me deal with my pain.

When I got home, my dad was in his favorite chair watching the news. Since Mom passed, he did his best to avoid their room whenever he could. He couldn't handle being in the space where she left, but he tried to hide that from us. I never said anything, but I noticed.

"What's up, Damian? Did y'all win?" He asked.

"No, sir. We got blown out. It was still cool, though."

"Well, I'm glad you had fun. What's up with those stains all over your clothes, though?"

I looked down, pretending like I didn't know what he meant.

"Oh, this? That was Destiny," I said, hoping that would be enough.

Then I remembered—I hadn't told him much about Destiny. That meant I had to explain who she was, and remind him what happened with Kamaria.

"Okay, so you talking to a new girl and she did that to you? Was it an accident?" He asked after I told him who she was.

I wanted to say something to make myself look better, but I wasn't about to lie to my father.

"Nah, she meant to do it. She saw me talkin' to another girl while I was gettin' her something to eat at the game. She called me out on it and threw the food at me."

"It makes sense, but still, why?"

"I don't know, I guess she just wanted me to—"

"No, son, I ain't asking why she did it. What was the point of talking to a girl when you were already there with somebody? You tryin' to prove ain't no woman gonna break you, huh?"

He was acting like he was asking questions, but he really wasn't.

"Yes," I said, lowering my head.

"Ain't nobody in the world gonna make it through life without havin' their heart broken. It ain't always gonna be 'cause they broke up with you, either. Look at me. Your mama just broke my heart into an infinite amount of pieces that I won't be able to put back together."

Pops was being vulnerable again. The way he spoke was almost poetic, and I could feel the beauty in his pain. His love for my mom was so deep, he felt like his heart was beyond repair. I hated we lost her, but I knew it was a miracle my father got to spend so much time with the woman God made for him.

Talking to Pops made me more comfortable with my pain. I started to think Destiny was a casualty in the love war with Kamaria I wasn't ready to waive the white flag for.

"Have you called her?" My father asked.

"Nah, I don't think Destiny tryin' to hear from me right now."

"No disrespect, but I ain't talkin' 'bout her. If you haven't tried to get at Kamaria recently, I think you need to do that."

"Oh okay, but what about you? You good?" I asked.

That was my way of telling him I agreed with what he wanted me to do, while still checking in on him.

"I ain't had no good days since she left, and I don't know if I ever will. That's why, if you feel like Kamaria's who you're supposed to be with, you gotta make sure you do all you can to make sure you've really tried. You get what I'm saying?"

"I love you, Pops. I know you'll never be the same, but you're not alone. I really wish you'd talk to someone, though."

"I told you how I feel about therapy, but I need to do somethin' 'cause if I gotta feel like this for the rest of my life, then God need to just take me, too. She's everywhere in this house. Our room, the living room, the kitchen... everywhere. I can't stand to see her memories jump out at me every time I take a step," he said as he started to cry.

With his tears flowing, I knew we had reached a stopping point. I understood everything he was telling me, and in that moment, there was nothing I could say to help him. So I just hugged him until it felt like it was no longer necessary. After about a minute or so, he sat up in the chair. He nodded to let me know, for the moment, he was okay.

It was getting late, but after talking with my dad, I had to reach out to Kamaria. For whatever reason, I got nervous again as I pulled out my calling card and dialed her number. When it stopped ringing, I didn't even wait for her to answer before I started talking.

"Hey, Kamaria. I..."

"Nah, this ain't Kamaria."

The voice on the other end was some guy—definitely not who I was expecting to pick up the phone.

"My bad, I must have the wrong number or something," I said, preparing to hang up.

"Nah, you got the right number, you just called it at the wrong time. This is Kamaria's phone, this just ain't her," the person told me.

I was really caught off guard hearing the stranger speak to me. I didn't know what I was supposed to do, but I ended up holding on the line until I figured it out.

"Hello," Kamaria eventually answered.

"Hey," I said, unenthusiastically.

"Damian, what's up? I've been meaning to call you 'cause you keep crossing my mind. How are you?"

She was acting like she didn't just have a guy answer her phone.

"I'm a'ight, but who was that?" I asked.

"Don't worry about it, that's not important," she told me.

I didn't know the guy who answered, but I felt like she was disrespecting both of us at the same time.

"Well, you keep telling me you've been busy. I guess I should've just listened. That probably would've saved me some pain, huh?"

"Like I said, don't trip. Anyway, how have you been?"

She wanted me to move past the fact that a guy answered her phone like it was nothing—but that wasn't something I could do.

"I'm not even about to get into it with you, but keep it real— is that who you with now?" I asked.

"No, Damian, I'm not with him. Adrian is a friend of mine, and he's in my study group. There's a bunch of us over here right now, and you caught us on a break."

Her story sounded good, but I didn't want to believe it. She said there were other people around, but I didn't hear anybody else. Kamaria had never been one to lie to me, but I guess college had changed her, too. And in spite of what she told me, I knew Adrian wasn't just some guy in one of her classes. He was way too comfortable answering her phone for that to be the case.

"Oh. Well, I was just calling to check on you. The last time we talked..."

"Yeah, our last few calls haven't been the greatest, but it's all good. We're still just trying to figure things out."

"Kamaria..."

"What's up, D?"

"Never mind, I ain't tryin' to come off as a sucka."

"What are you talkin' about? Just say what you gotta say, D."

I had to relearn how to breathe before I could keep speaking.

"Do you ever miss me, for real?" I asked.

I wanted an instant response, but that's not what I got. Nah,

Kamaria decided to give me an actual minute and a half of uninterrupted silence. I told her I didn't want to feel like a sucka, but that's exactly what ended up happening. Regret pulled up a seat beside me and made itself really comfortable while we waited to hear what she'd eventually say.

"I... I do. But I don't want to. Sometimes, I just want to be free. I want us both to be free. I don't want you to feel stuck 'cause you're thinkin' 'bout me, and I don't wanna be stuck 'cause I can only think about you."

"What if you're looking at it wrong. What if neither one of us is actually stuck? What if we're just equally yoked? What if, at this young age, we've already found what people spend their whole lives tryin' to find?"

I surprised myself with what I was saying. I was surprised because at some point, I stopped speaking with my mind and let my heart take over. My father had just told me his heart was broken because the love of his life was gone. I didn't want to move forward in my own life with my heart having questions for me I couldn't answer. Having it be broken because of chasing love would be different than having it broken because of lying to myself, or Kamaria.

"I'm pretty sure any other guy out there would be been happy if a girl told him to go out there and explore his new surroundings and find other women," she told me.

"Yeah, some guys may be happy with hearing that, but that ain't me. I don't wanna go after somethin' when I already have, my bad, I mean had, something better."

"I didn't know you was still feeling me like that, I really didn't. I thought you'd start goin' to Paul Quinn and forget about me as soon as you saw them other girls on campus."

"Forget about you? C'mon, Kamaria, that's impossible. Do you remember how many years I tried to get you to go out with me? How do you think I'm gonna forget about you that quick?"

"I guess you right. You were after me for a minute, huh?"

"Hey, I was just doing my part to be a good friend," I told her.

"Oh, that's what you were doing, D? Um-hmm," she said.

The little giggle she let out after that reminded me of how things used to be. It even gave me a little bit of hope until...

"Don't you think you done played with that dude's emotions long enough? He over here talking like he doing poetry and you just letting him talk like he still got a chance. I know this the one you were saying you used to talk to talk to in Dallas. He need to know you ain't in Dallas no more for a reason. Gon' let him get off the phone so we can get back to us. You over there talkin' 'bout we in a study group. Yeah, I got somethin' to study, alright," I heard Adrian say in the background.

"I gotta go, D. I'll talk to you later," she said, rushing off the phone.

I couldn't believe she did me like that, but maybe I should have. Since she went off to school, she had treated me wrong more times than she had treated me right. Evidently, I was too dumb to take the hints. The heartbreak I was feeling before the call returned with a vengeance, and I had more than enough of it for the night.

"A'ight, Pops. I think I'm gon' lay it down for the night," I yelled out after I got off of the phone.

"I know you betta not lay nothin' down with them dirty, cheese stained clothes you got on. I know you 'bout to go wash that stuff before you have this house smellin' like the Kraft headquarters," Pops joked.

It was as though he could sense my little phone conversation with Kamaria didn't go the way I wanted it to. He didn't say anything about it, but the way he told me to clean myself up almost served two purposes. First, I really did need to clean up because my clothes were not smelling good. Secondly, and most importantly, I felt like he was telling me to clean myself up. I don't mean that in the literal sense, but more like, washing the stench of disappointment and sadness off of me, at least for the night. Honestly, it was exactly what I needed to hear because it helped me have just enough peace of mind to get a little bit of rest.

12

I had a lot on my mind when I went to bed. I had a dream so realistic, I thought it really happened. It started off in a small room with about twenty-five chairs. At first, there was nobody there. Then, people started randomly filling the once-empty seats. Everyone had a face once they appeared, but they were almost out of focus, so I couldn't make out who anyone was.

I soon found myself walking from the back, alone. I looked around, trying to give everyone in the room equal attention. I stopped when I made it to the front. I didn't know what I was supposed to do. In the dream, I closed my eyes and allowed my spirit to guide my steps. When I opened them, I was standing beside my mother.

She had a glow around her. Her face was angelic. Her light brown eyes were full of life and joy. Her smile was like an eclipse I couldn't look at directly. Her scent, the one my father said he still smelled, filled the air. Then, she reached out to hold my hands.

As soon as she touched them, I saw all of our interactions flash before me. From my birth to her death; everything appeared in a matter of seconds, and I couldn't handle it. Just like the day of her funeral, I fell to the ground, sobbing uncontrollably. I balled up into a fetal position, and the only person who could console me was her.

"It's okay, baby. I promise you," she told me.

She hugged me until my tears evaporated like morning dew after sunrise. Then, she stood up and pulled me right along with her.

"I'm gone physically, but I will never leave you," she said.

She started to fade away, which made me believe I was waking up, but Mom wasn't finished talking to me.

"I need you to focus on what you need in your life, son."

That's when she pointed to the front corner of the room. I turned to where she pointed, and surprisingly, I saw Kamaria.

"She is what you need. They are just what you want," she said, pointing in the direction I'd already walked past.

I saw Destiny, Marie, and a bunch of other women I don't know if I had actually met.

"You'll have your fun, but you gotta make it right. Don't let life end without having the love God has for you," she said as I woke up.

The first thing I saw when I wiped my eyes was the clock showing it was three in the morning. As hard as I tried, I couldn't go back to sleep, nor could I forget what Mom said in the dream. I felt an unwavering urge to get out of bed, drop to my knees, and pray.

I talked to God often, but most of the time I was running my mouth more than I was listening. That night, well, morning, I said a few words before I shut my mouth.

"God, I don't know what I don't know. I've had my heart hurt by someone my mother is telling me I need to be with. I'm lost."

Like most people who go to God, I hoped for an immediate response that would clearly answer every question I had. That's not what usually happens, and it's not what happened then. Don't get me wrong, I heard from Him, but it wasn't in the way I expected.

"Be still more than you move. Listen more than you talk. And allow time to move forward. The clock eventually comes back around, but you'll only notice it when you're supposed to."

God spoke to me, almost in prose. I was thoroughly confused and had no idea what He meant. Clocks and time... listening and speaking, it didn't make any sense to me, but I wrote everything down. I wanted to be able to go back and review what God said, because at some point, I knew I'd understand.

I glanced over at the clock again and saw it was a little past five. I knew trying to fall asleep again was pointless, so I didn't even try. Still wearing my oversized Dallas Mavericks basketball shorts and hole-filled T-shirt, I went outside and sat on the stairs.

The crickets were loud as ever, like they were yelling at me for stepping outside when they normally had that time to themselves.

"My bad, y'all. I just had to get some fresh air. I promise this ain't gonna be an everyday thing," I told them.

Whether it was just coincidence, or they actually understood me, they quieted down after that. I took a deep breath and just sat there. The moon was getting ready to clock out, and the sun was waving from the other side—ready to start its shift.

There was no movement on the streets. No cars with busted speakers. No young folks walking by, cussin' in front of the elders as they yelled at them for stepping on their grass. There was nothing, and the quietness was refreshing. I wasn't used to seeing Oak Cliff like that. I wasn't accustomed to her being so quiet. I'm not saying her being quiet made her more attractive, it just allowed me to see the beauty I sometimes took for granted.

I leaned back on the stair that had become my seat. I got so relaxed, my eyelids turned into weights I couldn't lift. I felt my body catching up to the sleep that ran away hours earlier. Then, the sound of oncoming sirens snatched my ears and wouldn't let go.

I opened my eyes to see two cop cars flying down the street.

"Welp, back to reality," I told myself.

I got up, stretched, and took one last look around the neighborhood before heading back inside. My family was still sleeping, so I figured I'd be nice and whip up a world-class breakfast for them. It seemed like a good way to start the day.

I made some grits, bacon, cheese eggs, and toast. Families like ours, who never had a toaster, always had to decide whether to make toast in the oven, or in the skillet. In my house, we were always skillet-toast people—and nobody would've accepted anything else.

"A'ight, y'all, come get this breakfast! Don't let all this hard work be for nothin'," I yelled out.

I sounded just like our T-Jones did. Mom would wait for everyone to get to the table before she'd eat, but my stomach was rumbling too loud for that. I fixed a plate, blessed my food, and started eating.

"What do we have here?" My dad asked, rubbing his belly as he made it to the food.

"I know it ain't gonna be as good as Mom's, but I just wanted to make the fam a little somethin' to get the day going," I said.

"Well, I appreciate it, son. I really do," he told me.

He moved into the dining room and sat down across from me.

"You know, I had a dream about your mama last night," he said out of the blue.

"For real?"

"Yeah. She was far off, but I knew it was her. She was beautiful, D. The crazy thing is, I always told her she had a beautiful spirit, but I always said that because it's what I felt. That dream let me see it."

He had more to say, but he stopped himself. He sat there twirling the same forkful of eggs he'd picked up when he first sat down.

"You good?" I asked.

"Sometimes," he said.

We were all still trying to figure out how to live life without Mom —but for Dad, it was like he was being tortured. He loved us, but it often felt like he left us, too. It was like he didn't know how to function. When you get married, it's said "the two become one," but what happens when half of the equation is gone? That's what my dad was still trying to figure out.

After holding the fork a little longer, he finally took his first bite.

"You know how I said I appreciate you cookin'?" He asked.

"Yes, sir."

"I take that back. Boy, you need to stay faaaaar away from the kitchen, you hear me? You had me thinkin' I was 'bout to eat some good food—now you got my taste buds and stomach mad at me. I know I'mma have the bubble guts," he said, laughing so hard he snorted.

I was so happy to see my father laugh, I couldn't even be offended. Plus, I agreed with him. I had a full plate in front of me 'cause I thought it was nasty, too.

"Dang, bro, you made breakfast for us?" Elijah asked, sniffing the air.

Pops looked over and winked, telling me to follow his lead.

"Elijah, me and your brother was 'bout to tear all this food up. You and Lexi was gon' have to get whatever cereal's left in there. She still might if she don't hurry and get up," Pops told him.

Once he started eating, we figured he'd have the same reaction we did, but not Elijah. That boy ate like I was a five-star chef. The food wasn't good, but the fact that he cleaned the plate made me feel appreciated. It gave me a small sample of how Mom must've felt every day we tore up the food she made for us.

It made sense why she smiled so hard whenever she watched us eat. I could finally understand why she always wanted us gathered at the table together, whenever it was possible.

"Lexi! Hey, get in here!" I yelled out.

By the time she sat down with us, Pops was watching my younger siblings the same way I was. It was like Mom's calming spirit was sitting with us at the table.

"Thank you, D," Lexi said between bites.

"It's all good. Hey, so how's school goin' for y'all?" I asked.

They both looked up at me like they'd been waiting for me to ask.

"You know how folks'll clown you for bein' smart, or wantin' to study? It's not like that over there. We all nerdy in some kinda way, so ain't nobody really tripping, well, at least not about that," Elijah explained.

"That's cool, but please don't give into the stereotype that folks in other parts of Oak Cliff ain't smart, or don't care about learning— 'cause that's not true."

"What you mean?" Elijah asked.

"I've been to places outside The Cliff. When people found out where I'm from, their faces scrunched up like they smelled mediocrity in the air. That ain't us. Even at Kimball, our motto was 'We always seek the best.' Like I said, it's good y'all doing your thing over there, but please don't start thinking about folks outside of Townview the same way folks outside of O'Cliff think about us," I told them.

Insinuating we didn't allow each other to be comfortable enough to bask in our brilliance in our neighborhood kinda struck a nerve with me. Unfortunately, hearing people outside the hood think we're all unintelligent criminals had become almost normal, and I didn't want my siblings to add to the problem.

"You okay, D?" Lexi asked.

"Yeah. I know y'all didn't even say nothin' crazy. Just hearing how we be clownin' folks for being smart made me think—that might be why outsiders think we're dumb."

"My bad. I just meant stuff is a'ight. Folks sometimes bully me a little, but it ain't really that bad," Elijah said, apologetically.

"I wasn't trying to take your shine, lil' bro. I'm glad y'all are fitting in over there."

In hindsight, I know I overreacted. In that moment, I was triggered. It's possible my reaction came from all the times people made fun of me for "trying" too hard, mixed with the times I'd done the same thing to others. All throughout school, there were moments when people got better grades than me, and my jealousy made an appearance. I didn't want to see them celebrate, or watch others celebrate them, either. If anyone started clownin' them for what they worked hard for, instead of stopping it, I joined in.

When it came to intelligence, us making fun of one another wasn't like when we joked about other quirky stuff. Downplaying how smart someone is—or acting like it's wrong to work hard—is an issue that still runs free in our hood like a pit bull off its leash. It's vicious, and if you fall victim to it, the scars can last forever.

"Lexi, Elijah, can I tell y'all something?" I asked.

"Yeah, what up?"

"I've said it before, but I'm proud of y'all. I'm happy y'all are doing something you've never seen anybody do before. Don't get me wrong, I'm great, but y'all are greater. I don't know what God has planned for me, but if I can change the world, y'all gonna change galaxies."

The conversation about being smart stuck with me all day. When I looked at people, I really saw them—not just what they did. My professors weren't just teachers; they were mothers, fathers, husbands, wives—people with lives outside of the classroom. The students weren't just trying to pass classes; they were young adults, maybe the first in their families, trying to create legacies.

Later that day, I had to go to work at Mervyn's—the same department store I'd been shopping at forever. I'd only been working there a few months, but funny enough, I got that job through someone from Minyards who'd left and put me on. I worked at the one across from Redbird, right in the same area with Toys 'R Us.

Most breaks, I'd run to Toys 'R Us to look at, or play, whatever new games they had on display. I planned on doing the same that day, but as I started walking over, I had to stop and watch people—to imagine what made them who they were. The conversation I had with my family that morning was still playing in my head.

Everybody was rolling through the parking lot. I saw folks with big smiles, parking cars way worse than mine. I saw people in bubble-eye Lexuses—similar to what I drove to prom—looking like life did all it could to beat 'em down. Their scowls reminded me that money and material things don't equal happiness.

Then, my mind went back to stereotypes—about intellect, about decision-making. I realized there were times I'd see my people doing well and automatically assume they were dope boys, or into something illegal. And when I saw someone driving an old car, I'd think they were hardworking people, just a step away from a breakthrough.

Admittedly, my way of thinking was part of the problem. It's one thing to wonder about people—it's another to assume. That's the same thing I talked to my family about. If we wanted people to respect Oak Cliff, we had to start respecting ourselves. As much as I said I loved my neighborhood, standing there in that parking lot, I had to admit—I still had some toxic traits I needed to work on.

I checked my watch and saw it was just about time to go back. As I headed toward Mervyn's front door, I spotted Sterling—the same person who stopped to check on me when I was walking to school the first day of 10th grade. We'd had a class together, but he was older than me, and I hadn't seen him much since he left Kimball. Every now and then we'd cross paths around the neighborhood, but we were never close.

He didn't recognize me at first, but when I told him I was headed back to work, he asked me if we were hiring. When I told him we were, he briefly looked down, gripping a folder full of papers—probably copies of his résumé. He had on khakis and a button-down, which I remembered wasn't his usual style back in school.

I found it funny that someone I didn't really talk to was basically asking me to help him get a job. The same thing happened when I was at Minyards. For some reason, people thought I was the job plug.

"What you tryin' to do?" I asked.

"Bruh, at this point, I'm down for whateva. I'm just tryna do something legit to take care of my little girls, but it ain't easy out here."

"True. I ain't know you had kids."

"Yeah, me and my baby mama had twins my senior year."

"Congratulations."

"I 'preciate it, but it's rough. Since me and they mama ain't together, she make it difficult to see 'em because she said I ain't providing. I can't find no work, dawg, and I don't wanna do nothin' that can get me locked up, but it ain't like I got a choice."

God will show you examples of things you're questioning in your life. In this case, I'd just been thinking about intelligence and actions —how people sometimes do things they know are wrong. I already knew what would happen if Sterling couldn't find work. He'd end up sliding back toward the life he wanted to avoid. And if he got caught up, he could miss years of his daughters' lives, even though all he was trying to do was make a way for them.

If he made the wrong decision while trying to do right, he'd still be seen as a stereotype. So, I felt obligated to do something.

"I haven't been working here long, but walk in here with me. We can talk to my manager to see what he talkin' 'bout," I told him.

We walked into the store optimistically. Almost as soon as we stepped inside, I saw my manager, Bruce, getting yelled at by a lady trying to return something he clearly didn't wanna take back.

"This ain't your store, just gimmie my money back!"

"Ma'am, please calm down. You don't have a receipt, there are no tags, and the dress is torn. I'm sorry, but we can't take this back."

"You sorry a'ight," she said as she threw the dress and walked out.

Bruce was usually even-keeled. I'd never seen him get rattled. I don't know what he had going on, or what the lady said before I walked up, but I could tell he was close to losing it. When I asked him if he was okay, he went off on a tangent about being tired of people feeling entitled because they're on the other side of the register.

"I see this ain't a good time," Sterling said, starting to turn around.

"I'm sorry, who are you?" Bruce asked.

"Bruce, this my friend Sterling. We went to Kimball together. He's a good dude, a hard worker, and he's looking for work."

I stretched the truth by calling him my friend, and I didn't know if he was a hard worker or not, but I had the urge to say something positive. Even though the timing wasn't ideal, I saw an opportunity for Sterling to make a good first impression, so I vouched for him.

"What kind of work are you looking for?" Bruce wondered.

"Anything, sir. I just wanna work," Sterling said humbly.

As they talked, a customer walk up to the register, so I jumped in to help, giving them space to keep talking. When I came back, they were shaking hands and confirming Sterling's interview date. By that time, Bruce had cooled off. Before he walked away, he told me I had a few minutes to talk to Sterling before I got back to work. I agreed, and Sterling and I talked for a bit.

"Bro, you don't even know what that means. Since I had them kids, it feel like they the only ones on my side. E'rybody else been actin' like they just waitin' for me to fall. This the first time, in a long time, somebody grown said somethin' good about me."

"I'm sorry it's been like that for you, but it's gonna get better."

"I hope you right, but I'mma head out before you get in trouble. Hopefully, I'll be seein' you at work in a lil' bit," he said, before heading out.

13

I don't know why, but after the day I saw Sterling at work, I started paying more attention to the streets of Oak Cliff. I noticed how all sorts of businesses we used to support were closing down. It made me feel like my memories were starting to be taken away.

When more representations of your childhood start to disappear, you find yourself leaning more into adulthood—whether you're ready to or not. Childhood gives you a sense of optimism adulthood can sometimes take away. Regardless of what I was seeing around me, I was determined to not let the negativity of the hood outshine the positive, but sometimes it was a mountain of a task.

I remember going to work at Mervyn's on June 24th, 1998. I only know the date because it was the same night as the NBA Draft, and I requested an early shift so I could watch it with Pops. Work was going smoothly that day. Nobody went off on me, and I didn't go off on nobody. My co-workers were chill, management wasn't botherin' me, and I was getting ready to leave when I saw Sterling. Since he started working with me, he'd become my friend, and I could tell my boy was going through something.

I asked him what was going on, and he told me one of his kids had been in the hospital for two weeks. With no insurance, he didn't know how the bills would get taken care of. I felt bad, but there was nothing I could do. Without exactly saying it, he told me he may have done some things he shouldn't have to help his daughter.

"My family been in and outta prison my whole life. I said that wasn't gonna be me, but this ain't cuttin' it, bruh."

Since he got the job, I'd gotten to know who Sterling was. He was a good dude trying to do right by his family, but the job wasn't covering the bills. He was getting stressed, so he changed the subject and asked me if I was going to watch the NBA draft.

"I'm about to go watch it, but I had to make sure you were good."

"Gone and see who them Mavs get, even though y'all ain't gonna get nobody as good as my Clippers. We 'bout to change the game with this draft, watch," he said, smiling a little.

With that, I finally started leaving. I hoped it would be all good, but I had a sinking feeling it wouldn't be. I left work with my head down, not liking how I thought things would turn out. I headed back to the house I grew up in, and when I got there, Pops and Lexi were waiting on me.

Soon, David Stern, the NBA commissioner, walked on the stage and said, "With the sixth pick in the 1998 NBA Draft, the Dallas Mavericks select Robert Traylor from the University of Michigan."

"We gotta see what his work ethic looks like once he gets paid. Making it in college is one thing, but when you're a pro, you're goin' up against grown men," Lexi said, sounding like an expert.

"Where'd you get all that from?" I asked her.

She started rolling on the floor laughing in pure delight.

"Y'all should've seen your faces! I don't know what I was talkin' 'bout. I watched last year's draft, and that's the stuff they kept saying when somebody's name got called. I figured I'd just repeat as much as I could remember after they said who Dallas was gonna get."

"Yeah, baby girl, that was pretty good. You shol' sounded like you knew more than your big brother over there," Pops joked.

"Dang, why I gotta catch jabs?" I laughed.

We were havin' fun, then we heard our pick had been traded.

"Wait, so we tradin' the person we just picked? Why?" Lexi asked.

"Yeah, they trading Traylor to the Bucks for some dude from Germany named Dirk. I don't see that playing out well for us at all. Players from outside the US might be good, but ain't none of 'em gonna be good enough to dominate and help us get a ring," I said, feeling confident about my statement.

My father was disgusted by the trade. He started pacin' around the room like he was tryin' to figure out how to undo what happened.

"What if Dirk ends up bein' the greatest to ever play in Dallas and he ends up bein' the reason we win it all one day?" Lexi asked.

Her question made sense, but logic ain't a requirement for being a fan. Truth is, Pops didn't have anything against Dirk, he just wanted somebody we recognized. Instead, we got a kid we didn't know, but everybody said had skills.

Since our team's night was over, I started getting ready to go when my cell phone rung. We didn't have phones that were pocket-sized computers yet, but you couldn't tell me nothin' when I got that Nokia 3310. When I answered, my manager at Mervyn's told me Sterling got arrested while he was at work. The conversation ended without a trace of humanity or decency. It was colder than the nighttime wind blowing through the streets of Oak Cliff.

"What was that about?" Pops asked, clearly noticing the concern.

"They just told me the homie, Sterling, got caught up today. DPD came in while he was workin' and arrested him," I said.

"You ain't gotta give no details, but was he doin' somethin' he wasn't supposed to be doing?" Pops asked.

I didn't know how to respond, so I didn't. I just dropped my head.

"See... that look tells me all I need to know," Pops said.

"Yeah, but—"

"Ain't no 'but.' 'Wrong actions with the right intentions will still get you locked up,' that's what your granddaddy always told me."

It might've sounded harsh, but Pops was right. If Sterling made a choice — even for a good reason — he knew the risk that came with it. Understanding that didn't make me feel any better, though.

"D, are you okay?" My sister asked.

"Yeah, sis, but if Sterling gets locked up, I hope it ain't for too long. I don't want his lil' girls growin' up without their dad," I said quietly.

"Oh, he got kids and he risked his freedom — and time with his kids — just to get some extra paper?" Pops asked.

"It ain't like that, Pops. He wasn't just tryna make money to splurge. He told me one of his daughters was in the hospital, and they don't have the money to take care of the hospital bill."

My father shifted in his chair. His face changed from disgust to concern. Lexi was in tears when she found out Sterling had kids.

"I'm tired of us struggling so much we gotta do wrong just to survive. Now there's about to be two more girls who might grow up without their dad. Do you know how much that'll mess them up?"

She started to cry, and Pops hated to see Lexi cry. Her tears had a power over him nobody, except Mama, could ever match. He pulled her in for a hug as she continued to speak.

"I don't know Sterling or his girls. I just know how important y'all are to me, and I can't imagine not having you around. It's not fair so many Black men get taken from their families. What if something happens to y'all? I'm begging you — don't do anything that'll make you leave me. Mama's already gone... I can't lose y'all, too," she said.

In Oak Cliff — and hoods like it all across the country — Black and Brown folks are watched, judged, and targeted at a rate above others. I'm not saying everybody who's locked up is innocent because that ain't true. I'm also not saying every cop is out here profiling people because that ain't true, either. What is true, is this country's history of pulling Black men away from their families. Sterling was now at risk of becoming another statistic — and that sat heavy on me.

I had zoned out, not even reacting to my little sister's plea. She was pouring her heart out to two of the people she said meant the most to her — and when that hit me, I snapped back to reality.

"Can I join y'all's hug session?" I asked, walking to them.

She opened her arms, letting me know I was welcomed.

"We having family hugs and ain't nobody invite me? That's messed up," Elijah said as he joined us in the room, and in the hug.

After a few seconds of real family closeness, we let each other go.

"We just sharing love, or did I miss something?" Elijah asked.

"Yeah, we just got to talking about family and togetherness and stuff 'cause my friend got arrested," I said.

"Getting locked up really brings a family together," Elijah joked.

He was playing, but he wasn't wrong. One of the strange things about tragedy is how it pulls families together — even while it's tearing them apart. The duality of hood life can be beautifully ugly.

We hugged again before I headed out to my crib. I moved out of the family's crib a little while before, but I still lived in Oak Cliff. My spot wasn't the best, but it was mine — and I was proud of it. It was a gated community, but the gate stayed broken, so really, the gate was just for decoration.

After I got inside my apartment, I just sat there, listening to the sounds of the complex. I could hear people arguing just as clearly as I heard basketballs hitting the pavement. The thump of trunks filled with Kenwoods and Alpines rattled like the heartbeat of the neighborhood. The noise was chaotic, but that chaos was home.

It wasn't unusual for helicopters — or "ghetto birds," as we called 'em — to circle around loudly enough to make you think they were about to land on your roof. Like thunder follows lightning, whenever we heard the ghetto birds squawking, we knew those infamous red and blue lights weren't going to be very far behind.

When those neighborhood strobe lights started splashing cobalt and ruby across the complex, we all knew danger was close. The smart folks went inside. The ones who thought they were untouchable tried to get a better look. And for some reason — against my better judgment — I decided to be one of the latter.

I grabbed the rusty bars on my second floor balcony and looked around. I was surprised at how many people were still outside, but being nosey is a drug everybody in the hood seemed to be addicted to. The sirens stopped about three or four buildings down from me, which made me feel like I was meant to see what was going on.

My eyes got heavy, and my body told me I needed to, as Mama always said, "go sit down somewhere," but I went back downstairs, instead. Everyone was old enough to know how police operated in our neighborhood. I'm sure most of us had the same mindset: if anybody decided to use a weapon, it'd be the cops. Surprisingly, they moved cautiously that night, but the person driving the car didn't.

As soon as he saw an opening, he slammed on the the gas. The tires left scars on the street as he tried to get away. Before he could reach the gate, another cop car cut him off. Again, we all knew how things could end when a Black man tried to escape from police, but the people in the complex weren't about to let the worst-case scenario happen. So, once again, many of them put themselves in harm's way.

Most of the people probably had no idea what the man had been accused of doing, but that wasn't the point. Actually, the crime was almost irrelevant because they weren't out there trying to convince the police he was innocent. They were just doing what they could to make sure the population of Black people in our community didn't drop that night because of an interaction with an officer.

I wanted to move in closer, but I was already close enough to see what was going on, and far enough to run if I needed to. I stood back, watching the latest episode of Oak Cliff's reality show unfold right in front of me. The whole time, I was frightened just thinking about how it all might end. I was relieved we didn't have to witness anyone getting hurt, but I was saddened because the person ended up getting arrested. That meant, I learned about two Black men getting arrested that day. That might not mean much to some, but being that close to both situations made me see things from a different perspective.

I don't remember how long after that day it took, but word started traveling around Sterling had been sentenced to a few years behind bars. At work, Sterling was replaced within days, and his name was barely mentioned after that. It was a reminder of how inconsequential we really are, and how we have to fight to leave something behind that makes people remember we were even here.

I started reflecting more on what I wanted to do with my life, but the more I thought about it, the more lost I felt. I was trying my best in school, but my results didn't match my effort. I'd get tutoring, talk to professors, but sometimes, the information just refused to stay connected to my brain. Thoughts of quitting started creeping in, but I didn't tell anybody. I was starting to feel like I was in over my head.

I remember sitting in — I think it was a sociology class — when I started dozing off. I hadn't been out late or anything the night before, I was just tired for some reason. I didn't fall into a deep sleep, more like one of those moments when your eyes close just long enough for your body to relax and your head falls forward, waking you up again.

As my eyes stayed closed a little longer, I started to see something... someone. I couldn't tell who it was at first. Almost as soon as I realized it was my T-Jones paying me another visit, the dream started to end. Altogether, it couldn't have lasted more than ten seconds. She looked directly at me and said, "Help."

I woke up gasping for air. People asked if I was okay, but I couldn't get my words out, so I held up a finger to let them know I needed a minute. I gave myself permission to leave class. and I walked outside, still trying to figure out what had just happened.

"Help with what?" I asked myself, replaying what my mother said.

If she was telling me I needed help, I agreed, but I didn't know what to do about it. If she was asking me to help her, I didn't know how that was even possible, since she had already passed. Once again, I felt lost. So, I left out of the building. And like I'd done before, I found a patch of grass and made myself comfortable.

I grabbed my phone, half-expecting the numbers I was supposed to dial to jump out at me. Before I could think, my fingers started dialing Kamaria's number. The conversation we had that day flowed better than any we had since Kimball. It had to be going well because I wasn't even worried about using my minutes, which was major.

"I ain't deserve how you did me," I told her, as we talked.

"You've always done right by me, and I didn't do the same for you. I'm really sorry about the breakup and everything else..."

She tried to stop herself, but it was too late.

"What you mean?" I asked, hearing her breathing heavily.

"Never mind. I shouldn't have said anything. We can talk later."

That was her go-to line. Normally I'd let it slide, but not that time.

"We ain't doin' that. If you got something to say, just say it," I said.

"Please don't hate me, D. Please promise me you won't."

I didn't commit to things before I knew what I was promising, but she eventually continued speaking.

"I'm pregnant, Damian."

Ain't no way I heard what I thought I heard.

"Are you there?" She asked.

"Yeah, but what you want me to say?"

"I don't know. Just... say something, please."

She managed to stab me in the heart and the back at the same time. I was already wounded, but that new info ripped the old wounds open so wide my emotions had nowhere to hide.

"You the same chick who wouldn't even talk to me until I proved myself. What happened to that? Were you just playing me, or did your morals disappear once you left Oak Cliff? Now I see, all them times you said 'I love you,' you was just runnin' yo' mouth."

I didn't even know what I was saying. I didn't care if she was hurt or offended, either. She'd asked me not to hate her, but I was glad I didn't agree. She started crying, and I didn't care.

"I didn't mean for any of it to happen. It was a mistake," she said.

Hearing 'mistake' hit me hard. I wanted to stay mad, but I couldn't because I knew what it was like to be thought of as a mistake.

"Your child is not a mistake," I said as calmly as I could.

"What?" She asked.

"Your child isn't a mistake. If you're bringing a life into the world, you can't think of it like that. You don't wanna put that on your child."

"You still care, don't you?" She asked.

"What I said don't have nothing to do with you. I hope that child has a beautiful life, but don't feel obligated to tell me about it."

"I meant, how it happened was a mistake, not the child."

"You can spare me the details, Kamaria. You know how much time I wasted just trying to prove myself worthy of being with you, just for you to find your new man in DC and change everything? It was that dude, Adrian, right?"

"Yeah, but me and him ain't together, and we never were. I only met him 'cause I was doin' too much partying one night."

"It wasn't even a relationship? You made me wait for years, and you let somebody get at you on the first night?"

"Babe, I promise I didn't mean for any of it to happen. I'm sorry."

I couldn't tell if she slipped and called me "babe," or if she did it intentionally to get me to ease up on her.

"Look, I don't wish nothing bad on you or your lil' one, but..."

"I get it, you don't want nothing to do with me..."

"You the one who decided to go to D.C., not me. You the one who said you needed space. So, you can miss me with all that trying to sound innocent mess. That ain't gon' make it today."

"You can't be harder on me than I've been on myself. Someday, I hope you'll be able to forgive me, but I am genuinely sorry, and I want us to be cool. I know you won't believe me, but I still love you."

"Yeah, a'ight. Getting pregnant by somebody else is a good way to show you love me," I told her as I coldly ended the call.

My words were harsh, but I told myself I didn't care. I knew my delivery hurt Kamaria, but I was convinced she deserved it. She told me she loved me, and although I acted like it was a lie, I didn't actually doubt she meant it.

I walked to The SUB—the student union building, which is where people hung out on campus because it's where the cafeteria was. I needed a place where I could get a few minutes of peace, and it seemed like that would be it. When I stepped inside, I saw Dr. Weldon J. Walton, one of the dopest professors, advisors, and overall, one of the coolest people to ever walk Paul Quinn's campus.

"Hi, Dr. Walton. How are you?"

"Good, good. How are you?" He replied with a smile.

"I've seen better days," I said.

"That's the type of statement reserved for people much older than you. If you're saying it, that means you're dealing with something. I have a few minutes, if you're comfortable sharing," he told me.

Dr. Walton sat in a nearby chair and asked me to do the same. He glanced at his watch to gauge how much time we had to talk.

"I just don't know what I'm doing," I told him.

"Who does? We go through cycles of thinking we know everything, to realizing we don't know anything. It's okay to get lost in life—that's how you learn to navigate through it."

Like my parents, Doc was a person who always happily shared knowledge. When he spoke—whether to a class or to you directly—it was like you were getting insider info everyone else wasn't privy to.

"Can I be real with you, Doc?"

"As opposed to being fake? Absolutely."

"I'm not gonna go into crazy details, but part of what I'm dealing with is this dream I had. My mom passed a few years ago..."

"I'm sorry to hear that. My condolences to you and your family."

"Thanks. And so, every once in a while, I'll envision my mom. She doesn't always talk, but I saw her today and she just said, 'Help.' I don't even know what that's supposed to mean."

He looked at me, then looked off into the air, as if to analyze the information he'd just been given.

"I'm no dream expert," he said, "but maybe you're being told you need to be less self-serving and do more to help others—just as we are all purposed to do."

My fog of confusion started to clear up, but I was still unsure.

"But who am I supposed to help, and how?" I asked.

"Your answer might be found by reviewing who delivered the message," Dr. Walton told me.

I had my "aha" moment right then. The fog was completely lifted, and I could see more clearly than I thought I would.

"You've got this, young man," he said as he shook my hand firmly and walked away.

If I were to serve others, as he suggested, I had to think of what kind of help was needed, and what I could do about it. I also had to think about why Mama was the one used to bring me the message. It soon became so obvious I almost felt stupid for not realizing it earlier—Mama wanted me to help others who were dealing with cancer.

I wasn't comfortable with cancer being a vital part of my life's purpose, but it made sense because it always had been, I just didn't know it. In order to move forward, I had to figure out how our relationship would change. The brainstorming session started almost as soon as I left school. At first, I was gonna go home and be alone with my thoughts, but I decided to go chop it up with Pops for a few minutes.

I walked inside and sat on the floor with my back against the wall. I used to sit like that a lot when I was a kid, especially when me and my parents had to have a serious conversation.

"So, I kept falling asleep in class today. Don't worry, I wasn't out partying last night, and trust me, I'm not wasting your money," I said, answering every question I thought he'd have on his mind.

"Okay, good. Go 'head with your story, then," he told me.

"And I had a dream where Mama told me I need to help."

"Help who?" he asked, looking puzzled.

"At first, I ain't even know. Then, I had a talk with Dr. Walton and he helped me find an answer."

"So, what's up?" Pops asked.

"Somehow, I have to help people fight cancer."

Hearing the word connected with Mama's passing could've been a trigger for Pops, but it wasn't. He just gave me one of the most love-filled hugs I'd ever received, especially from him.

"D, I'm so proud of you. I've always wanted y'all to start walking your own path and attach some extra positivity to our last name."

"Yeah, I think I'm supposed to be a doctor so I can help people directly affected by cancer—and also do research so I can help a team figure out how to stop it altogether."

My father got excited and gave me a few playful pushes.

"Boy, that sounds amazing!"

No matter how old you get, you still wanna make your parents proud. Seeing the joy on my father's face confirmed I was moving in the right direction.

"I think I can really make a difference, Pops. Plus, if I'm able to get into research, I really believe God will put me in a position to make a breakthrough. Can you imagine how families will feel if they know cancer can actually be fought—especially if it's without chemo?"

"Talk that talk, Dr. Roberts," he said.

It was just my father hyping me up, but hearing Dr. Roberts for the first time made me believe I could become a doctor. After speaking with him a while longer, I left with a smile and got a burger from Short Stop. Then, I made my way over to Kiest Park.

I was enjoying my time until I saw a little kid playing with his mom. I was almost forced to think of Kamaria and her future child. It made me sad because I always imagined having a family with her. Overall, seeing people have fun at the park reminded me how heart-broken I was, and after about 30 minutes of it, I was ready to go.

When I got into my ride, I pressed my head on the steering wheel, causing the horn to go off. Soon, I started hearing laughter. I ignored it at first, but it not only continued—it got louder.

"Is you in the car cryin'?" Someone asked, pointing and laughing.

My ego wanted to get out and prove I was the baddest dude in Oak Cliff, even though I knew I was far from it. I also knew better than to step out of my vehicle, but egos don't care about common sense. With dried tears still on my face, I got out and looked at the person who was laughing at me, as well as his friends.

"Look, y'all—six feet of sadness got out his car."

Even though he was talking about me, I was laughing internally at that "six feet of sadness" comment. It was the most ridiculous, yet incredibly accurate description I'd heard about myself in a while.

"I know y'all ain't gonna do nothing with a bunch of women and kids passing by," I said, pointing out some of the people.

They all glanced at the people before turning their attention back to me.

"C'mon, y'all, leave Red alone," the guy who first talked about me said as they laughed and walked away.

At first, I was confused by the comment. My skin tone had been compared to a lot of things, but the color red had never been one of them. When I thought about what he said, I laughed so loudly they all turned around and looked at me.

"You got me," I yelled out.

He pointed, nodded, and they went on their way.

Red was a character in the movie Friday, that had come out a few years before. He was always thought of as being overly sensitive. After one incident, his friends Craig and Smokey joked that he was gonna "cry in the car." That's where the comparison to me came from.

Calling me Red had absolutely nothing to do with my skin tone, but everything to do with the fact that I was crying in the car. It was genius, honestly. Them laughing and walking off was the equivalent of dropping the mic after a good stand-up set, and they'd absolutely earned it.

Being dissed by some strangers should've put me in a worse mood, but it ended up having the opposite effect. It was one of those moments where laughing at my misfortunes kept me from continuing to cry about them. Lord knows I didn't wanna keep crying.

By the time I made it to back to my crib, I had a change of heart. I realized that, in spite of my pain, I needed to call Kamaria back and apologize. So that's what I did.

"I'll make this quick. I just wanted to say I'm sorry for how I talked to you earlier. I was hurt by what you told me, so I wanted to find a way to hurt you back. My bad."

Our conversation helped me clear my mind. When it was done, I unexpectedly decided to start looking into different doctors who dealt with cancer—the type of research they did, and what it would take to become one myself.

While we were talking, Kamaria told me she didn't wanna let her mom down, and I felt like that's exactly what I was gonna do. Maybe I'd misinterpreted what kind of help Mama was asking for. Maybe Elijah or Lexi were supposed to be doctors—'cause even as younger kids, I always felt like they were the smart ones. I told myself they were more intellectually equipped to handle the workload of becoming doctors, so Mama must've accidentally reached out to the wrong child.

"How do you see yourself, and how do you want others to see

you?" I asked the reflection looking back at me as I stared in the bathroom mirror.

With each passing second, my reflection seemed to grow more impatient with my inability to answer.

"I'm trying to make my family proud of me," I said.

"Cool story, bruh—but that ain't what I asked you," my reflection said, almost confrontationally.

"I want others to see me as a person working to make the community better. And I see myself as somebody who can do that—if I quit being scared."

"What are you scared of?" The reflection asked.

"I don't know... I'm pro'ly afraid of failing."

"So outside of Jesus, who ain't never failed?"

"Nobody," I told myself.

"Exactly. Don't get it twisted—I ain't saying you can't do something that hasn't been done before, 'cause you can. But my boy, if you really seeking perfection, that's a guaranteed L."

He... I mean, I was right in what I told myself. That session of "self-reflection" was unlike any I'd ever had before, but it was eye-opening. I actually gained some much-needed introspection, which helped me tremendously. I learned I was afraid to see how far I could go in life because I knew I'd be challenged. I tried to convince myself I was afraid of failure, but I think I was more afraid of success.

Actually, when you're from Oak Cliff—or from any hood—failure is expected. So while I lied and said I was scared of failing, I had a lifetime of experience doing it. I failed several times in school when my grades didn't meet expectations. I failed as a friend when I wasn't able to protect RaShawn. I failed as a boyfriend because, if I was any good, Kamaria wouldn't have broken up with me.

I eventually left my room of reflection and made my way to the apartment's only bedroom. I sat on the futon that doubled as my gaming chair and my bed. I turned on the 19-inch Zenith I had in the room, along with my PlayStation. With school, work, and visiting my family, I hardly ever touched either of them, but I needed a few minutes of mindless entertainment.

I kept trying to play, but my eyes were getting heavy. Before I knew it, I was waking up the next morning with the controller still in my hand, a sore neck from sleeping sitting up, and dried drool on my face. I got up because I coughed and caught a whiff of my own breath. There was no way I could keep sleeping with my breath stanking—not stinking—the way it was.

After brushing my teeth and getting ready for the day, I kept thinking about everything that happened the day before. Kamaria's situation crossed my mind for a few minutes, but I mostly thought about that mirror conversation I had. No matter how well things were going in my life, I always found a way to doubt who I was.

I usually started my mornings talking with God and praying, but that day, my spirit told me I needed to do more. I picked up my Bible and flipped the pages until I felt led to stop. Before I looked down at the page, I thanked God not only for the day, but also for whatever message He was about to deliver.

I stopped on Ephesians 2:10. I'm not a biblical scholar, so the message I read surprised me.

"For we are His workmanship, created in Christ Jesus for good works, which God prepared beforehand, that we should walk in them."

I read it over and over, not sure if I understood it—or what God was trying to tell me. Then I heard His voice speak to me directly:

"Don't overthink what I'm telling you. Read the words as written."

I slowed down and read the verse again, just like He said. Only then did I get it. God's living Word told me I was created and prepared to do good works. He made each of us for a purpose, and He knows His works. I couldn't doubt something written so perfectly, and so personally.

With that morning message in mind, my day went by beautifully. I studied, went to class, and enjoyed being present in every moment. As evening came, I started preparing myself for the follow-up conversation Kamaria asked for. When seven o'clock came, I made sure my phone was charged and ready. Then, eight o'clock came. Then, nine. Still nothing. By 10:45, I had called her a few times and started to get irritated because she still hadn't answered.

"Oh, she's back on that," I said under my breath.

I felt like I'd been played again. Her calling me babe and saying she still loved me was just a setup—a way to manipulate how I talked to her. Each passing hour, each day she didn't call back, I got angrier at her—but even more at myself.

Then, about three weeks later, she called late one Sunday night. I almost didn't answer, but curiosity got me.

"Yeah," I said flatly, not trying to show emotion.

"D, I know you're mad at me again, but please. You have to hear me out," she said.

Our conversations were starting to feel like they were stuck on a loop.

"Same ol', same ol'. We had one decent convo and you back to being D.C. Kamaria," I said.

She didn't say anything, but I could hear her breathing heavily.

"So, you ain't got nothin' to say?" I asked.

Still, nothing. I got even more upset.

"A'ight, so, this is a waste of time. I ain't gonna allow you to keep playin' me," I told her.

I was about to hang up on her when she finally broke the silence.

"My baby's gone!" She yelled.

"What?" I asked, barely believing it.

"My child... I... I can't... I don't..."

She couldn't pull enough words together to fully express what she was dealing with, and I couldn't pull my thoughts together to comfort her. I put my head down in shame. I was embarrassed for how I'd been acting, even though I had absolutely no understanding of all of the details behind Kamaria's silence.

"I lost him before I even got to know who he was," she said, her cries breaking free again.

When she said "him," I didn't know if that meant she'd actually found out the baby's gender, or if it was just something she felt in her spirit. Either way, it made sense why that little boy at the park made me think about her.

"That baby you never met is will always be a part of you," I said. "You didn't get the chance to meet him, but he met you. And that attachment you feel is the unbreakable bond y'all will always have."

"You always knew how to tell me what I needed to hear, D. I'm so grateful you didn't give up on me. Even my mama seemed like she done turned her back. That's why I haven't even told her about..."

Kamaria's mother had always been in her corner, guiding her since we were kids. She kept her away from me for a while because she thought I wasn't good for her. So, hearing that her mother turned her back was unexpected.

"You gotta tell your mom," I said.

"D, when I told her I was pregnant, she straight up told me I was just like everybody else, and I disappointed her. She said I ruined my life and not to come to her for help with my baby. My mama was like my best friend, and that broke my soul."

"I hate that happened, but your mom didn't mean that. I bet over time she'll realize how wrong she was."

"Yeah, maybe. But the damage is done. She changed what we had, and I don't know if it'll ever be the same. I can't even worry about that right now. I gotta figure out how to get back to life, and honestly, I don't know if I can. My heart hurts so much, Damian. For real... what am I supposed to do?"

"I don't know what you're supposed to do, but whatever you do, you won't be alone," I told her. "I ain't in the same city, but I'm always gonna be here for you. That's the promise we made, right?"

"It sure is. I love you so much, Damian. And I'm sorry for everything. I never thought this would be my life, but I really appreciate you for not turning your back on me, even though you had every right to."

"Yeah," I said, letting out a half-laugh. "I can't say 'Kamaria getting pregnant would bring us closer' was on my Bingo card, but apparently it was. I love you, too, but you already knew that."

And with that, we both said to each other what neither of us had said in a long time. In one of the worst moments of her life, Kamaria still managed to find a way to make my heart full again. I never thought I would be able to feel that way about her again.

Surprisingly, that phone call became another unexpected turning point for us. We had already survived a ton of ups and downs, but I honestly thought the pregnancy would be the end of any type of relationship between us. Obviously, God had another plan. At that point, neither of us could see what that plan was, but that's what walking by faith is all about.

14

———————

When Kamaria told me about losing her baby, all the negative feelings I had toward her vanished. The urge to look out for my friend came back. I told her I'd be there for her, but I didn't really know what that meant. After a lot of praying, I heard God tell me I needed to go see her. I definitely wanted to, but I didn't have the funds to make that happen.

See, me and money had a funny relationship back then. I always worked hard to see her, but whenever she came to see me, she said she had to leave—to go take care of Bill. I understood I wasn't the only one in her life, but I always felt disrespected by that.

On the real, I was hustling for extra hours at Mervyn's, trying to find some work-study hours, and overall, I was just looking for any way to bring in more cash. Nothing was working out, though. Fortunately, Southwest Airlines dropped a sale on some flights. I still had to spend money I didn't really have, but it was worth it.

I had never been out of the city, not for real. The furthest I'd ever been was Fort Worth when I was a kid, and I don't even remember why. So, I was a little nervous about flying, especially when I saw how busy Love Field, a Dallas airport, was when I left.

I dealt with long TSA lines, delays, overpriced food, and even an unexpected layover, but it was all a learning experience. I always prayed for a way to see more of the country, so when I started living in that prayer, I couldn't complain. Even when I found myself stuck in the middle seat, clutching two strangers' arms because I was scared to death during turbulence, it was still all good.

When I finally made it to Howard's campus, I had to stop and take it all in. Just like when I first visited Kamaria's house, it felt different than what I was used to—but still familiar. When you're Black, there are so many places in this country that seem designed to make you feel unwelcomed. So, being somewhere outside of home that instantly felt safe was special. That's the power of an HBCU.

After a few minutes, I called Kamaria and asked which dorm and room she stayed in. She sounded confused and wanted to know why I was asking, but I just told her I needed to send her something. As soon as she told me, I ran to the side of the dorm where I could see her window. I immediately started getting nervous.

Besides the clothes stuffed in my backpack, one of the few things I brought with me was a little battery-powered boombox I bought from a pawn shop. I had to have my moment like that dude in the movie, Say Anything. So, I pulled out my Lil' Keke CD, "Don't Mess wit Texas," put it in the tray, skipped to track eight, and hit play.

The song "Southside" is an undeniable Texas banger, and even though Kamaria had been away from the crib for a minute, I knew she'd recognize it. I blasted it until I saw her peek through the window I had been told was hers. She looked shocked, then started smiling as she made her way downstairs.

"D, is that really you? What are you doing here—playing 'Southside' in front of everybody?" She asked, grinning as she hugged me.

With the music still playing, I set the boombox on the ground. After the hug, she held onto me with one hand, and her stomach with the other. I took a moment to really look at her—because the picture of her I carried in my mind needed updating.

She didn't look the same. She was smaller than I remembered—definitely not what I expected. Her eyes were heavy with pain, and I could tell she hadn't been sleeping. She had on old track pants, a torn shirt, and house shoes that barely stayed on her feet.

People were staring, and I didn't want Kamaria to feel uncomfortable, so I turned the music off. I caught myself looking at her, noticing the confidence she'd always carried was gone.

"You are so beautiful," I told her.

"No, I'm not," she said quickly.

Neither her body language, nor her expression had the conviction I remembered. Adulthood had stolen pieces of who she used to be.

"I ain't gonna lie to you as soon as I get here," I said with a grin.

She hugged me again, then asked why I was there.

"You're dealing with some stuff, and I don't want you to be alone. When I said I'm here for you, I meant it. I wanted you to see I ain't just talking—I'm for real."

"Thank you, D."

I still had all of my things with me, but I asked Kamaria if we could walk around campus and talk. She said no at first because she had barely left her bed since getting back from the hospital. It took a few minutes, but eventually I convinced her to show me around.

Before we started walking, I put the boombox away and reached for her hand. I wanted her to feel a human connection so she would know she was loved. She hesitated, then took my hand. Our conversation began slowly, as if we were meeting who we'd become.

She tried to explain why she broke up with me, but I told her it wasn't necessary. No point rehashing what was already done. So instead, I just asked how she was doing.

"Some days are worse than others," she said. "I know you ain't supposed to, but after I lost my baby, I started questioning God. Like... why me? Why my baby?"

I squeezed her hand tighter. I wasn't about to toss out empty words just to sound wise. I just listened and let her release everything, without interruption.

"I don't think I'm above having bad things happen," she said quietly. "I know that's life. I just thought I saved up enough good deeds to keep me from this kinda stuff."

She paused and waited for me to respond.

"I get it. I don't think you deserved it, either, but what if we only got what we deserved?" I asked.

"That would be good, right?"

"Nah. I mean if we only got what we deserved—good and bad."

She stopped walking and thought about it.

"Oh, you mean if we only got the good and the bad we earned?"

"Exactly."

We—myself included—tend to focus on the bad things that happen. But even in our worst situations, the absolute worst doesn't always happen. Seeing RaShawn taken will forever be one of the most painful things I've ever experienced, but it could've been me, too. There was nothing RaShawn did that deserved death in that moment, and nothing I did made me more deserving of life.

It's like that for all of us, maybe not at that level, but the examples are there. That's what I wanted Kamaria to see. I told her I hated what she went through, and I was sorry it happened, but I also wanted her to see the good we don't deserve usually outweighs the bad we do. It was a good conversation that lasted about an hour as we walked around seeing her favorite spots on campus.

We tried to avoid talking about the bad times in our relationship while spending a little time remembering the good. At some point, I noticed she let go of her stomach, which was a small sign that she was feeling a little better. As it started to get late, I told Kamaria I was staying at a hotel that wasn't too far away.

"You just got here, though. You don't have to leave so early, and you definitely don't have to leave by yourself," she said.

When you're grieving, you can act in ways that may be outside of your character. I caught on right away to what she was saying, but I knew it came from a place of vulnerability. Don't get me wrong, I'm a man, so yeah, my mind went there for a second—but there was no way I was going to take advantage of someone I called a friend.

"I appreciate you wantin' to keep me company, but we'll talk tomorrow. I'm not set to leave until late, so I promise, we'll chop it up. Actually, we can grab breakfast or somethin' if you want," I suggested.

"I'd like that," she said softly.

I gave her a kiss on the cheek and let go of her hand.

"A'ight, cool. Lemme gon' get this map out so I can figure out how to get to where I'm goin'," I told her.

I gave her another hug and told her again that I was going to be there for her. I didn't really want to leave, but I didn't want either of us to think about, or do anything we might regret later.

"Thank you, D. Thank you for being my friend, even when I tried to push you away. This little surprise visit has meant everything to me," she said, finally showing a small smile.

"I got you, Kare Bear," I told her as I started to walk away.

I looked back a few times, and she was still watching me every step of the way. When we got to the point where we could barely see each other, we waved to say goodnight.

We spent most of the next day together. She told me more about how she met Adrian, the person who ended up getting her pregnant. It wasn't information I necessarily wanted to know, but I figured she'd never had the space to express herself. If she was going to start healing, she needed to let it out, so I listened.

Eventually, she started telling me about the moment she knew something wasn't right with her pregnancy. Water built up in her eyes as she stopped to catch her breath.

"My entire body was hurting. I was in so much pain, I could barely move. Every time I tried to get up, it was like my body pulled me back down," she said.

She was trying her best to keep going, but when she got to the part where she knew her child was gone, she couldn't control her emotions.

"I couldn't breathe. It was like I could feel my child's spirit leaving, and there was nothing I could do to keep him here with me."

All I could do was hold her while she relived that pain. She talked until she felt like she'd said everything she needed to say. Then, she cried until there were no tears left. When she was finally done, she exhaled deeply.

"I'm good," she said.

She wasn't saying it for me—she was saying it for herself, trying to convince her own heart. I understood that, even without her explaining it. She said she wanted to change the subject because she didn't want to keep reliving the trauma, so that's what we did.

"So, what's been up with you?" She asked.

"Man, I just been workin' and tryin' to figure out this medical school stuff."

"Hold up, what medical school stuff? What are you talkin' about?"

I said it really casually, forgetting we didn't talk often enough for her to know everything going on in my life. Plus, I hadn't done enough to think it was even a big deal.

"Yeah, I'm leanin' toward trying to go to medical school—because of a dream I had with my mom," I told her.

She looked at me with so much pride, you'd think I'd already graduated from the most prestigious medical school in the world.

"You saw Mama?" She asked, referring to my mother like she was her own.

"Yeah, not too long ago. I saw her in a dream."

"What did she say?"

"She just told me to help," I said.

She looked confused, the same way I did when it first happened. So, I explained the journey I went on to figure out what that dream really meant.

"That's what I'm talking about," she exclaimed.

"What?"

"You remember how I used to say I didn't want to talk to anybody who wasn't serious about their future, and how you started to change the way you looked at school and stuff?"

"Yeah, why?"

"I always knew you had this in you. You were just too scared to be who you were meant to be. I'm glad you finally kicking fear outta your life."

The word 'fear' loved making surprise appearances in people's thoughts and conversations. When Kamaria said it, it hit differently.

"I've feared fear for way too long. I think my life's runnin' outta space, so I really ain't got room for it no more," I said.

"Get it, Mr. Roberts. My bad, Dr. Roberts."

That was the second time someone called me Dr. Roberts, and I was starting to take ownership of it. The title was starting to fit, and I liked it.

"I'm still tryin' to figure things out," I said, "but at this point, I made a promise to my mom, and I ain't goin' back on that."

She was beaming. Just hearing me talk about my plans was enough to put a smile on her face, and that alone made me happy.

"When do you have to go back to the airport?" She asked suddenly.

"Dang, you tryin' to get rid of me?"

"No, it's not that at all. I was just gonna say, if you don't have a ride, I got my car. I can take you."

"I 'preciate that. I didn't know how I was gon' make it, for real, but I was gon' find a way. If you down for takin' me, I ain't got no issues with that."

We'd met somewhere between Howard and my hotel, so we made our way back to campus to get her car. After that, we went to the hotel so I could check out. Then, we finally headed to the airport.

"Damian, I'm really glad you came out here to visit me. You used to tell me you were scared to fly, so the fact you did that shows me you really care."

"Yeah, fa sho. Yo, me and flights didn't get off to the best start, but we cool now. I might have to fly back over here to check on you."

"The way things are going, I don't even know if I wanna stay. Don't get me wrong, I love Howard... "

"H-U! You know! That's how you do it, right?" I asked, cutting her off before she finished her sentence.

"D, never do that again. I mean... never," she laughed.

"I got you. I just figured I'd try—"

"No, sir. Just don't try."

"Okay, but for real, what were you saying about staying here?"

"I don't know if it's for me. I'm thinking about going back home."

Kamaria was always goal-oriented. When she set her mind on something, she didn't stop until she conquered it. So, hearing her say she was thinking about leaving Howard—even after everything she'd worked for—was surprising.

"It'd be cool to see you back in the 2-1-4," I said, "but you really gotta make sure that's what you need to do, not just what you want to do. Plus, you're almost done with undergrad. You sure you wanna transfer when you're this close?"

"I'm not even worried about that, for real. I might need to take some time off anyway, 'cause all of this has been draining."

We made it to the airport not long after she said that.

"Pray on everything before you make a final decision," I told her.

"I will."

"Well, it was good seein' you, Kamaria. I hope we're able to talk more now—and you won't just be avoidin' me," I said, leaning over to give her a hug.

"I really appreciate you visitin'. I don't know if I was battlin' depression, but that's how it felt. I'm a little better now, and I have you to thank for it. I really hope this is a new start for us," she said.

"Me too. And thank you for the ride out here. I'll let you know when I get back to Love Field."

I leaned over to give her another kiss on the cheek—just a small gesture to show we were good, even after that rough stretch between us. She didn't want that to be it, though. She gently grabbed my face with both hands and guided my lips to hers.

No lie, I'd been thinking about having that kind of connection with her again, but I didn't think it would happen right then.

"It's been a minute, but what made you do that?" I asked.

She was the one who started the kiss, but she looked just as surprised as I was.

"I'm sorry. I shouldn't have done that."

"It's all good," I said, moving in for a second one.

The awkwardness she felt disappeared the second I followed her lead.

"Damian... so what does this mean for us?" She asked.

"It means we don't know what we're doin', and we ain't got it together, but we gon' figure it out. I'll talk to you later, I promise."

When I finally got out of the car and back inside the airport, my pulse started racing, which was pretty much normal whenever I saw Kamaria. Once again, I started thinking about a future with her, and I convinced myself she was thinking the same about me. Still, I had to be real with myself. Maybe she only kissed me because she was still in that vulnerable space, and she just needed it in the moment.

It only took about two or three days to find out for sure, 'cause that's how long it was before she started calling me more often. The conversations started off being about us relearning each other; beyond the tragedy, beyond school, and beyond who we used to be.

If we were really gonna be friends again, we both had to make a conscious effort to learn who the twenty-something-year-old versions of Kamaria and Damian had become.

15

While Kamaria and I were relearning each other, my family was preparing for Lexi's graduation. It was hard for me to process the baby of the family was graduating. When it comes to younger siblings, it seems like time moves faster for them than it does for you.

When I graduated high school, I had both of my parents there to help me. When Elijah graduated, I helped when I could, but because of Mom's passing, Pops was still too emotionally unavailable to do a lot. Sadly, that meant Elijah was left to handle almost everything himself. We tried not to let that be the case for Lexi, but honestly, she didn't need much help. We chipped in here and there, but she knew what she had to do, so she did it.

On the day of her graduation, we had a great time celebrating her accomplishments. She was in the top 10% of her class and the family wouldn't have expected anything less, especially since Elijah did the same thing the year before. After the graduation, we went out as a family for a little while, then Lexi kicked it with her friends.

Soon after, she went into preparing for college, and we all went back to business as usual. For me, that meant focusing on everything

I needed to do for my own graduation and making sure Kamaria and I stayed committed to reconciling our relationship.

Growing up, I heard God could take a dead thing and bring it back, but I never thought that could apply to relationships. That's exactly what happened with Kamaria. I loved her, I hated her, and through conversation and growth, I ended up loving her again.

We didn't want to say we were a couple because we thought that came with too many expectations. Maybe even thinking about those expectations distracted me a little, which might've been one of the reasons I took longer to graduate than I planned. Life always be life'n, though. I controlled what I could, took responsibility for what I messed up, and dealt with everything that was beyond my control.

There was a brief period I was upset with myself for not graduating "on time," but eventually, I realized if God's plan for me was to finish later than I wanted, then there was a reason for it. His plan is always better than ours, whether we understand it or not.

By the time my celebration drew near, I almost had everything in order. Well, everything related to school. Things were moving along happily with Kamaria, so I was trying to figure out how to propose to her. I valued my family's opinion on marriage, so I asked them how the felt about me proposing.

My father gave his blessing, and eventually, Lexi and Elijah did, too. I knew they would because they all loved Kamaria, especially Lexi. Since I was still lost on how to propose, I asked God. I was hoping I'd get an answer as soon as I asked, but I should've known He never rushes anything just to meet our deadlines.

I hadn't heard anything from Him as my graduation got closer, so I just focused on last-minute details I'd overlooked. Out of nowhere, I was hit with thoughts of my mother as I looked over my invitation options. I hadn't realized how long it had been since she passed. I thought about how happy I was that she made it to my high school graduation, and how sad Elijah was she wasn't there for his.

Since Mama wasn't around, he almost didn't want to go to his graduation, but we convinced him to. When his name was called, Pops and I cheered from the crowd and Lexi joined in from her spot with the band. I know Elijah heard us because he looked our way as he moped across the stage.

That night at dinner, he told us why he didn't enjoy the moment.

"When they said my name, I was out of it. People had to tell me they were calling me. I knew Mama wasn't there, but I kept hoping I'd see her. When I didn't, I wondered why she didn't love me enough to stay and see me graduate like she did for you. I know she ain't have a choice, but I be thinking she could've fought harder," he said.

"Fought harder for who?" Lexi asked in between bites of her food.

"She could've fought hard for me, like she did for Damian."

His pain spread through all of us like an infection. Elijah worked hard to graduate from Townview, but we didn't talk much about it at the time. Even though we all knew it wasn't her decision to leave, Elijah was honest about how his battle with depression started when Mama died, and how it got worse after his graduation. I didn't realize how bad it was until I started preparing for my second graduation.

Days later, when I tried to go back to working on my invitations, the task felt trivial. I got smacked by a heavy wave of guilt. I had been so focused on myself, I drifted away from making sure my family was okay, and I knew Mama wouldn't have appreciated that. The guilt finally pushed me to grab my phone and call my brother.

"How are you? Don't just say 'a'ight,' either. Just keep it real."

"Bruh, you can't call here and tell me how to answer a question."

He was right, I couldn't tell him how to respond, but even with that, he had never been confrontational. Something triggered him, and I needed to figure out what and why.

"I'm sorry, Elijah, and I'll do better. But for real, are you okay?"

"Nope, and I'm tired of all y'all looking over me. Mama was the only one who had love just for me, and she ain't here. So, what am I supposed to do? Y'all didn't get all hyped up when I graduated like everyone did for Lexi, or they're doing for you," he said.

"I messed up. I should've hyped you up way more. Graduating from Townview, being in the National Honor Society, and finishing near the top of your class is major. I should've said that more. That's my bad, bro. I'm proud of you, and I love you."

As men, we sometimes struggle to tell other men we love them, even when it's our brother or father. We get caught up in this idea of masculinity that makes us think saying that four-letter word makes us less of a man. Even knowing that, it still felt strange saying it to him. His hesitation to respond told me it felt strange for him to hear.

"Bruh, I ain't even know I needed to hear that."

"We all need to hear it. So, if I gotta apologize a million more times and tell you I'm proud a billion times so it sticks, I'll do that. But I'm human, so if I mess up, don't give up on me."

"Oh, I hear you, and I appreciate it. Plus..."

"Plus, what?" I asked.

"Plus, I been around you my whole life. When it comes to messin' up, you are one of the best to ever do it. Remember how Mom and Pops said you almost flunked kindergarten?"

"Bro, chill," I said, laughing. "I didn't almost flunk. The teacher just suggested it might be in my best interest to repeat it."

"Yeah, like I said, you almost flunked kindergarten," he joked.

And just like that, my brother was back to being himself. I knew he was still holding onto pain from not getting attention, but hearing him throw out a joke let me know he was feeling a little better. Things seemed to be back on track until I asked him what he was doing to battle his depression. It was as if he was talking in code, which was frustrating. I kept pressing him to stop being secretive and just be real with me.

"I'm smokin'. There, is that what you needed to hear?"

He said it like he was mad at me. I knew I couldn't go at him with judgment, so I didn't.

"I don't wanna see you get caught up in nothin', " I told him.

"Everybody can't be perfect like you. Some people got problems they can't deal with and don't wanna talk to nobody about. Just be glad I'm just smokin' and not trying to take myself out again," he said.

I am far from perfect, but hearing Elijah open up, gave me more insight into why he felt like he couldn't talk to me about everything. On top of that, I had to deal with my brother talking about taking himself out again.

"Elijah, we need you here, bro. You can't—"

"You ain't gotta go there 'cause I'm cool now. Just keep checking on me. I'm gonna do me, and if you wanna make sure I'm cool, then that's all I need."

He hung up the phone without warning. I didn't understand how he went from saying he needed me to check on him, to just hanging up on me.

"So, you gonna tell your brother?" A voice asked.

I suddenly saw RaShawn, and he was asking me to make a decision about something I thought was behind me. The chorus from The Pharcyde's "Runnin'" started playing in my head, and I knew what I had to do. I called my brother back, hoping he'd answer.

"What?" He asked, sounding aggressive.

"I had a little time to think, and I get the whole 'image thing' you were talking about. I need to tell you something I've never told anyone before, not even Mama and Pops."

"I'm not one for secrets, but gon' say whatever you need to say."

What I was about to say could change everything, and I was terrified, not just of how he'd react, but of him being disappointed in me.

"You remember what happened to RaShawn, right?" I asked.

"Yeah, I do. The hood can take everything from you," he said.

"True, but I want you to know, me and RaShawn weren't as innocent as everybody thinks. Plus, we had actually seen them before."

"Okay, so you'd seen them around Oak Cliff before."

"Yeah, but we saw them because me and RaShawn was hustlin'. The same two dudes from the basketball court were watching us a week earlier. When we saw them at the court, we kinda already knew something was gonna pop off, but we tried to handle it."

"You and RaShawn was hustlin' when y'all first saw these dudes?"

Silence hung in the air for another minute or so before Elijah burst out laughing, louder than I'd heard from him in a while.

"C'mon, D, you can come up with something better than that. You know you weren't out there selling nothing. Maybe RaShawn was, but not you. You don't even sound right trying to talk about it."

I admit, it was probably just as strange for Elijah to hear me talk about it, as it was for me to say it. I wished I was lying, but I had to make sure Elijah knew I wasn't.

"Bro, you a fraud! You do all this talkin' 'bout being better, and you out there sellin' drugs. You can't use age as an excuse, either. We done all been sixteen, but you the only one dumb enough to think sellin' was the only way to get what you wanted."

He was harsh, but I couldn't deny anything he said. We discussed the details of what I did, and we both agreed on being more transparent with Lexi and Pops about our actions. So, I said I'd go to the house, and when I got there, I got right into it.

"Pops... I've tried to be a good son, but I ain't always done right by you and Mama. I did some things you wouldn't be proud of, but I can't keep them from you anymore."

My dad started squirming, already uncomfortable before he knew what was coming. Lexi's eyes were darting between me and Elijah like she was trying to guess what was about to go down.

"A'ight, let me get right to it. When I was around fifteen, I was hustlin', Pops," I said, lowering my head.

"We gotta hustle if we tryin' to get what we want," Pops told me.

"Pops, I was selling drugs, like hustlin', for real," I mumbled.

Before I could continue, my father slammed his fist on the table so hard, everything in the kitchen shook. He stood up, threw his chair to the ground, and got in my face. Before I could react, he grabbed my shirt and shoved me against the refrigerator with all his strength.

The physical part set me off. Without thinking, I pushed my father—not trying to hurt him, just to get him off of me. I lamented it as soon as it happened. I had never put my hands on my father before, and I saw his age as he hit the floor.

"I'm sorry. I didn't mean to do that, Pops. Let me help you," I said.

Lexi shoved me out of the way and helped him up. I looked at Elijah and he was just sitting there, watching the chaos unfold.

When I told them I stopped at 15, that got their attention again.

"So, you're tellin' us about stuff that happened like six or seven years ago?" Lexi asked.

"Yeah. I been done with that for a minute."

A sense of relief settled over the room. I could've easily said the real reason behind my need to come clean, but I wasn't about to dime my brother out and make him lose even more trust in me.

"Chill out for a minute, I got somethin' to say, too," Elijah said.

Everyone settled at the table. The attention slowly shifted from me to Elijah as he started to speak his truth.

"Look, I know y'all upset about D. We all do dumb stuff when we kids. Shoot, we keep doin' stupid stuff when we grown, too. You're supposed to live, learn, and get better, right?"

"I guess, but what are you tryin' to say? You out there selling, too?" Pops asked, hoping he didn't have two sons on the wrong path.

"Nah, but I been dealing with depression for a minute, so..."

"So, you not selling, you taking somethin', huh?" Pops asked.

"I'm just smokin' a little," Elijah said honestly.

Unlike when I told my truth, there was no burst of anger from Pops or Lexi. Neither of them looked happy, but they weren't mad, either. And I understood it. I told them I was harming the community and putting them in danger; Elijah told them he was smokin' to help with his depression. Neither one was good, but they weren't the same.

"Where did we go wrong?" Pops asked.

"I don't know what you gonna say, Elijah, but let me go on and get my explanation out the way," I said. "See, it ain't about what nobody, other than me, did wrong. You and Ma did everything y'all could to keep me on the right path. For a minute, I just got caught up with tryin' to look good. I convinced myself I had to do something. It was dumb, and I didn't think about the consequences, or about how my actions were hurting people. That's it."

"And what about you, Elijah?" Pops asked.

"Again, I ain't doin' nothing but smoking 'cause I need to stay calm. I been depressed for a while, but the closer I got to graduation last year, the worse it got. It ain't really got nothin' to do with what anybody did wrong, it's just me tryna deal with life so I don't try to take myself out of it."

Everyone sat quietly, letting his words sink in. Lexi left Pops's side and went to hug Elijah.

"I'm here with you every day. How come you never told me anything?" She asked.

"Lexi, what I look like telling my little sister I'm depressed? We all still dealing with Mama's death, so my issues ain't special. I'm just weaker than y'all 'cause I can't handle this stuff on my own."

Pops had been sitting in silence, but the moment he heard Elijah say he was weak, he got up.

"I cry every day about your mother," he said. "It's been years, and I still see her everywhere. I hear her voice when I'm tryin' to make a decision. I smell her perfume randomly in the room, so yeah, I get it. I don't know much about all this depression stuff 'cause my generation didn't talk about nothin' like that. And I don't know nothing about smoking reefer to take away your problems, either."

"Reefer? Dad, how old are you?" Lexi asked, laughing and momentarily ignoring everything else he said.

"That's what we used to call it, so that's what I'mma gonna keep calling it," Pops said. "I ain't worried about what it's called, anyway. That ain't even important. Elijah, wasn't you and D goin' to therapy? I actually thought about it for myself, but I ain't really about lettin' folks in my business like that."

"We was talking to people, but it's been a minute," Elijah said.

"It might be time for us both to go back," I told him.

When it came to therapy, I had fallen off. Either I convinced myself I didn't have time to talk to anybody, or I thought I had it all together. Either way, I was wrong. Talking with my family made that clear. Mama told me I had the responsibility of looking after everyone, so I had to do a better job of that.

"Can I be honest?" Lexi asked.

"Go for it," Pops said.

"As the only woman left in this family, I'm disappointed in y'all," she started. "Y'all supposed to be my role models—the ones I look to for guidance—and the type of men I compare others to. I love y'all, and I know y'all ain't bad people, but this ain't it. D sold drugs, Elijah smokes, and Dad—he's emotionally hurt every day, but still refuses to get help 'cause that ain't what other men his age are comfortable with. What are we even doing? Are we just tryna keep stereotypes alive? Is this what we want folks thinkin' about Black people, or people from Oak Cliff? I only been outta high school for a hot minute, so is this how y'all really wanna send me out into the world?"

I had to think about everything she said before responding. I had to set aside my feelings and just hear her. When I looked at Pops and Elijah, I saw we all had the same stunned expression. None of us could deny she was telling the truth.

"I get y'all on some 'do better' type stuff," Elijah said, "but outta everything goin' on, smoking don't even that bad. Would you rather me smoke, or feel like I want to end it all again? Let's be real."

"Why is it so hard for y'all to just talk to somebody?" Lexi asked. "Since y'all so scared to talk to a therapist, talk to your homies or somethin'. Talk to folks at the barbershop, or at work. I'm just asking that you don't keep everything to yourself."

Elijah didn't say another word, which gave me a moment to respond to what she'd said.

"Look, I'm flawed. Hustlin' ain't good, and I was terrible at it. I don't know how many people's lives I ruined, but I been tryna make up for it ever since. I only did what I did for a short time, but it ended up costin' my best friend his life, and now it's costin' me trust with my family. I let y'all down, and I been beating myself up way before y'all knew. Even when I try to forget, I can't 'cause it's part of my history.

Pops, my bad. I need you to know you didn't do nothing wrong—that was all on me. And I apologize for putting my hands on you. It won't happen again. Elijah, I'm sorry for not keepin' it a hundred with you, and for not bein' the big brother you needed. And Lexi, you're right. I was pushin' stereotypes, but I promise everybody in this room: I'll spend the rest of my life tryna be better and do better for me, all of us here, and for the community," I told them

I hoped they believed me, but I couldn't tell if they did. My ability to come across as truthful was irrelevant, though. I'd been working ever since RaShawn was taken, to be a better person, and like I told them, I was going to keep trying until my final days. I apologized again, and left, not knowing how my family felt about me.

That night's conversation was one I feared, but it gave me a great sense of relief once it was done. Sure, everyone saw me differently, but I was okay with that. I was never able to put my finger on it until that night, but before they knew about my brief stint as a dealer, I'd been put on a pedestal, and that never should've been the case. It was like they were looking at me as the golden child when I never did anything to earn that. After that night, I was just viewed as "regular," which took a huge amount of pressure off me.

As I made my way back to the crib, I started thinking about when I would tell Kamaria the same thing I told my family. We had just gotten back together, and I knew that kind of news could tear us apart again. But after that first conversation with Elijah, I also knew I had to be completely open with her. I wanted to go to her house and talk in person, but despite her concerns about staying in D.C. after her pregnancy, she ended up staying there.

I always hoped she'd come home, but at that point, she didn't think it would be best for her. That just meant I would have to call her, instead of telling her face-to-face. I didn't tell her that day, but I didn't wait long, either.

We skipped the small talk. I told her pretty quickly I had to say something that could change our relationship again.

"So, you're about to say something that could possibly break us up, and you're cool with that?" She asked.

"It's not that I'm cool with it at all," I said, "but I gotta make sure you know about me. I don't want nothing to be a surprise later on."

With that, I told her what I'd done in the past.

"Are you serious?" She asked.

"Yeah. Me and RaShawn were already trying to stop hustling before those guys saw us at the basketball court."

"Oh, so they targeted y'all?"

"Pro'lly, but I ain't sure 'cause we never interacted with them."

"Have you stopped, for real?" She asked directly.

"I stopped a long time ago, and I ain't tryin' to go back to that life."

She had the choice to believe me or not. Whatever she decided, I didn't want her to feel rushed, or influenced by me.

"If you need some more time, it's all good. You ain't gotta say nothin' now if you don't want to," I told her.

"I don't need more time, it's just kinda crazy you're telling me about this now because I just heard my brother's about to get out."

She hadn't talked about her brother in a while, so her news shocked me, probably just as much as my news shocked her.

"Word? How you feel 'bout that?" I asked.

"I don't know. Me and Mom really haven't talked to him since he's been locked up. I think it's 'cause he didn't wanna talk to us 'til he was free, but also 'cause we were leavin' home, and my mom didn't want him to know where we were goin'."

Without knowing it, my past connected me to the brother she hadn't seen since before we met.

"My bad, I wasn't trying to..."

"What? Remind me of my brother? I know you weren't. You had no idea, it's just crazy how things work."

"Yeah, it is. So... we good?" I asked, not really knowing what type of response I was about to hear.

"Look, I never would've suspected that was in your past. I don't like it at all, but you told me you're not goin' back, right?"

"Nah, I'm done with that. I've been done for a long time."

"I hate what you did and I wish you hadn't done it, but you can't change the past. You just gotta live with the results of your actions—and you know exactly what I mean without me even sayin' it."

"I hear you, and I appreciate that."

"Last thing I'mma say about this is—you been able to move past things I wish I did differently. You didn't hold stuff over my head when you could've, so I'd be a hypocrite if I didn't do the same."

I was surprised by how she handled it, and it made me appreciate her even more. Bringing that sort of information into a relationship could have destroyed everything. I'm very fortunate it didn't. With my past out of the way, I could, once again, focus on my future.

Over the next few days, I handled everything I needed to for my graduation, which was both exciting and nerve-wracking. It's strange how celebrating an accomplishment can bring tasks that cause stress.

It shouldn't be like that, but it usually is. I didn't stay stressed out about that for long, though. Once the graduation stuff was done, I started thinking about how I was going to propose to Kamaria again.

She told me she was gonna make it home for my graduation, but she didn't know how long she'd be able to stay. That meant I'd get to propose in person, but I wouldn't, necessarily, have a lot of time to do it. I also had to figure out what to do about her mom. Would Kamaria be okay if I invited her to my graduation, and would she automatically suspect something if she saw her mom there?

I had been waiting for God to order my steps when it came to proposal ideas. I expected something special to guarantee Kamaria would say yes when I asked, but God, being God, flipped the script.

"Keep it simple and ask," He told me.

That's all He said—and believe it or not, that was more than enough. His words told me to clear my mind of all the elaborate ideas Kamaria probably wouldn't have liked. She wasn't materialistic, and she didn't like being the center of attention. She generally chose to stay out of the spotlight. So, I had to keep that in mind.

I initially wanted to make some grand gesture to show how much I cared, but it wasn't necessary. Honestly, the things I was planning were more about showing off and feeding my ego, and that's not what proposing is supposed to be about. God knew my heart, and He knew what was needed, that's why He told me to keep it simple.

I was secretly saving for a ring since we were seniors in high school, but when Kamaria broke up with me, I started spending. When she told me she was pregnant, I spent a little more, but I never spent it all. I guess, no matter what was going on between us, I always thought we would get back together. Since my persistence and optimism paid off, all I needed to do was go get a ring.

You know how good advertising will stick with you, years after you've seen or heard it? That's what happened when I went ring shopping. There were jewelry stores all over Redbird, Irving Mall, NorthPark, and even Big T, but I only wanted to go to Kay Jewelers, the one we all called Kay's. Why? Well, it was because of their commercial: "Every kiss begins with Kay." That line stuck in my head.

I'm not a jewelry guy. When I stepped into Kay's, the saleslady started talking about natural stones and synthetics, diamond clarity, color, and carats. I was so lost, even if we had GPS back then, I wouldn't have found my way.

"I'm just tryin' to find a ring for my girl. I don't need all that fancy stuff," I told her.

"You may not need it, but doesn't your girl deserve it?" She asked.

She was good. She almost had me spend money I didn't have, using words I didn't understand, to describe stuff I didn't care about.

"Nah, I appreciate it, but she don't like fancy stuff, either. I just need a diamond ring. Something that looks good and shows I love her, but one that don't look like I'm tryin' to do too much."

"Oh, I get you."

I thought she was agreeing as part of her sales pitch to make me drop my guard. I'm glad it didn't end up being like that. She was trying to make a sale, but she listened to what I said and respected my budget. In less than an hour, I had something I was really happy with. I had a ring I felt fit Kamaria's personality perfectly.

That was one of the times it felt like everything was moving faster than usual. After buying the ring, it was time for graduation rehearsal. I couldn't believe how quickly time flew by. I stood in awe as I lined up with my classmates to see where we would be sitting on graduation day. Seeing all my peers preparing for the ceremony made me happy for everyone, even though most of the graduates were strangers to me. Being anti-social, I have to say, my lack of friends has way more to do with me than anything else.

Even without knowing them, I understood some of my classmates had an idea of what they wanted to do after school, while others were as unsure about their futures as they were before they started school. The difference was, with a degree, they had more options than when they first stepped onto Paul Quinn's campus. Some said they couldn't wait to leave Oak Cliff. Others had grown so attached to the community, they didn't want to go. I saw the pros and cons of both sides. I had been in Oak Cliff my entire life, but I didn't know where I stood.

If I stayed, I could immediately start giving back to my neighborhood, but would I be settling and staying because it was familiar? If I left, I'd gain new perspectives and experiences I wouldn't get at home. Then I wondered if I left, would it be like abandoning a loved one when you know they're sick, or would it be more like finding the best doctor when the help they need isn't available nearby?

Thinking about that, once again, reminded me of when the street preacher compared us to cancer. His words continued to stay with me. I still didn't agree with how harsh he'd been, but as "I got more life in my rear view mirror," as Kamaria's great aunt said, I understood it a little better. Maybe he shouldn't have called the people cancer, but maybe we could've all recognized the environment we lived in was sick. There's a difference.

"Mr. Roberts, you look a little lost. Do you have any questions?" Someone asked.

For the moment, I had to shift my focus from Oak Cliff and its people, back to the graduation.

"My bad. Nah, I'm good. Just kinda gettin' caught in the moment, I guess," I replied.

"Trust me, I get it. Just don't let it all overwhelm you. Everyone's worked hard to make it here, so celebrate yourself before worrying too much about what's next."

I didn't know him, but clearly, he had gone through enough graduations to know exactly how I felt. His advice helped me stay present, instead of trying to time travel through my past and future.

After practice was over, we all gathered outside of the building.

"So, what's up? You ready for tomorrow?" Someone asked.

"No doubt. You?"

"I can't even call it, but I think I am. We thought life started when we graduated high school, but it's 'bout to get real different."

"Fa sho, but us Tigers gon' be a'ight. We gon' go out and do some great things. We gon' change Oak Cliff, Dallas, and the world," I said.

"You on some 'We Over Me' stuff for real, huh?" He asked.

"That's what we 'bout 'round here, right?"

"True. Well, congrats," he said as he walked off.

Just like the person who gave me advice earlier, I didn't know the guy who talked to me after rehearsal. That didn't matter, though. If you had a connection to Paul Quinn, you were family. Being on a smaller campus, surrounded by people who cared, even when they didn't know you, was something I knew I'd miss. It's funny how you start to appreciate things when you realize they're about to change.

After rehearsal, I had to head to DFW Airport. Kamaria managed to get a last-minute ticket home, so I had to pick her up. Even though I had very little experience going to airports, I knew I hated going to DFW. Maybe it's the same at all airports, but there's just too much going on there. They have too many turns, exits, traffic signs, cars, people, just too much of everything. I put all that to the side for my baby, though.

When I got there, I had to circle around two or three times because her flight was delayed a little. I was already feelin' some kinda way, but when I finally pulled up to the Delta terminal and saw Kamaria standing outside waiting on me, all that frustration disappeared. My heart was full of nothing but happiness.

I pulled over and got out to grab her bags, trying to act like I wasn't excited to see her, but she knew I was frontin'.

"Put that bag down and hug me," she said, grinning ear-to-ear.

She had just gotten back in town, so I did what she said—just to make her happy. Nah, I'm joking. I dropped that bag quick than a mug and grabbed my girl. We had our little PDA moment before getting in the Tahoe and heading to my crib.

"Do you ever miss Ebony?" Kamaria asked randomly as we made our way to my place.

"Huh?" I asked, not even realizing what she was talking about.

"I know you still think about her, you have to," she told me as she started to laugh.

It took about three or four minutes to realize she was talking about the 88.

"I had no idea what you were talkin' about. Yeah, I miss my car, but she's still around. I had to retire her after she broke down on campus, but she's still around for nostalgia's sake."

When we pulled up to my apartments and drove through the

gate, which was broken again, she acted surprised because we weren't at my family's house.

"Oh, you got your own spot?" She asked.

"I been on my own for a minute. As hyped as I was when I got my crib, I know I had to tell you at some point."

"You probably did. We've been through so much stuff over the years, maybe that info just got lost in the conversations."

"That could've happened, but it's all good."

My furniture situation hadn't really been upgraded much since I moved into my spot, so I expected Kamaria to throw some subtle shade about my décor when we went inside, but she didn't.

"This is beautiful, D. You've been able to make this place your own, and you even brought over stuff from your childhood home. The posters you have on the wall, the pictures in frames, and the books all remind me of what I saw when I had the chance to visit your house back in the day. You can see who's influenced you and who's important to you. Your place is you... and you're amazing."

I almost felt like putting my head down with a sheepish grin, while kicking my feet out like the characters on old-school tv shows did when the girl they liked finally said something nice about them. Maybe that's doing too much, but what she said made me feel good.

"I really appreciate that," I told her.

She took some time to look around the crib a little more and soon found a framed picture she didn't know I had.

"D, out of all the years we've known each other, I have never seen this picture. How did you get it?" She asked.

She was looking at a picture from the first day we met. In the photo, we were all doing a group project, but she was in the foreground. Anyone who knew her could tell right away who it was. She'd never seen it because I only had it for a short time.

"Okay, you remember Mrs. Armstrong, right?"

"C'mon, D, how could I forget one of the greatest teachers ever?"

"You right, that was a dumb question. Anyway, I was at Kroger one day, trying to get some tv dinners, and something made me go down the coffee aisle. I stopped when I saw a lady, but at first, I didn't know who she was, or why I stopped."

"So... what happened?"

"Then it hit me. I yelled, 'Mrs. Armstrong, is that you?' so loud everybody in the store thought I was on somethin', but I didn't care. I knew students recognized her all the time, but that didn't mean she'd recognize them. So, I didn't really expect her to know who I was, but I stayed still while she looked at me for a minute. It was like she was analyzing me and running my face through a computer or something. After a while, she said, 'Damian Roberts, it's been a while.' I was so throwed off she recognized me, I didn't know what to do."

"Having her remember you turned you back into a kid, huh?"

"Already. It felt good to know somebody who impacted me so much still remembered me. I can't act like it didn't make me feel cared about and special, 'cause it did."

"That's cute, babe, but it don't explain how you got this picture."

"My bad, I almost forgot what I was talkin' 'bout. So, once I got over her remembering me, I asked if she'd seen anybody else from our class. She said she saw our classmates all the time. Then, she asked if I was still close with you and RaShawn. I almost broke down on a Folgers can when I told her what happened to him, but God helped me keep it together."

I stopped talking for a little bit because I could feel myself getting all choked up in real life as I recalled the story. It was crazy how often I found myself getting emotional as I got older, but that's how it was.

"You okay?" Kamaria asked.

"Yeah, so... when I told her about RaShawn, she gave me a nurturing Mama-type hug. She told me she kept pictures of all her classes and she regularly prayed for us. I got her contact info so I could check on her, and one day she just asked me if I wanted any of the pictures from my class. When I visited her, that's when I saw that picture. I told her about us, and I asked if I could have that picture."

"That's crazy. Wait... yooooo, look in the back," Kamaria said.

I looked at the picture, but I wasn't sure what she wanted me to see.

"Okay, what am I supposed to be looking at?" I asked.

"Babe, look way in the back. RaShawn is there clowning, like he always was."

I had looked at that picture at least a hundred times, but I was so focused on staring at Kamaria, I didn't even see my boy in the background. It was good to see my brother with a smile on his face again.

"Man, I didn't even see that. Thank you for pointing that out."

"He was always smiling and crackin' jokes," Kamaria mentioned.

"Yeah, he was. That old episode of The Simpsons where Rod and Todd were like, 'I got the joy, joy, joy, joy down in my heart,' that was him, for real. Whenever we dealt with something that wasn't good, he was able to brush it off. I still ain't got that skill," I said.

"Me, either. I be so in my feelings, I'll get stuck. But we all can't be the same. That ain't how God made us," she said.

Looking at the picture together let us reminisce on days past. It gave us the chance to talk more about RaShawn, who he was, what he meant to us, and who he could've been. Sometimes, when I talked about him, I tended to drift into the negativity of his death more than the joy that was divided up between himself and everyone else whose path he crossed. That night was refreshingly different.

Kamaria and I let that picture be the starting point of at least an hour-long conversation that had very little to do with us and was mostly about him. I talked about how RaShawn and I became friends because of some Fritos—a story I'm not sure she'd heard before. We talked about going to 6-12 the first day we all met in elementary school, and how she clowned me and RaShawn for our snacking preferences. We let the trip down memory lane take us all the way through our freshman year at Kimball.

We enjoyed trying to impersonate RaShawn's mannerisms, his joke-telling ability, and his unmistakable laugh. Just like in the conversation I had with Mr. Murphy in high school, I also talked about the things RaShawn said he was going to do with his life. My boy acted like he couldn't do anything one minute, then be convinced he could do everything the next. That latter way of thinking—that confidence—is the mindset I was trying to take on.

I hadn't seen many real-life examples of long-term success, but I had reached a point where I knew I had to eliminate the restrictions I placed on myself if I wanted to do anything noteworthy. I only started to understand that because the lessons I learned from everyone, and what I knew about God, started to impact me differently.

Speaking about our friend that night was something I didn't know I needed, but I'm glad it happened. It gave me freedom I didn't realize I was still seeking. When I woke up the next morning, the anxiousness I had about finding a way to propose to Kamaria, and the nervousness I had about graduation, were all but gone.

"Today's a big day. You ready?" Kamaria asked as we got up.

"No doubt. A lot is changing today, and I'm ready for it," I told her.

I almost slipped and said something about the proposal, but I kept it to myself. I still needed to take care of something, though.

"I wanted to invite your mom to graduation, if that's cool with you?"

"It's your graduation. If you want to, I'm not gonna stop you."

"Y'all were really close, and I know you miss that."

She slumped down on the futon and looked up at me.

"She's been acting like she disowned me after the pregnancy. It hurts, but I get it."

"Yo' mama loves me. If you give me the go-ahead, I'm gonna invite her to the graduation and help mend y'all's relationship. I'mma have y'all talking like you on Oprah or something. Is that cool?"

She didn't tell me not to do it, so I went ahead and made the call.

"Hi, Ms. Anderson, it's Damian," I told her when she answered.

"Oh, hey. It's been a while. How are you?"

"Yes, ma'am, it has. I'm good—how are you?"

"I've been better, but I'm okay."

"Good enough to be at my graduation today?" I asked.

At that point, I couldn't tell if Kamaria wanted to start getting ready, or if she was nervous about me talking to her mom, but she pointed to let me know she was headed to the restroom. I knew it was my chance to speak to her mom alone to ask about the proposal, in addition to the graduation. I took the call off speaker, moved around a little, and spoke quietly while Kamaria was occupied.

"Ms. Anderson, I'll be honored if you make it to my graduation, but that ain't the only thing I'm calling about. I'mma make this quick 'cause I don't know how much time I got on this call."

"Okay, I don't know what's going on, but go for it."

"This is gonna seem like it's comin' outta nowhere, but I love Kamaria and I'm asking for your blessing to marry her."

I stopped talking because I didn't want to come across like an overbearing car salesman. I wanted her to really think about it.

"I'm gonna be real with you," she finally said. "we ain't as close as we used to be. And, she's grown, so y'all don't need my blessing."

"I may not need it, but out of respect, it's something I'd like. Plus, I gotta make sure my future T-Jones-in-law is good."

She went quiet again for a few seconds.

"Okay, you have my blessing. Just take care of my baby."

"I will. And I don't have any major plans, but you'll be a part of how I ask her. Just make sure you don't say anything. So, do you think you'll be able to make it to the graduation?"

"If you want me there, I'll make it. Just give me the details."

As Kamaria came back, I gave Ms. Anderson the graduation info and ended the call. I was happy she said she'd go, but I was grateful I had her blessing to ask for Kamaria's hand in marriage.

"So, how did it go?" Kamaria asked.

"She was actin' like she wasn't feelin' it at first, but she loves me, so she's gonna be at at the graduation."

"That's cool and all, but does she know I'm here?" Kamaria asked.

"Not exactly," I told her.

That wasn't the answer she wanted to hear, but it was the truth.

"Well, it ain't like we got beef or nothin'. Things just might be a little awkward when we see each other," she said.

"Just call her and talk to her. Gon' get the awkwardness out the way so you won't have nothin' to worry about when you see her."

I hoped Kamaria would call her mom, but I was surprised how quickly she actually did. Before I finished a bowl of Fruity Pebbles (the greatest cereal ever), they were chatting it up like old times. It's amazing what some grace and a conversation will do. And she didn't say it, but the smile on Kamaria's face after the call told me they both needed to reconnect more than either of them wanted to admit.

I felt great about the day, but helping Kamaria made me feel even better. I only had a few hours before graduation, so as I started getting ready and called to make sure my family was doing the same.

"Hey, Pops. Y'all up?"

"I been up since 'bout five, people-watchin' on the porch—just bein' nosey like me and your mama used to do," he told me.

"You sound happy, Pops," I said.

"I am. All three of my kids done graduated high school, now you 'bout to graduate from Paul Quinn."

Over the years, my father continued to get better at expressing his feelings, but it was still surprising to hear him say he was happy. The conversation could've taken a turn, like it had so many times before, but it didn't. My father could've misconstrued what I was saying and reacted to what he assumed I meant.

"I've always been proud of y'all," he said, "but I'm getting older, D. I can't keep chasing joy away from me."

It took a turn, but not the one I expected. My father opened up about how he felt, and he even admitted how his lack of vulnerability over the years caused him to miss important moments with the family, especially with Mama.

"I ain't gonna be like y'all, but I'm working to be better. I know I said that a lot over the years, but I mean it. Today is another turning point, and I have you to thank. Plus, I can't be the grumpy old man. But enough about me—this is your day. You ready?"

"Yeah, but today ain't about me, either. It's about adding to our legacy. It's all about the last name, not the first."

"Boy, you a'ight wit' me," he said.

I didn't need FaceTime or WhatsApp (which were all still years away from existing) to see his smile. He told me he was glad he listened to Mama and saved for my college fund. Again, I had to think about the sacrifices they made to save money for me when we were struggling. They believed in their premie baby, even when they were probably told they shouldn't have. I am, grateful for that.

A few hours later, as all the family and friends of the graduates filled the Richard Allen Chapel, I took some time to look around for my people. I was searching through the crowd like a Where's Waldo book. When I spotted them, they were beaming with pride, hoping I'd see them. I was close to yelling out, but the ceremony started before I did. I had to sit down quickly before I made us all look bad. There was a prayer said near the beginning of the ceremony that caused a feeling of calmness to wash over me.

As the prayer ended, I kept my eyes closed. I didn't say anything —I just thought about my "village," and those who had gone to be with the ancestors. Nothing we do in this world is ever done alone, and that quiet moment reminded me of that. When my name was finally called, the imposter syndrome I used to feel whenever I accomplished something was gone, at least, for the moment.

Graduating from college didn't come easy. I struggled a lot, but I learned who I was, who I was becoming, and who I wanted to be. By the time we all threw our mortarboards in the air, I was thanking Paul Quinn for helping me grow up. I didn't know if that would be the last time I walked the campus, but if it was, I knew I had been changed for the better. Paul Quinn shaped me into the man I needed to be— the man ready to fulfill the promise I made in my dream.

I looked up and let my mom know I hadn't forgotten about her.

"We are on our way, Mama. I promise, I got you."

16

fter the graduation was over, it took me a minute to find my family again. When I did, I was surprised to see them, Kamaria, and Ms. Anderson all together.

"What's up, family?" I said, addressing everyone.

They all answered, but they also quickly made sure they congratulated me.

"Y'all lookin' good than a mug. My people showin' out," I said excitedly.

The smiles were universal as the feeling of success grasped onto all of us and wouldn't let go. I may have been the one who walked across the stage, but we all graduated that day. We were leaving behind one level of thoughts and expectations because together, we were able to see more.

As was our family tradition, we celebrated the graduation by going out to dinner. That day, we were joined by Kamaria and Ms. Anderson. As we all started receiving the meals we ordered, I heard God tell me it was time to propose to Kamaria. When Elijah told an unplanned joke, I made it obvious that I dropped my napkin on the ground so everyone would see my looking on the floor, but wouldn't think anything of it.

I quickly exhaled, looked up at God, and dropped to one knee with the ring in my hand. My heart was using my chest as a trampoline, and my nervous energy was about to make me change my mind, but then Kamaria turned back around and looked at me.

She almost looked away again when she noticed I didn't move. That's when she stared more intently. It was go time.

"When I met you, I knew you weren't like anybody I met before..."

She stood up, only to kneel down with me. She started to cry as I continued.

"You were there when my family needed you. You made me become a better version of myself, and when we weren't together, I knew it was only a matter of time before we would be. Kamaria Regina Roberts, will you marry me?"

Our hands trembled together as all of us waited on her to give an answer. Every second she was silent felt like a day, and so after what felt like a week, she finally gave an answer.

"Yes, a million times, yes," she finally said.

As I placed the ring on her finger, we stood up to a restaurant full of strangers cheering us on as if they knew us. Congratulations were being thrown from every direction like confetti at a New Year's Eve party. And with that, we were engaged.

The rest of dinner was almost unnecessary because I had overindulged in joy and love. With graduation, dinner, and the proposal, it was beautiful to have a few hours of peace without being inundated with the troubles that can be connected with the hood.

I asked myself how I could have a similar experience everyday, and if I would have to leave Oak Cliff to get it. I had asked myself similar questions over the years, but when I was able to reach a conclusion, it was usually just based on what I wanted. Being a newly engaged man, I had to consider how things could impact my fiancé, even if she didn't know it.

The longer you live, the more times you meet up with moments that change your life, or maybe those moments are the ones God uses to get you back on track. Either way, that day was one of them. Before getting engaged, and before graduating, one thought that occupied a lot of my time was where I wanted to go for grad school. After that day, it was as though the decision was starting to be made for me.

In spite of going through a time when she thought she was done with living in DC, Kamaria was still there. As far as I knew, she was no longer even considering leaving, even though she was taking a break from school.

"What if I moved to DC?" I asked randomly one day.

"That would be great. I just never thought I'd ever hear you say you'd leave Oak Cliff, I mean, not for real."

"Me, either, but things are different now. If we plan on spending our lives together, we might actually need to be together to do that, feel me?"

"Yeah. It would be so good to have you here," she told me.

Truthfully, I had been taking steps to get into a school out that way for a while, even before discussing it with Kamaria, or anyone else. The back and forth discussions of leaving Dallas had been ongoing in my mind since I was at Kimball, maybe even before, but they became more frequent the closer I got to graduating from Paul Quinn.

When the first acceptance letter I received was from Howard, even though it was one of the last schools I applied to, God provided the clearest sign he could have possibly given to me. I immediately told Kamaria. She was shocked that things were happening so quickly, but she was happy.

With my family, important information was normally shared in-person. So, when everyone was available, I met them at the house. In my mind, I thought they would have issues with me leaving Oak Cliff, but in reality, they acted as though I was the last one to figure out I'd be leaving. They said if my fiancé wasn't about to move back, they knew it was only a matter of time.

Since they were already cool with the idea of me moving away, we got to spend time together as a family playing dominoes, Uno, and a bunch of board games we hadn't touched in years. We listened to music each of us liked. Pops clowned us because he couldn't understand our music, and we made fun of his music because most of it sounded like a bunch of begging and whining. Overall, we had a good night just being in each other's company.

I left the house happy, but I got choked up when I drove off. I realized the days of us being in the same room, laughing and joking on a consistent basis, were about to become far more infrequent. I looked at the crib I had lived in for the majority of my life in my mirror and it became symbolic of me getting ready to leave Oak Cliff.

When I made it back home, all I wanted to do was sit outside on the porch and talk to God. With my legs stretched out against my gate, I leaned back and looked at the night sky. The stars seemed like they glistened brighter than before, and the moon was shining like it was trying to show the world it was more than just the sun's sidekick.

I was outside to talk to God, but I ended up just listening. There was no need for me to speak because He addressed the concerns of my heart faster than my brain could formulate questions. He told me not to worry about moving to a new city because I couldn't move forward if I stayed still. He reminded me that I couldn't provide the help my mother asked for if I never learned what help the world needed. Lastly, He told me the pain I'd endured in the past — and the pain I'd meet in the future — might scare me, but I should never be fearful because He was always with me.

When God told me what I needed to hear, I called it a night. I went to bed for eight hours, but somehow, it felt like I didn't wake up until it was time to move. By then, the crib had been packed up. Since I had to drive my stuff to D.C., I picked up a U-Haul truck early that morning and waited for my dad and brother to come over and help me load everything.

"I'ma keep it real with you, son — I'm kinda sad. I know you a twenty-something-year-old, six-foot-tall, grown man, but every once in a while, I'll look at you and still see that little premie baby we had to stay in the hospital with. I know you don't need me to protect you anymore, but as your father, that's a job I'll never retire from," Pops told me.

"Yes, sir, I get it."

"And I don't even know if I'm sad or not," Elijah said, "but it's gonna be weird knowin' you're not right down the street. That's gonna take some gettin' used to."

"It might take a minute for all of us to get used to, but I'm just a call away. I'm keepin' my 2-1-4 number, so just hit me up," I said.

We talked more about how to stay connected despite the distance. After a few more subject changes, we got everything into the U-Haul and hooked the Tahoe to the back of it. I was seemingly ready to go, but I questioned if I really was.

I gave them both a hug.

"I love y'all, and please hug Lexi for me," I said, getting into the truck.

"We got you. You know she wanted to see you off, but her band's got a gig in Houston today," Pops said.

"She told me. I ain't trippin'. When she said why she started playin' them drums, I knew music would be in her life forever."

After dapping them up, I got in the truck.

"A'ight, y'all. It's time for the next chapter."

"You got it, bro," Elijah yelled out as I started to drive off.

My dad didn't say anything else, but when I looked in the mirror, I saw Elijah put his arm around him as they both wiped their eyes. My heart was punching my chest like subwoofers in the trunk because after all those years of wondering how life would be if I ever left Oak Cliff, I was finally on the road to finding out.

Getting on the freeway and passing the spots I'd known all my life had me reliving my entire story. The positive memories far outweighed the negative ones. It was sad leaving the only city I had ever known, but I knew it was for the best.

A little under twenty-four hours after I left, I was pulling up to Kamaria's — I mean, our apartment. As soon as I got there, I let Kamaria know I made it.

"After all the years we've known each other, we're really about to start living together," she said once she made it outside.

Thinking about it was a trip, but it was even crazier to hear her say it. It got more surreal as we unloaded the truck. When we finished, I wanted to sit down, relax, and start getting used to my new home, but I didn't have time.

After I got cleaned up, Kamaria and I went out to grab something to eat. We talked about how our lives would immediately start to change, and when we made it back home, I started unpacking.

"Don't you wanna sit and chill for a minute?" She asked.

"I gotta get stuff cleaned up. I don't wanna mess your crib up."

"Mess up what?" She asked.

"Your... I mean, our crib," I said, chuckling.

It took a while, but by the time I was a few years into grad school, D.C. was actually starting to feel like home. The environment was different than what I was used to, though. It was common to see Black people doing well, and that's what I wanted for Oak Cliff. More people there were thriving, while back at the crib, we were surviving.

Like everywhere else, D.C. had its issues, but as an outsider, they didn't seem as bad as they were at home. Maybe I hadn't been there long enough to see how things really were, or maybe I just wasn't in an area dealing with the same problems we had in Oak Cliff — but stuff was different. I'm not gonna say it was better, 'cause ain't no place like home, but it definitely wasn't the same. Even with that, I still found myself getting homesick every once in a while.

"You okay, D?" Kamaria asked one day while I was at home studying when she'd just gotten back from work.

"I'm good. I just miss the crib."

The hug she gave me reminded me why I felt comfortable enough to leave my home — the only neighborhood I'd ever known — to live with her. That embrace made us start talking about our goals and the path we planned to take to get there. Kamaria told me about her mom, and how guilty she felt for still not finishing school.

She always said she wanted to take care of her mother, and since she hadn't been able to do that, she often questioned a lot of her decisions. She told me when she was at her lowest points, that's when she missed being home the most. It was surprising to hear her say that, but I understood it.

For the first time I could remember, she explained one of the reasons she didn't want to come back home after losing her child was because she hadn't completed her mission. She said she had a specific reason for leaving home, and she'd consider herself a failure if she returned before taking care of it.

"I miss home all the time," she said, "but I can't go back until I can go back — if that makes sense."

"So, let's get you back in school. Let's finish what you started."

She showed all her teeth when she smiled, obviously happy about what I said.

"For real? You think I should go back?" She asked.

I did all I could to show how sincere I was about wanting her to go back, especially after hearing how much it meant to her. And hearing her say she missed home actually made me feel better about missing home, too. She got up and went to the 3-disc CD changer she kept on the built-in bookshelf.

She didn't tell me what she was about to play, but she was already dancing before the music even started. A few seconds later, I heard the famous words that transported me right back home:

"Yeaaaah, Oak Cliff, that's my hood—" the song started.

"Oak Cliff, That's My Hood" was birthed by Young Nino and other Oak Cliff artists to show love for the same hood I grew up in — and we ran that song back at least four times. That song was the exact medicine we needed to cure our case of homesickness.

It wasn't long after our conversation about Kamaria finishing school that I found out she had actually re-enrolled in classes. When Kamaria set her mind on something, she found a way to make it happen. And as if she hadn't missed any time at all, she jumped right back into being one of the best students in all of her classes.

I, on the other hand, was persevering, in spite of struggling. The math seemed nonsensical, the science was happy flying over my head, and even the English classes felt foreign. I was second-guessing myself almost every day. I asked Kamaria if I made a mistake thinking I could become a doctor. She responded by asking me if my parents ever struggled, and if they quit.

They had struggled, but they never gave up. Kamaria told me

she'd been asking herself the same things about her mom. We both realized sulking wouldn't get us anywhere, and talking would only do so much. If we really wanted to reach our goals and build legacies, we had to be 'bout that work.

So we threw out our excuses like it was trash day, and for the next few years, we both kept a laser-level focus. While I was still grinding through my classes, Kamaria graduated with a degree in finance — with honors, of course. When I reached my next graduation, I was just honored God let me make it.

Our lives were moving fast, but we made sure we were really living. While we were earning more degrees and settling into our careers, we always made time for each other. We lived together, but I still asked Kamaria out on dates — never taking a "yes" for granted. It kept us connected, and as we got closer to the wedding we'd been planning for over a year, it confirmed we were making the right choice.

While we were both at Howard, we used to ask each other when we wanted to get married. After a bunch of talks, we decided to wait until I had "Dr." in front of my name. At first, getting a doctorate seemed like a million-step journey. In a lot of ways, it was — but when I stopped looking way ahead at the last step and just focused on the one right in front of me, things started to feel a little less daunting.

17

Becoming Dr. Roberts was a dream come true, but it couldn't compete with becoming a husband. Since our family was back in Dallas, there was no question the wedding would be there, too. Kamaria and I didn't want to feel rushed, so we caught a flight a week before the wedding to take care of the last minute details. I tried to help, but Kamaria and her mom basically told me they had everything under control.

They took care of the floral arrangements, Kamaria's dress, the colors, and everything else that would've had me confused. I just had to try on my tux, sample the cakes, and agree to the location. If it were up to me, I would've worn a Nike tracksuit, had a German chocolate cake, and had the wedding at the crib, but I knew that wouldn't happen.

One thing that was left up to me, was knowing who my best man would be. Before Kamaria and I had any details on the wedding, my brother was the only person I considered for the job. Since he was an introvert, he generally strayed away from anything that caused him to be the center of attention. Fortunately, he was willing to step out of his comfort zone for my wedding.

Neither of us were really the wildin' out type, so he didn't throw a crazy bachelor party for me. He just invited some people I was cool with to the crib and we played spades, dominos, and watched sports. I know it ain't what most fellas would've done on their "last day of freedom," but I was cool with keeping it simple. Plus, I had to make sure I'd be good on my wedding day because I had to get up early and meet my barber at the venue so I could get a fresh cut.

The day of the wedding, I thought I was good. There were no nerves or cold feet, just good vibes. When I got to the venue, it all changed. I got a bad case of the bubble guts that didn't calm down until I was walking through the doors at the start of the wedding. Since Kamaria and I decided not to have a big wedding party, I just had my brother with me, making sure I was good.

He walked behind me to the front of the church, and we stood there, waiting for Kamaria's entry music to play. When I saw her, I almost couldn't believe she was there to marry me. Like the first day we met, she had long braids that swayed as she moved. I, once again, became that 8-year-old boy who was smitten by her.

Her mother walked her down the aisle, and Nadia, a longtime friend, was making sure her wedding dress train was straight. When she made it to her spot, the preacher got started. A few minutes later, she was repeating her portion of the vows.

I tried to stay focused, but I was captivated by her. The lights could've been turned off and her smile would have lit the room. When Elijah handed me the ring, and I placed it on her finger, we broke down. I didn't care what anybody thought about it, either. We had gone through a lot, and God allowed us to be together. Any tears we shed were earned.

After we were officially married, and went into the reception hall, I took the time to scan the room. I wanted to see everyone who was there to celebrate our love, which is something I didn't do during the wedding. It didn't matter if we knew the people for a year, or our entire lives, everyone genuinely seemed happy.

The conversations happening around the room ended when Elijah asked for everyone's attention.

"I appreciate everyone showing up for my brother and Kamaria. I love my brother, and from day one, we knew he loved Kamaria. Bro, things won't always go the way you want them to in a relationship, but knowing the kinda person you are, I know you'll do all you can to get things right when they go wrong. Kamaria, me and Lexi have always liked having you around, so it's cool you're now officially part of the squad. I love y'all and D, I'm proud of you. Congratulations to you both."

Elijah said he was proud of me, but I was more proud of him. He had conquered his fear of public speaking, handled all of his best man duties, and he even told me and Kamaria he loved us without feeling ashamed. All of the talks and the therapy sessions were paying off, and it was good to witness his progression, and to see his growth as a man.

After Elijah's speech, Lexi stood up. She hadn't said much to me that day, but she formed a heart with her hands, and went behind a curtain I hadn't even noticed. When it opened, she was with the jazz band she formed after she got out of high school. I heard plenty of their music, but I hadn't seen them perform live until then.

"Let's get it, lil' sister," I yelled out.

Lexi was sitting behind the drum set, but she was also leading the group. After she counted down, the group started off by playing Method Man and Mary J. Blige, "All I Need." When Kamaria heard that, she practically drug me to the dance floor.

"There's no way we're not gonna dance to this. C'mon, husband, let's get our first dance on," she told me.

Method and Mary was the first song we danced to when we went to Kamaria's family's get together back in the day, so it had always been "our song," and the fact that Lexi knew that, even though I didn't remember ever telling her, was absolutely amazing. They played the song almost identically to how it sounded on the radio. They even had someone rapping, and another person singing.

They played it so well, I would've been cool if that was the only song they played, but they followed it up by going into Stevie Wonder's, "As," which in my opinion, is one of the greatest songs ever written. It had all of the couples in there reliving their glory years, and it was beautiful to see. After that, Lexi said they were about to end their performance for the night.

We all thought they would play another R&B or love song to end the night, but they completely flipped the script and played Big Tuck's, "Southside Da Realist." Man, it was crazy than a mug seeing everybody get hyped, lit, crunk, or whatever you want to call it, in suits and dresses. Lexi's band did their thing and they made sure the vibes were right before the DJ took over.

When the group finished, Kamaria and I thanked each one of them before we had some time to speak to my sister.

"Man, y'all were on one out there, Lexi. Thank you so much for being here, and for playing," I told her.

"You don't have to thank me. There was no way I was gonna miss your wedding," she said.

"Yeah, thank you little sister. You looked so beautiful leading that talented group of musicians," Kamaria added.

Lexi paused before she looked at us and reached out to hold one of Kamaria's hands.

"I love my brothers with all of my heart, but there were so many times growing up I wished I had a big sister, especially after Mom died. Hearing you say that—"

"Girl, I get it. I always wanted a little sister, too. I have a brother, but I was basically an only child my whole life. I love you, and if you ever need to talk, your big sister is here," Kamaria told her with a smile, as she gave her a hug.

With that, two of the most important women remaining in my life cemented an unbreakable sisterhood. We all moved over towards my father who was sitting down, just watching everything happen around him.

"Look at my son and his wife. This is beautiful, y'all," he told us.

"Thanks, Pops. You okay?" I asked.

"Yeah, son, I'm good. I'm just happy for y'all, for my family."

I looked up, and it was like I saw my mom holding onto him. Right then, Pops put his hands on his on shoulders as if he felt her presence. He didn't say anything, and neither did I, but it was one of the many awe-inspiring moments that happened throughout the day.

Elijah soon joined us, and we all spent a few more minutes conversing. Then, Kamaria and I excused ourselves to spend a few minutes with everyone who had taken time out of their schedules to be with us on our special day. One of the last people we had the chance to talk to was Kamaria's mom. It wasn't that she was sitting by herself, or she was mad, or anything like that. The reason why she was last was because we just couldn't get to her.

Mama Anderson was on the dance floor cuttin' up as soon as music started playing. Even after all the music stopped, she was still moving. It was like the echoes of sound waves was enough to keep her going. Kamaria was so excited to see her mother full of joy, she was beside herself.

"I love you seeing you like this, Mama," Kamaria told her.

"My baby got married today, and she has herself a good man. God is good, and I ain't got no complaints," she told us.

When the reception was over, and everyone had gone their separate ways, my wife and I had some time to sit down and talk amongst ourselves.

"How are you, Mrs. Roberts?"

"I'm great. How are you?"

"Chillin'. I just got married today. I got a beautiful wife, and I heard there's gonna be a nice lil' private after party for the two guests of honor later on tonight," I joked.

"You heard about an after party, huh?"

"Yeah, it's supposed to very exclusive."

"It sure is, and I know you gonna enjoy yourself," she told me.

"Girl, don't threaten me with a good time. We can go right now," I joked.

We were both laughing, but I meant what I said. Before we got up, I looked around once again and imagined all of the people who just filled the room. I looked at the table in front of the room where Kamaria, me, Nadia, and Elijah sat. I looked down at the end and I saw RaShawn standing there. He was excitedly walking around in a circle like he just heard me spit some incredible bars in the world's best rap cypher.

"You see him, huh?" Kamaria asked.

"Who?"

"RaShawn."

"Huh. How did you…"

"I'm your wife, babe. I can just tell. Are you okay, though?"

"Yeah, I'm good. It's just crazy to think the dude who got us talkin' ain't here for our wedding."

"Not here? Nah, RaShawn's spirit was definitely here today."

"How you know?"

"Babe, you didn't see how hard folks were laughing all day? If you don't believe that was RaShawn showing out like he always did, I don't know what to tell you," she said.

Her words game me solace. So, when she was ready to leave, I was, too. Our lives changed forever that day, but marriage wasn't the end of change. The marriage just gave change a more united platform to show up to. We all have to make adjustments as we navigate through life, it's just easier to pivot when you have the perfect partner to pivot with you.

18

Since we already lived together, Kamaria and I didn't have many issues getting back to reality after we got married. The main problem we had was making ourselves leave our honeymoon destination. After that, things were pretty easy.

Kamaria was working with a financial organization she absolutely loved. While I was incredibly grateful to be working in my field, I can't say I was feeling fulfilled. At first, I was okay with it, but a few years into our marriage, when we found out Kamaria was pregnant, I started feeling the pressure to do better financially. The pressure wasn't brought on by Kamaria, it was self-prescribed.

For so many years I talked to my family about therapy, but as I started running into adult problems, it no longer seemed like a viable option. I started feeling like a hypocrite and I didn't know what to do about it. With so many great things going for me, I foolishly decided I needed to start going to the bar to get help.

I wasn't a drinker, so I was getting anything. I was just trying to have a few minutes where the pressure was non-existent. And as our child was growing, I would sometimes hear Kamaria pray our baby didn't have the same fate as her first child. She was doing all she could to stay happy and calm, while I was drinking more and more.

By the time we reached the seventh month of pregnancy, Kamaria told me to get myself together, or expect for our marriage to end, and for me to not be able to see our child. That was all I needed to hear. I started going to AA meetings, found a new therapist, and by the time we reached the end of the 8th month, I was completely sober and thankfully, I had made my way back into Kamaria's good graces.

"I think it's time," Kamaria calmly said one evening.

When I understood what she was saying, I started running around like I was lost. I knew we had bags packed in our closet, but I couldn't figure out how to turn the door knob. We had her birth plan hanging on the fridge, but I couldn't find the kitchen. All the while, Kamaria was gathering all of the things I was looking for.

"We're ready. Just get us there safely," she told me.

I made sure she was comfortable in the car, and we were on our way. She glanced at me silently to tell me to slow down. The police sirens I eventually heard, let me know I should have listened.

With all that has happened with police and Black people, I got nervous. Kamaria was upset because I didn't slow down like she wanted, but she didn't say anything. The officer knocked on my window and told me why we got pulled over. I tried to remain calm as I explained why I was driving so quickly.

"Congrats, but you still shouldn't be driving like that," he told us.

"I'm just tryin' to get us to the hospital before this baby is born."

"The best way to do that is to let me be your escort," he told us.

When he got back into his car, he turned the siren on, and pulled up beside us. He said we needed to follow him. We made it to hospital so quickly, I had to thank God because His favor is real!

We parked, got checked in, and for a while, we just sat there. I thought we might have come to the hospital a bit prematurely, but I didn't say anything about it.

"You got this, Kare Bear," I told her, as I held her hand.

"I'm kinda scared, babe. I don't want what happened before—"

I knew what she was saying, but I didn't want those words in the atmosphere. It seemed like prayer was needed, so I prayed.

"Father God, we're here because you allowed us to be. We pray

the hands of every nurse and doctor who step foot into this room are
anointed. We pray the birth plan Kamaria has will be followed, and
her safety will be a top priority. We are praying for the safe delivery of
a healthy baby. We pray our child is not rushed, but still knows we
are here waiting. In the name of Jesus we pray, amen."

She was relaxed after the prayer, and that was all I could ask for.
The room's tv was on one of those game show channels because I
knew it would help keep her mind at ease. The atmosphere
changed when a nurse told Kamaria she had gone into active labor,
though.

Kamaria pushed and followed every instruction she was given.
After about 30 hours, she looked down and told our child, "It's time,"
just as she had told me. Moments later, we were being told we were
minutes away from seeing our baby.

We went through the entire pregnancy not knowing the gender of
our child. So, when I heard, "It's a boy," I almost passed out. Our son
was silent, and that scared me. So, I had to make sure he was okay.

"It's okay to cry, son, I don't care what anyone says," I told him.

I wanted to immediately break generational curses, and right
after I said those words, he cried so loudly, we had to cover our ears.

"There you go, my boy," I told him, as the nurses cleaned him up
and placed him in Kamaria's hands.

"Hey, baby. I'm your mama. I love you," she told him.

Hearing her say she loved him brought on our son's very first
smile. She smiled, just as he did. She was holding him for the first
time, but she was a pro. Motherhood already looked great on her.

"What's his name?" She asked in a whisper.

We had been throwing out names for months, but nothing stuck.
Prior to him being born, there was no way I would've thought she
would let me name him, so I didn't have an answer.

"Who are you?" I asked him, as I held his hand for the first time.

My son looked at us, then he just giggled, and turned his head.
Making everyone laugh is what helped me come up with a name.

"I think I got it. What about Shawn Clifford Roberts?" I asked.

She thought about it briefly.

"That's so cute, and I get it. His first name is a tribute to RaShawn. That's a beautiful, Damian."

I was relieved because I didn't know how she was going to react.

"Do you get where his middle name comes from?" I wondered.

"Not really?"

"Where are we from?"

"Dallas," she said.

"No, where are we really from?"

"Oak Cliff. Oh, shoot. Cliff. Only you would come up with a name like that. I really like it!"

"We'd like to introduce you to our son, Shawn Clifford Roberts," I told everybody in the room.

They all clapped for us, and started telling us how to take care of him. After three days, they let us take him home. I still can't believe that happened. Trying to put him in the car seat for the first time took a degree in mechanical engineering, and I wasn't ready for that. Kamaria and a nurse ended up getting it situated because I was lost.

A day or so after we got settled, I called Pops to let him know he was a grandfather. I also called Lexi and Elijah to let them know they had a nephew. When Kamaria told her mom, she immediately asked if she could come out to help. We hadn't considered having anyone over to help us out, but seeing how worn out we were, we were willing to take all the help we could get.

I also thought it was necessary to call RaShawn's parents, who had always served as parental figures, to let them know about the family's new addition. They were both happy for us, but when I told them his name, they were almost in disbelief. I made sure they remembered I made a promise to them to keep RaShawn's memory alive, and they thanked me for still caring about their son.

A few days later, we flew all of our family out to meet Shawn. Everyone fell in love immediately. We let them have their time with him, as one of us watched, while the other got some rest. It was good to get some sleep, but it was even better to have the family around.

"What y'all think about DC?" I asked everyone.

"It seems cool, but I don't think I could stay out here," Lexi said.

"Well, we don't think we can, either. That's why we're moving back home," I told them.

A few days before we went to the hospital, I received a random call from a 972 number asking me if I'd be willing to relocate to Dallas for an employment opportunity. They explained everything about the job, but I couldn't make the decision without Kamaria. Since she finished school, she was open to moving back home.

The family wanted to help us pack right then, but things didn't move that quickly. Fortunately, I ended up getting an upgraded offer to relocate, even before our home was sold. When that happened, we thought the transition back home would be easy, but it wasn't.

Initially, the company that hired me tried to get us to move to the suburbs, not actually in Dallas, for some reason. When I told them we wanted to go to Oak Cliff, they were surprised.

"Oak Cliff is an up-and-coming area. I've seen land in potentially great areas, sell for low prices. If you're willing to wait it out, moving there could be a good investment," I was told.

He was talking about gentrification, the same thing Pops told me about over a decade before. He told me how it was going to play out, and it was crazy to know it was happening. I didn't like it, but I figured if anyone deserved to profit off of an ascending Oak Cliff, it should be someone who was already invested in it.

After a long search, we found a nice spot in the Kessler Park area, and that's when we officially moved back. One day, when Kamaria and I were both off, and Shawn was with his grandmother, I asked her if she wanted to go to Paul Quinn with me. Neither of us knew why we were going, but we went anyway. I showed her around campus and we headed over to The SUB. When we were walking, I saw someone I felt I was supposed to say something to.

People say when you have that strong feeling of intuition, it's God telling you something, so you're not supposed to go against what you're told.

"Hey, what's up, bro, how are you?"

"I'm good, what's going on?" He asked.

"My name's Damian. This may sound crazy, but I graduated from here, and I feel like I'm supposed do something to help the community. Is there anyone you know of who can help?"

"What's going on, Damian. My name is Kenneth, and I'm actually the Chief of Staff here. We're always looking for volunteers and mentors to help with events in the city."

We talked for a few minutes before Ken said he had to go. He gave me his contact info and told me to reach out to have a real convo, if I was serious about helping the community. So, after we finished walking the campus, and we got back home, I made the call that changed my coarse of actions.

It only took a few days before Ken's connections had me speaking to kids about my educational journey, and how I got into my new job of doing cancer research. That speaking engagement helped me get others, and soon, I was able to grab ahold of the fulfillment I'd been seeking. Ironically, once I found more things to do outside of work, I started to get more research opportunities.

A few years in, we were finding more about cancer and ways we could eliminate it. Through a network of people I had become a part of because of the meeting with Kenneth at Paul Quinn, I started working with people in the community to understand how cancer impacted them. Almost everyone I talked to had stories similar to what happened with Mom, and I felt sorry for my people. There was no way so many of us should have been connected by cancer.

The connection of the neighborhood and cancer made me think about the street preacher I saw when I was younger again. The reason became more clear in one of my meetings with new community members. I was speaking to everyone when one of the people started looking familiar. I tried to recognize him, I couldn't.

I walked around the room, creating an opportunity to speak to everyone more closely. When I reached the familiar face, my brain went through the photo album of my life's interactions. Then, I imagined what the person I was talking to looked like when he was younger, before the sickness reached him. That's when I knew who he was. I was staring at one of the people who took RaShawn's life.

He and his friend escaped the justice system, but life had gotten ahold of him. Not only did he have some form of cancer, but I could see the track marks on his arms, so I knew he had a relationship with drugs, at least at some point. Looking at the withered face of RaShawn's killer made the petty side of me want to taunt him for his condition. The other side didn't want me to say anything because I vowed to help people, and I promised to do all I could to stop the people of Oak Cliff from being thought of as cancers. If I taunted him, I would be going against it all. God also told me to keep my mouth shut, but my flesh won over my spirit.

"RaShawn didn't deserve what he got, but you do" I told him as I walked away.

I was wrong for saying what I did, I know it, but I'm human. I begged God for forgiveness and made sure He knew, regardless of the hatred I had in my heart for that person, I would do all I could to help him. Unlike with my mom, if it was God's will to take him away that minute, I would have been okay with it, though.

When I went home, I had to remove the negativity on me and remember my purpose. Cancer became a topic I spoke about a lot at home. Kamaria and Shawn gave me different perspectives on what it meant to be sick, and how lives could be improved, even if the disease wasn't gone. I felt like I was getting closer to a breakthrough which made me feel good because I was inching towards providing the help my mother asked of me.

Then, on the day we made a discovery that could possibly change cancer forever, I got a call from my doctor with results from a recent visit. He wanted me to go in, but I was able to convince him to tell me over the phone. As it turned out, I was researching something I had. I was told I had stage 2 colon cancer. Was my diagnosis the result of God knowing I wouldn't listen to Him and kick someone when they were down? I'll never know, but as my guilt kept getting the best of me, I received another call. I was told I would be the winner of a Community Award for the work I was doing.

Telling my family about the award was easy. They showed their excitement as they asked every question they could think of. As for the other news, it took me a few days to tell them about that. I didn't know how Kamaria would take it, but she handled it brilliantly.

"And this too shall pass. Evidently God made you do research for a reason. You're going to do everything to take care of your health, and we are going to beat it," she told me.

That was all I needed to hear, so that's how I approached each day. A month later, it was time for the awards show. When we got there, my family and Ms. Anderson had reserved seats they were escorted to while I went backstage since I was going to be one of the first people honored.

Suddenly...

"We're honored to have our first winner here tonight. He's one of the doctors leading the way in cancer research. Please give a round of applause to Dallas' own, Dr. Damian T. Roberts."

Before the event, I was asked what music I wanted to walk out to. There was only one song that could properly introduce me to the crowd. The song's piano-led introduction rang throughout the theater as the words soon bellowed out.

"Yeeeeeaaaaaahhhh, Oak Cliff...that's my hood..."

I knew Young Nino's, "Oak Cliff, That's My Hood," was the perfect song for me. It connected me and my neighborhood, and it was something I needed to hear. When I walked from behind the curtain, I looked around one more time before adjusted the microphone.

"Hi, everyone. First, I want to thank God. I'm supposed to talk about my research, but I'm taking a detour. If you don't know where I'm from, then seeing where I am won't mean as much.

I'd also like to thank my family. Kamaria, you changed my life for the better and I love you. To my son, Shawn, I appreciate you believing in me and making me feel like a superhero. My brother, Elijah, witnessing you grow into who you are has been an honor. If people think my testimony is something, wait until they hear yours.

Lexi, I know you'll inspire others as you drum to your own beat. Pops, you've been a great role model to me. I'm glad I got to see your imperfections because they showed me I was able to mess up, too."

"To Ms. Anderson, my T-Lady-in-law, I want to thank you. I'm grateful to have you in my life."

Then, I made it to an emotionally challenging part of the speech.

"Let me talk about these tears. These are for the people who should be filling those empty seats next to my father. Those were saved in memory of two important people who are no longer here. My friend RaShawn. We met because of Chili Cheese Fritos, and he quickly became my brother. Losing my friend is still tough for me. Throughout my journey, his parents reminded me to keep my hope."

Being in the crowd, I had to give his parents their flowers.

"I'm glad y'all made it. I heard RaShawn's voice when I was dealing with my issues, and hyping me up whenever I accomplished something. I thank y'all for raising him the way you did."

Talking about RaShawn was difficult, but I knew talking about my mother had the potential to break me down completely.

"The other chair is for my mom who lost her battle with cancer. I got into this field because of her. Even in death, she is still helping me make decisions to impact the world. Mama, I hope you keep helping me reach the places God wants me to go. I love you forever."

The audience patiently waited as I took a few seconds for myself.

"Many people doubted me because I'm from the hood, and I know how it made me feel when people told me what I couldn't do. I want us to see what God can do when we have faith. We're all here to help others, and I'm so glad my mother reminded me of that.

Whatever I do, Oak Cliff is right here with me. When people see me, and any good thing I'm able to do, they will see us. Kamaria told me God put greatness inside us all, so I'm making sure we're able to show that to the world."

I stopped myself and reached into my pocket to pull out the grill I purchased when I was a teenager. I wiped it off and I snapped it on.

"Let me give you a visual of what I'm saying. When I was younger, Kamaria and I got grills from Big T Bazaar. Mama said we carried a light that shined with our purpose. So, even when we're surrounded by darkness, we could always, 'shine.' This grill represents me keeping a promise to keep shinin', no matter what."

I tried to keep speaking the prepared words, but I started dealing with a sense of gratitude that was almost too much for me to handle. I looked up at God and stopped talking. I had to be quiet because I didn't want to speak while God was talking to me.

Pins dropping on a cotton floor would've been louder than the auditorium as God conversed with me. People probably thought my nerves had gotten the best of me, and in a way they had. I suddenly became nervous about properly representing what I was doing.

"Please forgive me. I have to speak from my spirit. Is that okay?"

I was quiet as I got myself together, once again.

"This award isn't about me. This award, whether you know it or not, is about God. That's why you've heard me talk more about Him than I have about any of the doctoral stuff I'm being honored for.

Only God can see a kid in Oak Cliff, who was never the brightest in class, and decide that's who He was going to use. Since I was a child, I've learned being chosen doesn't mean you'll be spared from pain. In fact, being chosen means you're pretty much guaranteed to have to endure things God knows others aren't built to handle."

As I spoke about God, it felt almost as though His hand was on my back, pushing me to keep going, so I did.

"I lost my best friend, I lost my mother, and I had a brief battle with alcoholism. I've seen my soulmate become a person I hated, only to be guided right back to her. I don't know what you've endured in your relationships, but I know we feel the way we do today because we've been tested like a Scantron.

If you told me I'd be a doctor when I was younger, I would've called you a lie, not a liar, but a straight-up lie. God's purpose will take you on such an atmospheric rise, it'll make it hard to breathe. You'll feel like the air has been taken from your lungs until you get acclimated with ascension.

When I was younger, we used to use the word 'already.' Growing up, it was a slang, but I look at it differently now. Perhaps we used it because our spirits already knew God had destined us to be great. And over the years, I've heard many negative things that tried to take me away from that greatness.

One of those things was when I heard a preacher, when referring to the people of Oak Cliff, say we were the cancers plaguing our society. When I found out what he meant, I was hurt, but the words stayed with me. People of Oak Cliff, let's be real for a minute. That preacher wasn't the only one who thinks of us as cancers, and we know that. So, instead of acting in ways people may view as cancerous, let's work together to become the cure. Thank you God for believing in me, and trusting me to be in this position. I now understand my pain has helped me realize my gain, and I'm grateful.

OC, we did it. I've said we're in a toxic relationship, but that was before I understood who you are and what you mean to me. I forgive you for the wrong you've done to me, and I hope you can do the same. When I left you, I knew we both needed some space to grow."

I got off of the stage not uttering a word about my diagnosis because I was in a room full of my people and collectively, we had a rare moment where we could all experience joy together. That night was about what God did throughout my life. It was about what my parents and the community did, and what we were looking forward to doing in the future. Many of us grew up in areas surrounded by clouds of darkness and that night gave us light, that hope RaShawn's parents begged me never to lose. There's no way I was going to be selfish and take any of that light from them.

My speech was said knowing I may not even get to see the final results of the things I was being honored for. If that's God's will, I am okay with it. The work was being done for those who would follow, anyway. I always hoped God would continue to find me worthy of being used as a light to shine on His kingdom, my family, and the community I grew up in.

When you know you're sick, you don't necessarily put out a welcome mat for death, but you do make sure your house is in order. Regardless of when my time is up, I pray I've done enough for the people of Oak Cliff to do just like Mama said against anyone who doubts them, and "shine on 'em." As long as that happens, no matter when my journey ends, every step has been worth it. Already!

www.ingramcontent.com/pod-product-compliance
Lightning Source LLC
Chambersburg PA
CBHW032233050726
47591CB00001B/380